KINGS OF CONFLICT

BOOK 4 THE BRUNANBURH SERIES

M J PORTER

B

First published in Great Britain in 2024 by Boldwood Books Ltd.

Copyright © MJ Porter, 2024

Cover Design by Head Design Ltd

Cover Photography: iStock

Map designed by Flintlock Covers

The moral right of MJ Porter to be identified as the author of this work has been asserted in accordance with the Copyright, Designs and Patents Act 1988.

All rights reserved. No part of this book may be reproduced in any form or by any electronic or mechanical means, including information storage and retrieval systems, without written permission from the author, except for the use of brief quotations in a book review.

This book is a work of fiction and, except in the case of historical fact, any resemblance to actual persons, living or dead, is purely coincidental.

Every effort has been made to obtain the necessary permissions with reference to copyright material, both illustrative and quoted. We apologise for any omissions in this respect and will be pleased to make the appropriate acknowledgements in any future edition.

A CIP catalogue record for this book is available from the British Library.

Paperback ISBN 978-1-83751-228-7

Large Print ISBN 978-1-83751-229-4

Hardback ISBN 978-1-83751-227-0

Ebook ISBN 978-1-83751-230-0

Kindle ISBN 978-1-83751-231-7

Audio CD ISBN 978-1-83751-222-5

MP3 CD ISBN 978-1-83751-223-2

Digital audio download ISBN 978-1-83751-226-3

Boldwood Books Ltd
23 Bowerdean Street
London SW6 3TN
www.boldwoodbooks.com

For my brother, JC. For doing what all big brothers should do – putting up with me, being supportive, and encouraging me to do things I might not otherwise do. Thank you.

The Family of Alfred the Great

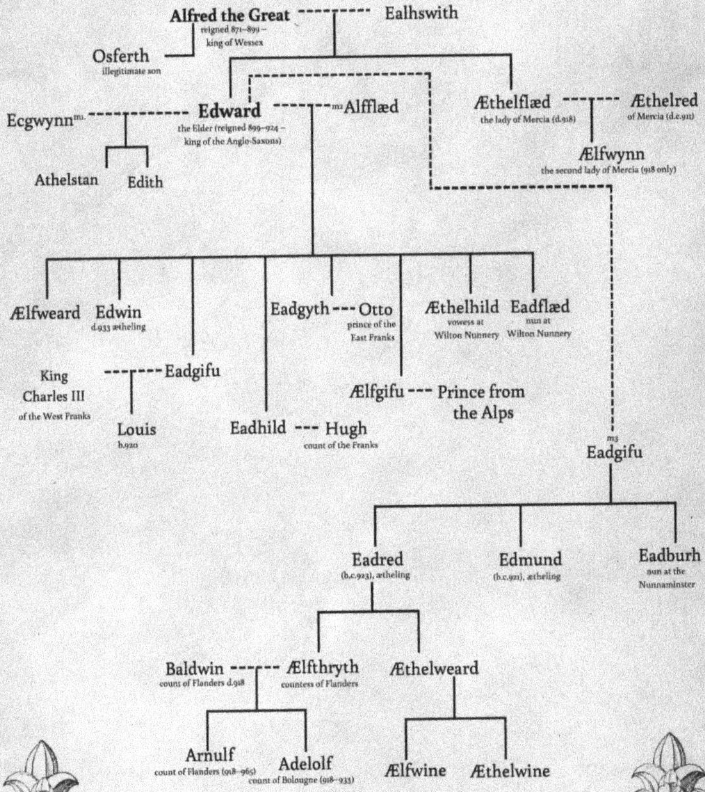

Alfred the Great (reigned 871–899 – king of Wessex) ---- Ealhswith

- Osferth (illegitimate son)
- **Edward** the Elder (reigned 899–924 – king of the Anglo-Saxons) m2 Alfflæd
  - m1 Ecgwynn
    - Athelstan
    - Edith
- Æthelflæd the lady of Mercia (d.918) ---- Æthelred of Mercia (d.c.911)
  - Ælfwynn the second lady of Mercia (918 only)

Children of Edward:

- Ælfweard
- Edwin (d.933 ætheling)
- Eadgifu ---- King Charles III of the West Franks
  - Louis (b.920)
- Eadgyth ---- Otto prince of the East Franks
- Eadhild ---- Hugh count of the Franks
- Ælfgifu ---- Prince from the Alps
- Æthelhild vowess at Wilton Nunnery
- Eadflæd nun at Wilton Nunnery
- m3 Eadgifu
  - Eadred (b.c.923), ætheling
  - Edmund (b.c.921), ætheling
  - Eadburh nun at the Nunnaminster

Edmund's children:
- Ælfthryth countess of Flanders ---- Baldwin count of Flanders d.918
  - Arnulf count of Flanders (918–965)
  - Adelolf count of Boluogne (918–933)
- Æthelweard
  - Ælfwine
  - Æthelwine

CAST OF CHARACTERS
(ALL HISTORICAL UNLESS UNDERLINED AND THEN FICTIONAL CHARACTERS)

The English
The Family of Alfred the Great (reigned 871–899 – king of Wessex)
m. Ealhswith
Æthelflæd, the lady of Mercia (d.918)
m. Æthelred of Mercia (d.c.911)
Ælfwynn, the second lady of Mercia (918 only)
Edward the Elder (reigned 899–924 – king of the Anglo-Saxons)
m1. Ecgwynn
Athelstan, initially king of Mercia from 924 and then king of the English with an 'imperium' over Britain
Edith – Athelstan's only full sister – married King Sihtric of York (Sihtric ua Ívarr), but she was repudiated, and Sihtric died in 926
m2. Ælfflæd
Ælfweard ruled Wessex for only days until his death in 925
Edwin (d.933), ætheling
Eadgifu married King Charles III of the West Franks (Charles the Simple) in 918
Their son, Louis b.920
Eadhild married Hugh, count of the Franks (died 937)

Eadgyth married Otto, prince of the East Franks
Ælfgifu married a prince from the Alps
m3. Eadgifu
Eadburh, nun at the Nunnaminster
Edmund (b.c.921), king of the English (939–)
m1. Ælfgifu, Edmund's first wife – their sons are Eadwig and Edgar (the youngest, Edgar, is fostered by Athelstan the ealdorman and his wife, Ælfwynn)
m2. Æthelflæd, Edmund's second wife
Eadred (b.c.923), ætheling of the English

The English ealdormen
Ealdorman Wulfgar
Ealdorman Athelstan of the East Angles (from 932), married to Ælfwynn, the lady of Mercia's daughter
Ealdorman Eadric, Ealdorman Athelstan's brother
Ealdorman Æthelwald, Ealdorman Athelstan's brother
Ealdorman Guthrum, now dead
Ealdorman Uhtred
Ealdorman Ealhhelm
Ealdorman Æthelmund
Ealdorman Athelstan (another one)
Wulfstan, archbishop of York
Oda, archbishop of Canterbury
<u>Wihtred, King Athelstan's messenger</u>
<u>Taliesen, scop</u>
Halfdene, Edmund's warrior
Ordhelm, Edmund's commander
Eglaf, man with the trained dogs
Oslac, Edmund's man

The Scots

The succession strictly alternated between two noble lines
Constantin, son of Aed, king of the Scots (reigned 900 to c.942)
Ildulb, son
<u>Giric – Ildulb's man</u>
Amlaib, grandson, son of Ildulb, died at Cait in 934
Cellach, illegitimate son, died at Brunanburh
<u>Alpin, son, was hostage at the English king's court, murdered</u>
<u>Mael Muire, daughter of Constantin (name is fictional, although we know she existed)</u>
<u>Her son with Gothfrith Gothfrithson</u>
Mael Coluim, son of Domnall, king of the Scots from c.942
Dub, Mael Coluim's son

Strathclyde
Dyfnwal, the king (known as Dyfnwal III in sources for the period)
Owain, Dyfnwal's father and predecessor (dies at Brunanburh)
Owain, Dyfnwal's son

The Welsh kings
Hywel, king of the South Welsh (Deheubarth), known as Hywel Dda
Owain ap Hywel, Rhodri ap Hywel and Edwin ap Hywel, Hywel's sons
Morgan ap Owain, king of Gwent
Cadfan, king of Glywysing

The independent kingdom of Bamburgh
Ealdred, king of Bamburgh (died 934)
<u>Ealdwulf, his son (might not be his son, but his brother)</u>
<u>Hild, Ealdred's wife</u>

The Dublin Norse and their allies

All claimed to be descended from Ívarr the Boneless, the Viking raider who led the Great Heathen Army of the 860s. Some would have been grandsons, others perhaps great-grandsons. The genealogy is particularly complicated.

Sihtric, king of York (Sihtric ua Ívarr/Sihtric Ívarrson), died c.926, married Athelstan's only natural sister, Edith

Anlaf Sihtricson, his son, not the son of Edith

Rognavaldr Anlafson, Anlaf Sihtricson's son

Haraldr Sihtricson, Anlaf's brother, now dead

Gothfrith, king of Dublin, grandson of Ívarr, died in 934

Olaf Gothfrithson, son of Gothfrith, great-grandson of Ívarr, died in 941

Camman, Olaf Gothfrithson's son

Rognavaldr Gothfrithson, Olaf Gothfrithson's brother, died at Brunanburh

Blakari Gothfrithson, Olaf Gothfrithson's brother

<u>Gothfrith, Olaf Gothfrithson's brother, king of Dublin</u>

Misc

Congalach Cnogba – high king of Ireland

Bishop Cathroe – missionary bishop from Metz. A 'life' was written about him c.1000

<u>Brother Cuthbert – member of his entourage</u>

Hakon, king of Norway – foster son to King Athelstan

Eirik Bloodaxe – see historical notes

Gunnhild, the wife of Eirik Bloodaxe

Denewulf – messenger

NOTE ON NAMES

The unwary traveller to this period will be faced with a profusion of names for the men and women in this story. Names may be given in Welsh, Gallic, Old Norse, Old English or with modern spellings. As such, you may find Olaf/Anlaf/Amlaib and be surprised to discover these are all the same person. You may find the name Eadward used, although the most common form is Edward. Equally, Æthelstan is the correct form of Athelstan. You will find names used interchangeably if you consult different sources, and secondary sources. The choice taken will depend, quite often, on the main sources the writer uses and on their own personal preference. I have attempted to use the names that are most recognisable for the individuals involved. Welsh and Norse convention usually names someone as the son of their father, e.g. Olaf Gothfrithson is Gothfrith's son; Owain ap Hywel is the son of Hywel. Names are often reused throughout the generations in all societies and, in England, families often name all of their children with names that begin with similar letters, e.g. Athelstan, Athelwald, etc.

All quotes from the Anglo-Saxon Chronicle are taken from *The*

Anglo-Saxon Chronicles, M. Swanton ed. and trans. All quotes from the Chronicle of the Kings of Alba are taken from *From Pictland to Alba* by Alex Woolf.

PROLOGUE

942, WINCHESTER, THE KINGDOM OF THE ENGLISH

Eadgifu, the lady of Wessex

My son, King Edmund, has been returned to me from the far northern extent of his kingdom. He's lauded by his witan as wise, just and a victorious warrior. The forts, or burhs as they're known, stretch across the land that's still disputed between the Norse kingdom of Jorvik and England's most northern reaches, a permanent bastion against anything the Norse of Jorvik might think to attempt. The Five Boroughs of Nottingham, Lincoln, Stamford, Derby and Leicester remain in the hands of the English.

King Edmund is triumphant.

I'm proud of all he's accomplished.

Now Edmund allows the warmth of good wine and the hearth to add a gentle flush to his cheeks while he sits with his wife, Ælfgifu, and young son, Eadwig. I smile to myself as I watch them laughing and joking.

There was a time I thought my son would never settle into family life. I feared that, like his father before him, he'd father children with many women and that on his death there'd be uproar and unease about who would succeed him. That will not now happen.

'Mother.'

I turn to my youngest son, Eadred, where he waits to refill my goblet. I offer him a smile of thanks. I might have ensured Edmund is the king of the English he should be, but Eadred is another matter entirely. He's still young, I know that, with fewer than twenty summers to his name, and yet he's often beset with illness. I fear it's like the ill health his grandfather, King Alfred, endured. As such, Eadred refrains from indulging in rich wine. At least, I reason, I'll never be forced to drag him from the stables with hay in his hair, and his trews around his ankles, as I've had to do with Edmund.

With a smile I recall when Edmund and Louis, now king of the West Franks, were caught drinking and forced to endure a long ceremony under the knowing gaze of King Athelstan. Those days seem decades ago now. I can't imagine King Edmund ever being found in such a position.

'My thanks, son,' I offer, mindful that Eadred does well to serve me wine while drinking boiled water himself, flavoured with sweet-smelling herbs to aid his belly. He eats food that's not as rich as others. He doesn't seem to suffer from failing to indulge as much as I might do. I'm used to the ways of the court. And the fine food. All the same, despite his more restricted diet, Eadred is becoming an excellent warrior.

'Does he truly not realise?' Eadred questions, jutting his chin towards his brother. Edmund sits before the men and women of his court. He's relaxed, wrapped in a thick cloak with fur-lined boots upon his feet. Athelstan ran a more formal court, but as we celebrate Christ's Mass in much more comfort than three winters ago when news of Olaf Gothfrithson's seizure of York ran rife through the court after the tragic and unexpected death of Athelstan, everyone is at their ease.

England's safe and secure. The burh walls of Mexburh, Kexburh and Coningsburh are garrisoned. Anlaf Sihtricson is quiet in his kingdom, licking his wounds after failing to emulate Olaf Gothfrithson, and there's nothing to fear. We can enjoy the season. We can luxuriate in the warmth and fine food. We can, dare I say it, relax for the first time in my many years at the West Saxon court knowing that the enemy are not about to attack.

'No, Edmund suspects nothing. He even saw the scop, Taliesen, this morning and didn't make the connection. No doubt, he thinks Taliesen will narrate the victory he and Athelstan accomplished at the battle of Brunanburh against Constantin of the Scots and Olaf Gothfrithson of the Dublin Norse, and nothing else.'

'Then, Mother, it's to be hoped Taliesen's written a song as good as that to recount to us.'

I smile at my son, resisting the temptation to run my hand through his tousled hair. After all, he's a man now. I should remember that. That he shows no remorse for not being included alongside his brother is a testament to his nature. He didn't fight beside Edmund. With only a small son, and his brother who could become king had Edmund perished, Eadred was forced to remain in Winchester while his brother found triumph against the enemy.

'It is, yes. He must extol Edmund's virtues,' I agree. I consider the scop, Taliesen. There was a time I didn't trust him and felt King Athelstan erred in doing so after he was brought before him by King Hywel of the Welsh, as the cause of the unease amongst the Welsh, the Norse and the people of the Scots. But, in the last five years, Taliesen has proven himself a loyal supporter of Athelstan and then Edmund. I know the words he'll speak today are inspiring. When men and women hear of Edmund's victory over the Norse last year, they'll forget the attack ended in a truce. In time, that truce will not matter. There will be war. Soon. Anlaf Sihtricson is weak. Edmund is not. He merely needs time to prepare for such a huge offensive against the Norse.

For now, we can enjoy the peace of the winter season, warm in our beds, secure in the knowledge that Edmund's task of once more uniting the Danish Five Boroughs with England will not need to be done again. Even now, the court abounds with men and women who hold influence within Derby, Stamford, Leicester, Nottingham and Lincoln. There's a gabble of voices from many places, Frankish, Norse, some from even further afield. Like his brother, Edmund presides over a court that's rich and vibrant.

The problem of York, and the fact that Anlaf Sihtricson is still king there, will resolve itself shortly.

Gurgling laughter has me gazing at my grandson. It's a strange feeling to know that one day Eadwig will hopefully rule England. He's so small, I can't imagine men and women will ever obey his every command, but that's how it will be. It was the same with Edmund.

Eadred nudges me, and with eyes alight, I watch Taliesen bow to Edmund and his wife, to me and Eadred, for Eadred remains his brother's successor, an ætheling beside Eadwig, until Eadwig becomes a man. Both Eadred and Eadwig are the sons of kings.

Taliesen then turns to the wider audience and bows to them. A hush greets his actions. All know that Taliesen is a man with great skill for evoking the glory of battle.

With a serious expression on his face, he strums his lyre and begins to sing.

> *Here King Edmund, lord of the English,*
> *guardian of his kinsmen, beloved instigator of deeds*
> *Conquered Mercia, bounded by The Dore,*
> *Whitwell Gap and Humber river,*
> *broad ocean-stream; five boroughs:*

Leicester and Lincoln,
and Nottingham, likewise Stamford also
And Derby. Earlier the Danes were
under Northmen, subjected by force
in heathens' captive fetters,
for a long time until they were ransomed again.
To the honour of Edward's son,
Protector of warriors, King Edmund.

I smile with pleasure at hearing this new scop song singing the praises of my son. Those lucky enough to be within the hall roar their approval, raising drinking goblets to toast the triumph of their king. King Edmund inclines his head towards me, and towards Taliesen. His face is even more flushed.

We've heard the song of Edmund and Athelstan's victory at Brunanburh on many occasions. As monumental as it was, as delighted as we were by the words that Taliesen composed on that occasion, it's time for King Edmund, my son, and the second king of the English, to take the acclaim of the men and women of England. His brother had years to succeed, Edmund has had barely three to accomplish the same dominance over his enemies.

I raise my wine goblet, shimmering beneath the bright lights of the candles, as Taliesen strums his lyre softly, as pleased with the reception as Edmund. Edmund mirrors my action. We share a moment of triumph.

King Edmund didn't take kindly to having the kingship thrust on his shoulders when Athelstan died.

I know he'd still rather Athelstan was king, but time can't be rewritten. England is his to rule.

'Long live the king,' I chorus, adding my voice to the rightful acclaim my son has earned.

PART I

Earlier the Danes were
>under Northmen, subjected by force
>in heathens' captive fetters,
>for a long time until they were ransomed again.
>To the honour of Edward's son,
>Protector of warriors, King Edmund.

>— ANGLO-SAXON CHRONICLE, A TEXT, FOR 942

1

943, SCONE, THE KINGDOM OF THE SCOTS

Ildulb, prince of the Scots

I eye Mael Coluim with contempt that I try to keep from showing. We've long been enemies and allies. My father's lengthy reign made us uneasy with one another. If my father never dies, then how could Mael Coluim become king and then die himself, opening the way for me?

This new development, my father's abdication, forced upon him by Mael Coluim, in a moment of weakness, has placed me in an awkward position. Should I hate Mael Coluim for my father's sake or rejoice that I'm now a step closer to the kingship I've so long coveted? I'm not sure what to think. While my father still lives, I don't believe anything has truly changed.

If Mael Coluim should die, men will bray for my father's return. It's my father they trust so much they've turned it to hate. The anger at his failure against the English has made it too easy for them to accept another as king. But that battle, between the English and the Norse, disintegrated almost before it had started. It did little but make the men of Jorvik look weak and, by association, myself. And by implication, my father, who gave me the permission to become involved. Mael Coluim used that to his advantage to have my father ejected from the kingship.

Am I, after all, to blame for my father's abdication? Did Mael Coluim play me and allow me to get too deeply involved in politics and bloodshed beyond our borders, only to watch gleefully as it all went hideously wrong? Or was he just opportunistic? I suspect the latter. Mael Coluim can only find his nose because it's on his ugly face.

'My lord, Ildulb,' my new king calls to me. I present myself to Mael Coluim with the same arrogance he showed my father before ousting him from power. I'm the heir to the kingdom, no matter that my father yet lives. It is the way of our people that the kingship passes from cousin to cousin, and not from father to son. I will show Mael Coluim respect while presenting myself to the rest of the court as his worthy successor. If he should fall at the first problem, I must be the man they consider, not my ageing father.

'My lord king?' I enquire. It's painful to offer the man my respect as he sits in my father's chair at the front of our royal settlement in Scone. My father lives in banishment and exile at St Andrew's. He'll pray until his knees and mouth both run to dust. His constant exhortations to our Lord God are for the souls of those who've gone before him, my son killed at Cait by King Edmund when he was little more than a boy, his son, Cellach, killed at Brunanburh, and his other son, Alpin, murdered by my sister when mad with grief. What a family we are. Perhaps he's cursed to live so long? Maybe God's punishing him with such a long life? I wonder if he considers living through so many winters a torment.

'Your father's settled?' Mael Coluim questions, his rich voice grating. He wears beautiful clothes, bright with thrice-dyed cloth and thread. His soft hands caress the great wooden chair my father used to sit within. But his familiar face is hard. His mouth has always been mean and measly, no matter that he tries to hide it behind a full moustache. There's more hair on his chin than on his head these days.

It was my responsibility to ensure my father, Constantin, made his way to St Andrew's. It was my responsibility to safeguard his compliance with the enforced change in kingship. That was Mael Coluim's way of punishing me while testing my loyalty. I was tempted not to do it, to refuse to be complicit in my father's disgrace, but my father begged me to fulfil my new king's orders. I couldn't deny his request. He is still my father and the rightful king of the kingdom of the Scots.

Even with Constantin's grief-hooded eyes and sagging shoulders, so sunken to have his power ripped from him, my father is a wiser man than I'll ever be. He didn't contest the delegation led by Mael Coluim and his supporters. Not that he went like a meek lamb to the slaughter, but neither did he fight for his kingship. I wondered about that at the time, considering if he was as old and tired as Mael Coluim implied.

I know better now. I've seen the rod of implacable iron that holds Constantin upright in the face of such an affront, accomplished with words and weapons. I know that whatever happens, my father is more than aware of everything. I know he'll fight for his kingship when the time is right. He's not given up. If anything, he's even more determined now.

'My father's pleased to be where he can pray and offer his uninterrupted worship to his Lord God,' I reply pleasantly. My father ordered me to speak these words when I returned to the court. From the flash of fury in Mael Coluim's eyes, once more my father has read the situation better than I have, and he's not even here.

'He was pleased?' he repeats, the inflexion revealing anger that my father might be happy with his new occupation. Mael Coluim believes my family should be wrathful for Constantin's removal from the kingship. He little understands my father, even though he's known him far longer than even I have. Mael Coluim's a physical embodiment of the vast length of my father's reign, with his greying hair, gaunt face and slightly protruding belly lying heavily on him within the royal chair. Not even thrice-dyed cloth can mask that.

I nod, just enough to show that I'm honouring him as my king while agreeing with my initial words. His eyes flash again, greeted by a wave of sound moving through his body of counsellors who number many, many more than my father would ever allow power within his court. This is why Mael Coluim's coup worked. My father was of iron resolve and a true force to counter. He made the decisions for his kingdom. He didn't allow the self-interests of others to temper his actions.

Some would say he didn't listen, was too egotistical and thought he could rule alone. Some might say that.

Even I might have but age, time and watching my father lose what he's held for so long has made me appreciate his decisions. Already, these other men, dressed in finery or war gear, hold more menace in the court than my father ever allowed. The court isn't so much a place of firm governance but a hotspot for angry words and even more enraged retaliations. I've been gone a month, but I know what's happened in my absence. Mael Coluim might just have bitten off more than he can comfortably swallow.

The men intend to take action. They aim for those actions to be seen. But they are not united in that purpose. I envisage a kingdom riven by the rivalries that once split this land into more than one kingdom. I see a return to the status quo that existed before my father came to rule, when we weren't Scots, but the men of Alba or the men of Pictland. When we were not united. When we allowed ourselves to fight amongst ourselves and allowed our enemies to triumph.

'My father's an old man. He's outlived many of his contemporaries. He hopes to spend more time praying for their souls and those of his family. I thought you'd be content, my lord king?' I add enough nuance to make it a question and a censure.

My father demanded I add this into the conversation at some point, Mael Coluim's words when he ousted my father ringing loudly in his ears. I can hear every pointed statement now, sounding in my head as I pretend to be a loyal servant of the new king. Mael Coluim spoke words that should never have been said aloud. My father has cajoled me into repeating them as often and as frequently as I can, now that he has no place at the court because Mael Coluim has taken it from him.

Constantin also taught me how to carry myself. How to stand aloof from this kingship because he foresees nothing but trouble. Constantin sees portents that only age can allow a man to have. I feel as though he holds more power than the seers that live in their hallowed caves and pretend to see a man's future, the men my father would revile for their unchristian ways.

He either taught me or, for the first time in my life, I allowed myself to listen. My father's changed position has made me more amenable to him. I no longer have to fight him for every position of power I want. No, now I have to become entangled with Mael Coluim. I thought my father was the greater menace, but Mael Coluim eyes me with condescension and lines his grown sons up against me. The sudden reversal of fortune is dizzying.

Why only now do I fully appreciate my father's power and how great he was? Why only now am I capable of having the skills he always decried me for lacking?

Mael Coluim, his eyes black as night, doesn't know how to react to my report. I can tell. He opens his mouth to continue to berate me, and yet what can he say? They're his words, not mine. To keep the illusion for the court, he must accept that my father is indeed happy and is doing what Mael Coluim demanded from him upon removing him from the kingship.

The gaggle of men at his side divide their attention between him and me. I consider what they're thinking.

I'm forcibly reminded of that day, only a month ago, when Mael Coluim marched into my father's hall and spoke the fateful words with his little moths fluttering after him. They reminded me of sheep following their shepherd. I'd love to be the wolf running among them, taking a bite where and when I will, allowing my instinct and nature to override all good reason. But again, my father has cautioned me against doing that.

It was a dark day when Mael Coluim came before my father, wearing his warrior clothing for all that the Scots were at war with no one after the unsatisfactory conclusion to my trip south. I watched in horrified shock, my father with only mild interest. He had, to all intents and purposes, been sleeping soundly in his royal chair. He'd woken, eyes repeatedly blinking as Mael Coluim stepped directly into his line of sight. To all who watched, he appeared as an old man, shrunken and unkinglike. Lost and without anyone to defend him.

I understood then that my father knew about Mael Coluim's intentions.

Still, my eyes narrowed as I watched. Mael Coluim, his gaze alight with far more than just the glow of the candles and the fire burning at the hall's centre, set about usurping my father. I knew pure hate for him, a foreboding infecting me and making my hand subconsciously seek out the weapons I usually stored at my waist. But I was not wearing them before the king, as my father had earlier dictated.

I realised then that my father had known how I'd react, and he'd been right. I'd have sliced Mael Coluim's neck from his shoulders and relished the thrill of his blood sliding over my face and across my hands, slick like water in the river. I might even have been tempted to lick some of it from my hands, turning my teeth battle red and grimacing at the fluttering moths who forced Mael Coluim's hand. It was they who'd finally managed to rile Mael Coluim enough to take irreversible action against their holy king, my father.

'My lord king,' he mockingly called, my father jumping at his shouted voice, intended to reach everyone within the great hall. At once, all actions within the room stopped, even the bloody hounds realising that something monumental was being played out before them, and leaving their bones unlicked on the floor.

'My lord, Mael Coluim?' my father offered tiredly, his hands shaking as he pulled his fur across his chill knees. It was a cold day, but even I was surprised by my father's skills in deception. I wished I'd been able to see Mael Coluim's response, but I'd been watching my father. Since then, I've imagined the gleeful look on the bastard's face. More and more armed men entered the king's hall, their hands menacingly enclosed around swords and seaxes, their stances angry and purposeful.

That was it. They'd come to kill my father.

Only then did my father's eyes rake me in, his gaze firm, meaningful, challenging me to not act, as I wanted. Just daring me to throttle the man before me. I took a firm breath, tried to cool myself, but I was not able to stay my hand completely. I walked to stand as close to my father as Mael Coluim, taking up my position beside his shoulder.

Mael Coluim twisted then, his eyes on his co-conspirators, not noticing me, jumping with fear when faced with my anger on turning back around. I don't know what expression I wore. I imagine it was murderous.

'My lord king,' Mael Coluim shouted once more, spittle flowing from his mouth with his uncontained triumph. No one stood with me to protect my father. I'd like to think everyone else was frozen into inaction with shock. 'I've come to take your kingdom. You're old and weak, more fitted to be a monk than a king. You spend too much time on your knees, too much time away from the court in St Andrew's. The men of our land have spoken, demanded, as is rightful, that I should take the kingdom under my protective wing.' Mael Coluim affected an incline of his head towards those supporting him. My heart turned to stone as I realised who'd betrayed my father. A mix between those I'd long counted as his loyal followers and those who'd sell their mother for a prized cow. Some surprised me. Others annoyed me with their predictability.

Barely drawing breath, Mael Coluim continued as my ire swelled.

'Your failures against the English kings, not just Athelstan but also Edmund. Your failure to protect our land from the depravations of the Norse raiders even when you ally with them and have a grandson who shares their blood. They will not stand. Your insistence on controlling the religious life of our people will no longer be tolerated. Your sons have no support.'

I wanted to argue at that, but I bit my tongue.

'I possess that support, and I'll be king now. I demand, and I have the backing of the great men within this hall who escort me, that you stand, hand me the accoutrements of your kingship, and take yourself to your beloved St Andrew's. Go where you can pray and offer your uninterrupted worship to your Lord God. Ask him to forgive your failures, for the people of the Scots will no longer do so.' His tone was contemptuous. I knew real hatred then, cursing through every finger, every toe, to the very top of my head. I don't know how I didn't kill him. I still don't.

My father watched him, mouth opening and closing silently, playing the part of the old, weak man, unable to mount any response to Mael Coluim's demands. But I saw his eyes darting around, looking, taking it all in. He'd marked every man there, every small boy and every babe at the breast. Constantin licked his dry lips. I expected, even though I should have known better, that, at any moment, his battle voice would issue from his mouth, ring from the rafters and shake the spiders from their webs.

What I hadn't expected was nothing. Not a single thing.

Constantin simply stood, bowed his head and walked from the hall. He reached out his hand, no longer shaking but firm and steady, and grasped mine. In that touch was a word of caution, an entreaty to hold my peace, and not take any action I might regret. Sadness touched his hard eyes. I swallowed and allowed him to go with not one word of denial.

In that action, I understood a great deal about my father. An old man he might have been, even to me, his son, but he knew more than everyone else in that hall. As people had held their breath, waiting, as I had, for him to deny Mael Coluim, to make a war of the hall, to start a battle that would see his family annihilated by the supporters of Mael Coluim, he'd won an even greater battle.

He'd given Mael Coluim nothing. He'd simply gone.

He did what Mael Coluim asked of him, but not at all what Mael Coluim had wanted. Even now, the defeated look on Mael Coluim's face brings a smile to mine. It should have been his moment of triumph, his greatest achievement in over forty winters. But while he'd hoped to gain, he'd simply lost more than he'd ever had.

He'd lost the opportunity to kill my father's family, to belittle him, to take blade and iron and hold it against my neck, that of my new sons, that of Olaf Gothfrithson's small son, still firmly in my sister's arms.

A beat, a pause, as everyone in that hall listened to the slow shuffle of an old man walking away from his kingship without even a look behind him.

What did that say to Mael Coluim's followers? What sort of message did that send to the kingdom? Was it my father's ultimate betrayal?

Wrong-footed and deprived of the drama he'd hoped to enact, Mael Coluim fixed his gaze on me. In that look, I saw his worries and fears laid bare, saw him for a fool. All of his life, all of it since he'd realised what breed of man he was, what he was heir to, he'd railed against my father and his laws, restrictions and expectations. Suddenly, he was alone, bereft. Who did he have to fight now? Who would guide his steps?

I smirked at him, enjoying his moment of triumph turned to despair. Others might have misinterpreted it and seen in my smile an acceptance of what had happened, a delight that my father was no longer king, that I was one step closer to the kingship. Let them think what they wanted.

I turned to follow my father, his footsteps finally fading into the distance.

'My lord Ildulb,' Mael Coluim had said, his voice small and quiet and not at all the conquering king as it had been only moments before.

'My lord king?' I enquired, somehow ensuring the words didn't convey my distaste for him.

'Take him to St Andrew's. Ensure he stays there.'

'My lord king?' I asked again, surprised by the task. His eyes blazed. Did he expect me to kill my father? To ensure something befell my father to make his seizure of the kingship somehow serendipitous?

Mael Coluim sighed deeply.

'Ensure it's done well and with due respect. Your father was a great king.'

I nodded and resumed my escape from the hall, the centre of my father's power, or so Mael Coluim thought. In my wake, my children, my tormented sister, her delightful son and anyone else who was firmly of my father's line exited the hall. There was no need for any of us to witness Mael Coluim's greatest mistake.

Watching him now, I know that the last month has been much less than he'd thought it would be. I hold my amusement in check.

He needs my father to have done something, anything, to make him appear strong against my father's weaker nature. He needs my father to have shown himself to be self-interested and to be working against the Scots, perhaps with the Norse. He'll not gain that. My father, pretending meekness and illness, a feigned infirmity, has ensured that Mael Coluim holds the kingdom, but with growing unease. It's unnatural for Mael Coluim to claim the kingship while the previous king still lives.

He's miscalculated. Badly.

In St Andrew's, my father pretends to his meekness, but he's scheming. He'll rise again. I know it.

Mael Coluim knows it.

It's only a matter of time before Mael Coluim finds himself without a kingdom.

I could laugh.

Mael Coluim's actions have made him weaker than he's ever been. In the reflected light of that, my father is a greater man, an even mightier man – a true king of the kingdom of the Scots.

Mael Coluim's days are numbered, but until then, well, I'll be attentive to him and play the part of heir-in-waiting as he once did in my father's court.

I doubt he's spent a single comfortable night since he became king.

The bloody fool!

2

943, THE KINGDOM OF JORVIK

Anlaf Sihtricson, king of Jorvik

Blakari Gothfrithson struts about the great hall as though he owns the place. I've heard the rumours. I'm not such a fool as to think my treaty with the English king has been well received amongst my fellow Norse. I know something's coming. I need to determine where the real menace lies. Is it Blakari, with his drinking and love of women and his resolve to revel in battle lust, or is it the other great man of Jorvik, Archbishop Wulfstan? The one is more English in his outlook than the other, and yet he's decided to cause as many problems as possible for the English king from his privileged position outside his reach. Archbishop Wulfstan's master is the pope, not King Edmund.

I almost think Archbishop Wulfstan was more upset with the peace arrangement agreed at Lincoln than I was. I believe he fancies himself a greater warrior than me. It couldn't be more amusing. Wulfstan's a fat little duck, waddling everywhere, stinking of grease and sweat, stuffing his face with anything he can find, and yet he thinks himself a warrior. Perhaps not a fighter in the sense that I infer it, with blades as weapons, but certainly a warrior of his God. And, if I'm not mistaken, of his bloody ambitions. Archbishop Wulfstan sees himself as a missionary amongst the people of Jorvik, and as such wins the acclaim of the pope.

I find it more likely he's a troublemaker. In the past, I've not let it upset my plans, but then, I always used to be a part of his plans. Now I feel the menace emanating from him. He means me harm. It's not a comforting thought. I might have warriors at my command, but Archbishop Wulfstan has the confidence of his faith.

My loyal men tell me Blakari, a man who detests the fat little scrunched-up face of Wulfstan, is regularly in contact with him. Do the pair plot against me? Or does Wulfstan mean to cause unease between us by having me question Blakari's loyalty? Does Wulfstan seek to undermine my ability to rule Jorvik? I'd like to see him do better.

It's a pretty little conundrum I've given myself. My alliance with the English king has allowed me to return to Jorvik, while keeping some of the gains made into the northern reaches of his kingdom by Olaf Gothfrithson. Admittedly, not many of them. Olaf Gothfrithson was well connected. Blakari was his brother, and he was related to Constantin of the Scots through marriage.

I knew it would be difficult to convince my followers of the need for the new alliance with the English king. I did not anticipate it would be this difficult. They allow the ignobility of the alliance to plague them, and turn away from me. Whether they look to Blakari or Archbishop Wulfstan, I'm unsure.

I see the truth of it on their faces. I don't need those who remain loyal telling tales. I sense my power waxes. But, until I know who my enemy is, I can't counter the threat.

I admit, it's long been the curse of the Norse. There's always another who looks shinier than a fresh-struck silver dirham to take their allegiance and promise them more.

I suspect it's Blakari Gothfrithson who'll take Jorvik from my control. I believe he'll do it soon with the support of Archbishop Wulfstan. I'd like to think Blakari allows himself to be led, either willingly or unwillingly, towards the kingship of Jorvik by Archbishop Wulfstan, but I'm far from convinced.

Blakari's always resented my place here. He thinks Jorvik should simply have been his on his brother's murder. But that's not the way of our people. I reigned alongside his brother, not him. The kingdom was mine to rule, not his, when his brother died. Only on my death will Jorvik become his. And only if he can hold it against the ravages of the English king and the unease that infects the borderlands with the English holding firm not far to the south of Jorvik.

I also harbour suspicions about current events in the kingdom of the Scots.

It was Olaf Gothfrithson who forged an alliance with Constantin. It should have crumbled on his death, but the presence of Constantin's grandchild, Olaf's son, in the Scots kingdom has ensured the old hoary bastard looks to interfere in my kingdom. I know where his ambitions lead him.

In the past, Constantin saw this land as a buffer zone between the English and his new kingdom united for a few years more than England. That strategy had helped and hindered my predecessor. Sending his son, Ildulb, and his likely successor, Mael Coluim, south to assist in my attack against Edmund had been a stroke of genius. At the time, I'd taken it as a positive that Constantin intended to continue to support me, no matter Olaf's death. In the wake of my failure, I'm no longer sure it was support. Perhaps it was a tacit acceptance of the inevitable triumph of the reinvigorated English. Maybe it was just an attempt to kill off Mael Coluim once and for all and allow his son, Ildulb, the kingship. If it was that, it failed.

The English are like bloody hunting hounds. They won't relax their jaws until the prey is well and truly dead. I don't like being anyone's prey, let alone King Edmund of the English.

News from across the border with Constantin's homeland is suspiciously quiet. I'm confident I'll be sent word if the old king dies. But I've heard nothing.

The interplay of individuals in Constantin's kingdom delights me with its confusing nature. It's almost akin to how my people are ruled. I find it hard to believe that after more than forty winters, Constantin has lost his kingdom to a usurper. Neither can I completely shake the feeling that this is what's happened.

Mael Coluim's a slippery character. I more tolerated him and chaffed at his comments than warmed to his abrasive nature. For a man who's known all his life he would one day rule, he lacks the easy way men need to earn the respect of others.

Ildulb's little better. I find him hard to befriend. Of course, I know the man's history, his grudge against the English king being far more personal than anyone else's because Edmund killed his son many years ago when both of them were mere boys.

The men of my family, with all of its twisting branches and strange forks, are challenging and contrary. The sons, grandsons, nephews and cousins of past kings, of either Dublin or Jorvik, all wear their entitlement to kingdoms and allegiances as though born with them. That knowledge has always formed a part of our very beings. I know becoming a leader of men such as this takes great skill, diplomacy and a willingness to turn to bloody means with the slightest hint of trouble. I have those skills. I've lived long enough to enforce my claims to rule. I'm not about to lose everything because of a little piggy Englishman who shouldn't even be allowed into

Jorvik, let alone permitted to sit and eat in the same hall as I do, but gains admission because of his faith.

'What ails you?' Blakari questions. He sits beside me at the front of the great hall, the central hearth warming our faces, not our arses. His voice is filled with wry amusement.

I wrench my thoughts from my worries and glare at him. He's interrupted my deliberations just when I might have been about to resolve my problems. I imagine he knows as much, and that's why he's done so. Sometimes, it's better to have enemies rather than allies dressed up as enemies.

'Nothing, just considering what's happening in the land of the Scots.' This seems to be the least contentious matter to discuss. After all, Blakari is my subordinate. He knows much that I do.

'Why, do you think the old bugger's finally dead?' Blakari queries, his eyes narrowing. I wish he'd learn to mask his thoughts. The raw ambition suddenly evident on his face is unpleasant to behold.

'I don't know, but the silence is unnerving.'

'What silence? We had a messenger only the other day. When was it? Monday, Tuesday? I can't keep bloody track.'

'Tuesday,' I mutter, filling in the information for him. And that's another thing. Blakari's no tactician. He remembers little or nothing, and the past is a place he only ever considers when someone tries to question his parentage, and his right to be a king above that of others. He sees what else has happened before as irrelevant and focuses only on what he hopes to gain. Whether he truly mourns his brother or not, he uses it when it's important, and the rest of the time could happily forget Olaf Gothfrithson's existence.

'Tuesday then,' Blakari repeats, reaching out to take a cup of ale and swill it around his mouth. Not for the first time, I realise how much more congenial it would be to have his brother sitting beside me. Olaf Gothfrithson might have been the more senior of the two of us, but I know I'm a cunning and devious man, unlike Blakari. I see little in Blakari's future but more wine and ale, and more little bastards running around with his likeness. I can only guess how many sons and daughters he has haunting Jorvik.

Sourly, I acknowledge this is exactly the reason the kingship of my ancestry has been diluted. If any – and I mean *any* – of my ancestors, had managed to do less shagging and more ruling, Jorvik itself would be far more secure. At the moment, there are too many people claiming descent from Ívarr the Boneless. There are too few kingdoms to share with so many claimants.

I shift uneasily. My thoughts are dark and unpleasant for so early in the day. But I can't dismiss them. Last night my dreams were disturbed. Today, my contemplations are just as troubled.

Not for the first time, I wish I could ship those who don't respect me back to their homeland in the north or off to Iceland or the outer isles, Greenland, the Faroes. Anywhere would be better than having them here, trying to leapfrog each other to become king when I've won the position by stint of ambition and no small amount of brilliance.

'The messenger said nothing on Tuesday about King Constantin's health or position,' Blakari continues, dragging me back to the reality of here and now.

'Exactly,' I say, feeling my ire rise at the man's inability to think beyond the obvious.

'Does he usually?' Blakari presses. He attempts to sound interested but fails as he eyes up the slave girl bringing food to the table. She wears little and sweats copiously in the heat from the massive fire driving back the cold of winter. He licks his lips, and anyone who watches him knows where his urges have taken him. The girl understands he watches her and, no doubt, in a matter of moments, he'll leave me and ride her.

'You'd know if you kept your cock in your trews,' I huff in frustration.

Blakari chuckles darkly. He loves women, all women. He sees beauty in anyone. I'm far pickier in the women I choose to bed.

'I normally get some hint of what's happening at the court of the kingdom of the Scots, but not this time. Something's happened, and they're not prepared to tell us yet.'

'You worry too much,' Blakari quips, his attention almost wholly focused on the young woman's sweating cleavage and shapely curves. He licks his lips with more than delight. The woman won't be keeping her clothes on for much longer.

I've a sudden thought that the slaves take it in turn to entice Blakari away from his duties. Lying in his bed must be better than working in the kitchen or being forced to sew all day to ensure the men of the hall are always adequately clothed. It might give them some enjoyment as well. Blakari's had so much practice; he must know how to please his partners.

I stop myself from a tetchy reply. I've repeatedly bickered with Blakari about his need to pay more attention. All it gets me is more and more of his disdain. I should let him make an arse of himself. Blakari's welcome to the girl, and she to him. I've other worries to consume me.

My thoughts return to the king of the Scots. Am I allowing my fears to overwhelm me? Surely someone as strong as Constantin would never lose his kingdom? But if he's been removed from the kingship, it doesn't bode well for me.

Resolved, I stand. It's much better to ride north and find out what's happening than waste my time worrying about it.

Leaving has a dual purpose. If Blakari intends to steal my kingdom with the help of Archbishop Wulfstan, I'd rather he did it while I was away. In that case, I'll never know the identity of the traitors.

As I rise, I hear the noise I've been dreading and anticipating. Whatever Blakari's been conducting with the slave girl, he stands before me with the insufferable Archbishop Wulfstan at his side. The slave girl has slunk unhappily from the hall. I wish I could do the same.

I slump to my seat. I've no intention of making this easy for them. They might think they're the intelligent ones and the men who've thought of every eventuality. Something, however, will happen to make them rue their decision here. I'm convinced of it.

'King Anlaf,' Archbishop Wulfstan announces in his insufferably annoying voice. Cynically, I notice he's made some effort to look the part of the man of God he always pretends to be. I've always known he cloaks himself in layers of deceit and lies. I'd not realised it extended down to his very clothes. He's been hiding things from me for longer than I thought.

Now Archbishop Wulfstan wears a thick cloak even though it's stiflingly warm in the hall. The red flashing fur of a fox expertly rims its collar. I appreciate the irony. The sly fox is being worn by the artful archbishop. An amused smirk touches my face despite everything.

'Archbishop Wulfstan,' I offer, with no hint of a question.

'The people of Jorvik have spoken. They've told me of their fears you can no longer lead them and reward them as they expect. Not only are you a beaten man, you don't follow the same God these people pray to in their church. They demand, as do I, with the full authority of the Christian church behind me, that you leave the kingdom.'

'Just who are these people?' I rebuff. Now I'm betrayed, I want to know their identity. That way, I can exact my revenge when I return. I already know I'm leaving Jorvik today. Tomorrow, and the next day, well, they're both days that hold the promise of retribution.

'The people of Jorvik, your warriors, Blakari's warriors, even the new king of the Scots, Mael Coluim, have offered our humble contingent their support.'

Ah, finally the truth emerges. Blakari has been aware all along. Or has he? The raising of the man's eyebrows as Archbishop Wulfstan speaks makes me wonder if this is news to him. Just how many men does Wulfstan communicate with as an equal? I've long suspected him of being in contact with the English king, and certainly the Archbishop of Canterbury. I've underestimated the web of connections and lies he weaves with his fat little fingers. I wonder how he has the stamina for it.

'Bring them before me. I wish to see them.' Arrogantly, I look behind Archbishop Wulfstan, as if seeking out these other men, for Wulfstan and Blakari stand alone. I begin to hope the support they think they have is more a figment of their imagination.

Blakari shifts on his feet. He looks regal but uncomfortable. What has he bartered for his chance to sit where his brother once did? I imagine he's converted to Archbishop Wulfstan's Christian God. How else could Wulfstan speak with the authority of his 'Christian church'? Conversion is a primary tactic for these religious men. Conversion makes idiots see everything the way the holy men wish it to be seen. I could almost pity Blakari, only this is an ancient game of power. The words of Archbishop Wulfstan mean little to me. It's the threat of violence that Blakari brings to their unholy alliance that makes it powerful.

Archbishop Wulfstan's wheedling ways might well work with the English king and his desire to be seen as fervently in his beliefs as his dead older brother. In Jorvik, the men and women, the majority not sharing any kinship with the English king, view religion in a different light.

Archbishop Wulfstan's Christianity is as much of a weapon as a blade and just as pointed and sharp, only with the possibility of a significant reversal. It's easier to stop being a bloody Christian than it is to stop being dead.

The image brings a smirk to my face – Archbishop Wulfstan peers at me from behind his fat little cheeks in surprise.

He thinks he knows the ways of Norse men and women, but he doesn't. There's no permanence to our arrangements. There has never been. We're opportunistic, not kings for life. Not like the English and their 'royal' Wessex dynasty.

Archbishop Wulfstan will learn, hopefully at the end of my seax or sword. Then, his Christian church will have no means of protecting him.

Blakari will certainly learn the folly of his actions on the edge of my blade.

3

943, WINCHESTER, THE KINGDOM OF THE ENGLISH

Edmund, king of the English

My ealdormen are before me, Athelstan, Æthelwald, Eadric, Uhtred, Wulfgar, Ealhhelm, another Athelstan and Æthelmund. I've gained the respect of all of them since my encounter with the Norse.

I don't know what my supporters expected from me, but it seems it wasn't such an effective response against our enemy. Men have died, men have been wounded and alliances have been frayed or broken, and yet the number of my supporters remains firm and has, indeed, grown. After all, it's not I who made a fool of myself and overextended my resources deep into enemy territory. No, it was Anlaf Sihtricson who did that.

Not that it makes my position any easier. Another bloodthirsty and land-hungry Norse bastard has replaced Anlaf. And yet. Well, I hold out the hope that my actions might have done even more harm than so far seems apparent.

My encounter with Anlaf Sihtricson weakened him. Blakari Gothfrithson stands in his place, but Blakari's also vulnerable. He's dependent on the goodwill of Wulfstan, Archbishop of York, and Wulfstan is a problem for Blakari. Wulfstan doesn't consider himself subject to my commands, as York lies outside my control. He says the pope is his master, but the pope is far distant from England, and York, and so really Wulfstan believes he has no master.

That will be his undoing. And, by association, also Blakari's.

The peace agreed with Anlaf has had catastrophic reverberations in the kingdom of the Scots. King Constantin, the long-lived hoary old bastard, has 'retired' to a monastery. Using the word 'retired' brings a smirk to my lips. It doesn't mean what it implies. While Constantin wasn't directly involved in Anlaf's move against the English, sending his son, Ildulb, and his acknowledged successor, Mael Coluim, in his stead, the treaty agreed with Anlaf has left Mael Coluim the stronger man. Tired of waiting for the king to die, and with the support of his countrymen, he's usurped Constantin's power.

Both Mael Coluim and Blakari have other, better men waiting to claw back their kingdoms when they lose the support of those who placed them in the position of king. I don't foresee much security for either kingdom. And now my ealdormen attend upon me. We must exploit this precarious situation in the neighbouring kingdoms.

Ealdorman Athelstan's grown in stature since his actions near Mexburh and the responsibility I placed on his shoulders to hold against the threat of the Norse of Jorvik. So have his brothers, Æthelwald and Eadric. The win, even if it was ultimately formalised in a treaty, has made us stronger and more secure in our abilities.

The ignominy of the first attacks on my kingdom has been erased. It needed to be if I were ever to earn the respect and trust that King Athelstan once held. Olaf Gothfrithson raided far and wide into England while my brother was barely cold in his grave. His murder in the lands that border the Scots and Bamburgh couldn't have happened to a nicer man.

Being a king, having a kingdom thrust onto my shoulders, wasn't the easiest way of coming to terms with Athelstan's unexpected death. When the time comes for a successor to take my place, either my son or my brother, should my son still be a child, I hope they're better prepared than I was. In that one way, my older half-brother coached me poorly. But then, his death was abrupt and unexpected. I thought he'd rule for many winters longer. So did he, it appears.

Ealdorman Athelstan meets my eye, a wry grin on his lips. He watches his brother, Eadric, pace the room. Eadric doesn't like to sit still, or stand still, or let his body stop at all. He's a man of constant action. He'd be marching on the weakened Norse kingdom of York if he could. In his mind, he's probably already at the gates of York.

I return Ealdorman Athelstan's grin. I might spend much of my time pretending to be a noble king, holier than any other, raised above them all by my anointing at my coronation, but I know I'm just a man, given to bleed and sickness just as any other. Athelstan is my oldest friend, as are his brothers. If I can't let my guard down before them, I'll always have to wear the mask of kingship, just as King Athelstan did.

Athelstan, I now realise, had even more to prove than I did when he became king. Overlooked by our father and unwanted by the men of the kingdom of Wessex, he worked hard to become the leader they thought they should have, an embodiment of our grandfather, King Alfred, the greatest king who ever lived. I smirk at that thought.

My grandfather, King Alfred. Men and women speak about him in hushed voices, almost as though he were a holy man, only to be mentioned in the vaguest terms and with the utmost respect. They speak of my father in normal tones, and my brother, well, they too think he was almost holy, but I happen to share their opinion. It doesn't annoy me as much as when they speak of my grandfather in such a way.

I never knew my grandfather. He was long dead when my father whelped me on his third wife. That my mother still lives while my father has been interred in his grave for over a decade and a half is a testament to her youth and my father's age at their marriage. It's not the most pleasant of thoughts, but I'm grateful to have my mother at my side.

King Edward liked women and littered the kingdom with a selection of sons and daughters. Some were far more suitable to rule than others. A few were fit for nothing but abandonment in a monastery or a nunnery. Others have enjoyed long lives while some perished before their time. I find it strange how so many different-tempered children could come from the same father.

I hope one day to see for myself, should I be blessed to be the father to more than one child.

Ealdorman Athelstan quirks his head to one side as he catches my smirk. I shake my head slightly. He doesn't have to know all my thoughts. I wouldn't want him to think that his brother only serves as amusement for me.

'We will wait,' I finally say into the superheated atmosphere. I think we should, and Ealdorman Athelstan's small nod indicates his agreement. We've only recently secured the treaty with the Norse kingdom of York. We should savour it. It allows us time to rebuild.

'My lord king?' Ealdorman Eadric queries, his face creased in unhappiness. 'The men and women of York, just as in the Five Boroughs before them, want you to be their king.' His voice is pleasant, but firm resolve makes it sound hard, as though it were a weapon in and of itself. He's an implacable man, convinced his thoughts are the correct ones.

I nod in understanding. This isn't a new argument. The men and women of York have long thought of themselves as falling outside the command of the English king. Yet, under my brother's kingship, they were content. They send almost daily letters demanding that I take them back, by force if necessary. That most of them are written in Archbishop Wulfstan's language, and as such echo his sentiment, has never been without question. He's a clever man to play both sides of the poorly formed Norse-struck coins. I don't deny that.

'We aren't abandoning them,' I state. I've spoken these words more often than I like to remember. The problem of York has exercised my mind many times over the last few months. Ever since the treaty was signed at Lincoln, I've longed to travel north and finish the work I started, but I cautioned myself to be patient. It was clear Anlaf Sihtricson wasn't as powerful as he thought. I needed to wait for his weakness to become pronounced.

I believed his kingship would be contested. Now I need to bide my time and see what occurs next. If Blakari Gothfrithson proves to be as ineffectual as Anlaf Sihtricson, York will be under my control within a year.

'We're waiting to see what happens. Blakari lacks the power Anlaf possessed. I hear it's a wonder he can stay sober from one meal to the next.'

'Then how has he expelled Anlaf and taken his kingdom?' Eadric demands angrily. I don't mind. My supporters should understand my thinking even if they don't agree with it.

'Only with the help of Archbishop Wulfstan,' I clarify. Still, Eadric furrows his heavy eyebrows.

'Who does the archbishop of York work for at the moment? Himself, the pope, his God or for you?' As the sentence continues,

Eadric's voice trails away. He narrows his eyes and glares at me. He believes I have more to do with this than I do. I weigh up the value of telling him as much. It'd be pleasant if my men thought me more far-sighted than I am. But what if Wulfstan turns against me again? It would be difficult to unpick the lies then.

'Wulfstan labours only for himself,' I reaffirm. I must be clear about that. 'He has no loyalty to the Wessex royal family, and little to the archbishopric of Canterbury. His master is the pope, and no one else.'

'The man should be gelded,' Ealdorman Eadric complains. I laugh aloud. Archbishop Wulfstan accounts for himself only to God, and even then, he seems to have an enormous amount of leeway compared to other men who lack his implied religious fervour.

'He should, yes, but he might be useful in the future.'

'What of the kingdom of the Scots?' Eadric presses.

'What of them?' I query.

'We should attack them. King Mael Coluim is weak, his new kingship only just beginning.'

'What of the House of Bamburgh?' Ealdorman Uhtred interjects roughly.

'Bamburgh will fall when York does,' Eadric mutters moodily. He's unhappy today. His ill humour must be something other than a need to take action. Ealdorman Athelstan's shaking head is enough of a warning for me to bite my tongue and not question Eadric in front of my other ealdormen.

'Bamburgh won't fall when York does,' Uhtred retorts. 'It's been a stronghold on its own for years and years, much longer than York. It'll only fall when it's attacked, and right now, a young man sits on the throne. He took it when Ealdorman Guthrum died. We should reclaim it for England now.' Affairs in Bamburgh are a reminder that not everyone lost something in the skirmishes on the borderlands between York and England. Young Ealdwulf used quick thinking to take back the stronghold when Ealdorman Guthrum died, and we were all looking the other way fearing an attack on England, not one on Bamburgh.

'If we attack Bamburgh, Blakari Gothfrithson and Mael Coluim will be roused to action,' I state. 'At the moment, there's no alliance between them. Blakari's more likely to ally with Constantin than Mael Coluim. His brother was married to Constantin's daughter before his death, and his nephew is kept in the kingdom of the Scots. We need to keep them apart, not draw them together.'

Uhtred's unhappy at my words, but I know he'll agree.

'What of Strathclyde then?' Ealdorman Athelstan queries. This is something we've discussed before. Strathclyde's a tantalising little kingdom that can very easily upset the kingdom of the Scots. Since Owain's death at Brunanburh on the edge of my blade, Constantin has largely run the kingdom of Strathclyde. One of Owain's sons is king there but Dyfnwal's a puppet of Constantin.

I don't know if Strathclyde should be an enemy or an ally. It's so close to the kingdom of the Scots that it could be used to great effect if the English gained an agreement with Dyfnwal. I'm undecided on my plans for Strathclyde.

'Strathclyde's at peace with us,' I offer. It's the truth. But then, the kingdom of the Scots is also at peace with England.

'King Dyfnwal is Constantin's creature,' Eadric mutters moodily. He's not to be happy today until I demand he go and kill someone.

'Perhaps, but with Constantin gone, we've no idea of the current relationship between the two kingdoms.'

'Surely he'll be subject to Mael Coluim?' Eadric interjects. He's not considered all the nuances of the new situation. They're appearing before him while he argues his way to my point of view. Eadric might think slowly sometimes, but he does at least bother to think.

'Why would he be? Does he owe his kingship to Mael Coluim or Constantin?'

'He owes it to the death of his father,' Eadric continues darkly. Only then does his furrowed brow clear, and he laughs aloud at his contrariness. 'Apologies,' he says to everyone in the hall, offering me a small nod as a further apology. I wave it aside. It's not that I'm displeased to receive it, but I need men who speak their minds. Grumpy or not, Eadric always speaks his.

'We need to watch and be ready to strike when we can,' I say meaningfully, sitting forwards, my hands resting on the arms of the chair I sit within. The kingdom should never be left unprotected again. I've learned from what happened after my brother's death.

'Should we amass our warriors?' Ealdorman Uhtred asks.

'I believe we have time yet. We must weigh the advantage of moving quickly when the opportunity presents itself.'

Ealdorman Athelstan interrupts me. 'We could create the opportunity.' His voice is quiet but insistent. I know he's thinking of Archbishop Wulfstan in York, as well as Dyfnwal in Strathclyde. Dyfnwal's kingship is almost as recent as mine, while Archbishop Wulfstan can be turned to any cause provided he believes the gain will be his.

'What is it that he wants?' I ask my ealdormen.

'To meddle,' Ealdorman Athelstan is quick to answer. We share the same opinion of Archbishop Wulfstan. He's a troublemaker, a mischievous creature from the ancient pagan tales, for all he's supposed to be a good Christian man.

'He always wants something?' I question.

Ealdorman Athelstan's nodding. 'He does. We should determine what that is. A few spies?' he enquires.

I nod. He'll have some men he can send to York to find out the truth of the matter.

'And Dyfnwal?' Ealdorman Uhtred presses.

'Can we do the same with Dyfnwal?' I press. The men of Strathclyde aren't as mixed as those in York, where Norse and English live side by side. It might be harder to blend in if we send someone to Strathclyde. For a start, they must speak their guttural language.

'No, but we can still find out,' Ealdorman Uhtred announces with finality. I don't press him. He has his own contacts.

'Then it's decided,' I announce. 'We'll seek greater intelligence, and amass our supplies, but we'll not strike yet.' The ealdormen glance at me. Some of my counsellors have decided not to enter the conversation. Their thoughts mirror the men they stand beside.

Athelstan and Eadric, brother ealdormen, are opposites, and yet they have a common desire to rule in my name. It's their brother, Æthelwald, who sticks to the middle between the rasher Eadric and the almost too sedate Athelstan. Uhtred knows his mind and shares it with all or keeps it to himself. The other men, Æthelmund, Ealhhelm, the older Wulfgar and another Athelstan, are either too new to their positions or too long in the tooth to offer more than the others.

Not that I expect any of them to have any further advice. It's simple to me. Attack or wait. I can see the benefit of being the aggressor, but my kingdom is being rebuilt. It needs more time, perhaps only half a year, to feel united. The men and women of the Danelaw, the recently returned territories, see themselves as my subjects already. I don't wish to offer them the opportunity to look to another, not while I honour their laws and lords.

I don't miss the significant look that passes between Ealdorman Athelstan and his brothers. They're a mighty force behind me. I must keep them close to me. They could potentially be a threat. They hold a large amount of land in my name. I could have been wiser to share the spoils differently, but they're like family. Ealdorman Athelstan's married to my cousin, Ælfwynn, the daughter of the lady of Mercia. Their children will be loved by my children in years to come.

Yet, as I know only too well, family can be the greatest of all enemies. I need only look to the Norse and the Scots to appreciate that, and indeed, to East and West Frankia where my half-sisters create problems for one another. I don't have King Athelstan's stamina to contend with them. I've become as involved as I can. There's little more I can offer them now that Louis, my childhood friend, is no longer a prisoner of my other half-sister's husband. I shake my head at the thought of the strife they cause one another. I'll not allow such discord to ripple through my kingdom. One day, my son will rule. And after him, his son. It's the way it should be.

4

943, DUMBARTON ROCK

Dyfnwal, king of Strathclyde

The messenger eyes me with distaste. It's clear he doesn't care for me. Mael Coluim should have sent someone who can pretend to greater respect. Antipathy pours from him. I could drown in it. Already, I don't wish to hear his message.

If Mael Coluim wishes to be my ally, he should have come himself, not sent a messenger who hates me. I consider what I've done to cause such ire to him.

However, the news he carries is welcome. I'm pleased Constantin has been removed from power, both him and his bloody son, Ildulb. For too long, Constantin tried to sway events in my kingdom. I've only held it for a handspan of winters. He named me king here, as though it was his right to do so. But I'm the son of the previous king, Owain, who was killed fighting at Brunanburh, and it's my right. Not, I admit, that I mourn for my ineffectual father.

'King Mael Coluim of the kingdom of the Scots requests your presence at his inauguration in four weeks' time,' the messenger continues. I barely prevent myself from spitting out my drink in amusement. The man's voice is deep and rich. It's also filled with contempt. I can see it in his eyes as they shift around the room, taking in the huge roaring fire and the weapons hanging menacingly on the walls. He doesn't need to know that their edges are blunt and more likely to swat a fly than hack someone's head from their shoulders.

If I attended Mael Coluim's coronation, it would be a fine opportunity for him to attempt to exert his control over me. I won't allow that to happen.

'You must send my apologies,' I offer, with the sincerity of a violent fart. My voice is glib, and my response is too quickly given.

The man's beady little eyes watch my every move. I've an overwhelming desire to smack the disdain from his face. Mael Coluim chose poorly or well, depending on what he hoped to achieve. Perhaps he doesn't want me to travel to his inauguration? Maybe he wishes to have an excuse to attack my lands, and it will begin with my failure to acknowledge the change in kingship? I must think before I speak. I'm the king here, not this jumped-up little messenger with his ill humour and bad manners.

'He was most insistent... my lord king.'

The 'my lord king' is an afterthought. Now I'm considering what Mael Coluim intends. Constantin showed some respect in his dealings with me. This man seems determined to cause outrage rather than seek reconciliation.

'And I insist I won't attend,' I state boldly. I tire of speaking to him. I wish to be alone to consider the implications of the change in the kingdom of the Scots. He's not the usual messenger from Constantin, the man who used to bring his demands but couch them in such terms that the possibility of refusing was always there. This messenger, I forget his name, simply speaks as though I'm his to command.

It was a terrible choice if Mael Coluim wishes to maintain friendly relations.

'I'll send my messenger if you're unhappy with the response.' I try a new approach.

His unhappiness is easy to see. I wonder what he's promised the new king. It was all lies, whatever is was.

'It's not me who'll be unhappy... my lord king,' he says, again the 'my lord king' a late addition to the sentence. The pause between his words and my honorific is enough to ensure I know it's purposefully done. My anger stirs. This messenger is determined to earn my wrath. But perhaps that's his plan all along. Maybe he wants me to act irrationally and provide Mael Coluim with an opportunity to strike against me and my kingship.

I reconsider my stubbornness. It would, perhaps, be better if I did as Mael Coluim requested. That way, he'll have no excuse to attack me.

The messenger turns to leave. I raise my voice.

'Tell your king I'll be pleased to attend. It'll be good to see him and talk with him again. We have past discussions that will require resolving now he's king.'

The man stops and turns. His face is half hidden in shadow, but his slumped shoulders tell me all I need to know.

He was sent to infuriate me and make me irrational. He was to provide Mael Coluim with an excuse to attack me. I'm pleased I've seen through such weak efforts to antagonise me.

Attending Mael Coluim's inauguration will allow me to experience the atmosphere at his court first-hand. It might prove to be invaluable. Hopefully, I'll see Ildulb. I'd enjoy witnessing his reaction to his father's forced abdication.

The messenger shuffles from my presence, taking his arrogance and bad manners. Immediately, my advisors surround me. Questions tumble from their mouths. None of them surprises me.

'His insults were well practised,' one offers. I nod slowly as I meet the eyes of my son. He's a bright lad sharing my father's name, not yet quite a man, but it won't be long. He'll rule after me, provided I can hold the kingdom together long enough to bequeath it to him. With Constantin gone, that task might have become much easier.

'He meant to incite me, force my hand.' I may as well point this out because it seems some weren't close enough or paying the correct amount of attention to our short exchange.

'Mael Coluim intends to follow Constantin's policy of claiming the land of other men,' my son continues. He sounds wizened. When did my son gain such insight? 'We should ally with the English king. He'll counteract Mael Coluim's influence.'

'We'll never ally with the English,' one of my allies states as though it's his right to make policy within the kingdom. Some of my closest supporters eye him in surprise, others in consternation.

'Why not ally with the men of Jorvik?' I ask, ignoring him and concentrating on my son. I'm always keen to discover his thoughts.

'They're unstable. Even now, they fight over who rules the lands south of here and who Dublin and Limerick. They're fools and bloodthirsty ones. Family means everything and nothing to them. They say one thing and do another.'

This is a sophisticated view of the Norse. For nearly a century now, they've played havoc in the lands of the Britons and the Irish. I hope they'll leave, maybe travel to Iceland, or perhaps return to their homeland. I certainly want them gone from here. Possibly they'll even go to the rumoured lands far to the west. No man has yet returned from there, so it seems like the perfect destination for the bastards.

'I agree. We should approach the English,' I interject before any can belittle my son. 'It'll depend on the terms, of course,' I announce, my decision final. I've been to the English king's court, or rather, his brother's court. I know how to prostrate myself before the English. They pretend that the intrigue and betrayal the Norse use is a peculiarity to them. It's not, but I'll play their games if it makes my kingdom more secure.

'You would even speak with the man?' Still, one of my councillors complains.

'I would speak with the man until I know what Mael Coluim has planned for my kingdom. We must be patient,' I snap, the juxtaposition of my words and their tone not lost on me. 'My son will remain in my absence. We must show Mael Coluim that Strathclyde isn't to be toyed with by him.' I speak calmly and nod at my son, who takes the news with surprise that only I can decipher. He has a face of stone. He'll make an excellent king one day.

I glance at the rest of my council. With Constantin in seclusion at his monastery, I need to be careful. I can trust no one but my son. Certainly, I can't trust the English, or the bloody Norse, for that matter.

I'll bide my time, but there's much to be gained from Mael Coluim's hasty removal of Constantin. For the first time since I came to the kingship, I feel I'm truly in control of my destiny. I can decide on whether to approach Mael Coluim or Edmund.

Long may it continue.

5

943, ST ANDREW'S, THE KINGDOM OF THE SCOTS

Constantin, deposed king of the Scots

The soft scratching of cloth over the smooth wooden floorboards is the only indication that my meditation is to be disturbed. My curiosity, dulled by the days and weeks I've spent kneeling in the church, acknowledges the sound. There's no need for my old head to swivel on my thinning neck. Not any more.

Since my abdication six months ago, age has descended on me like a ravenous raven after a battle. It gnaws at me, little by little, and the result is that I'm left desiccated and stick-thin, all knobbly bones and no skin at all. My more fleshy parts are gone, my arms hanging useless at my sides, and my muscles entirely disintegrated.

It'll be Ildulb who thinks to disturb me. He's a good son. He visits me despite the unpopularity it causes with Mael Coluim – the bastard.

Once more, I pray Mael Coluim's reign is short and marred by uprisings and war. He took what wasn't his. In my eyes, he's worse than any aggressor, any Norse warrior. They at least have the decency to come in their battle glory to attack my people and my land.

Mael Coluim's the fox in the henhouse. I hate and admire him in equal measure.

'Constantin.' The voice is rough and quiet at my side. I turn slowly, my mind trying to process what I hear, because it's not Olaf's voice, which is impossible. Olaf Gothfrithson has been dead for two years. I shouldn't hear his voice, even in my church, haunted by the members of my family who were struck down too young.

In the muted light from the candles, shadows stretch and tease, making it hard to focus as I turn to assure myself a spectral vision hasn't decided to visit me. I narrow my eyes, gasping at the apparition. A smirk touches my face. I'm an old man of whimsy and superstition, prone to the same stray thoughts that mar every person who prays to our Lord God.

'Yes?' I murmur, because the person who stands before me is real. He's no figment of my prayers and tortured mind.

'I'm Blakari, Blakari Gothfrithson.' The words are edged by the Norse tongue.

'I know who you are,' I offer in a voice lacking warmth. I've been sent here to die by Mael Coluim. I'm not to interfere in the kingdom's affairs. Blakari's presence is a compliment as well as an annoyance. Briefly, my heart flares, despite my thoughts. Outside the four walls of my prison, my reputation marks me as a man worth seeking. I'm relieved that men continue to believe I possess the power to help them and shape the events that befall this island of warriors and fighters – this island of constant kingly conflict. 'Go away,' I reject him. I don't think I want him to leave, but instead, test his resolve.

'Lord Ildulb said this would be your response,' he offers lightly, a smile on his lips. When he speaks, he sounds so like his brother that if I closed my eyes, I'd truly think it was Olaf Gothfrithson after all, the man I allowed to wed my precious only daughter, Mael Muire. It wasn't a good decision.

'You spoke with my son?' I question sharply. I don't want Ildulb to be caught up in any controversy that might affect his relationship with Mael Coluim. I was firm with him about that.

'Only outside,' Blakari offers with a shrug of his wide shoulders, which neither reassures nor sets my mind at rest. Why has Ildulb allowed Blakari to speak to me?

I push myself to my feet with effort. I've been here since before dawn, when the land was cloaked in grey mist. I can tell through the small stained-glass windows that it must be close to midday. Where does the time go? Surely, each breath should be treasured and remembered when I know I have so few left. Instead, time flies, each day merging into the next at a dizzying speed.

I've almost forgotten how long I've been here and how long Mael Coluim has had possession of my kingdom. Almost. Or so I lie to myself.

'Why have you come here, to St Andrew's, to see a man who is no longer a king?' I suspect the answer to my question.

It's quiet inside the church. Even though this is my establishment, I appreciate that Mael Coluim has spies everywhere, listening to everything I do and say. He banished me, and did me the honour of not killing me to gain the kingship. Every day, I believe he laments that decision, wishing he'd been able to end my life so there was no one to stand against his rule.

Mael Coluim's not the most far-sighted of men, even though he's been waiting to be king for four decades. No doubt that's why it took him over twenty years to build up the courage to move against me.

I gesture that we should walk from the church, but Blakari's reluctant to go outside, even as he considers how to answer my question.

'It's safer to speak in the clear air, near the cliffs.' I explain my desires. With a grimace of unhappiness, he saunters beside me. A walking stick would aid my movement, but I refuse and will continue to resist when the object is offered. I might feel like a crippled old man, and my body may act like I'm one, but there's no need for others to see it laid bare before them. I know I'm old and weak. There's no requirement to labour the point.

Standing proudly, I push my shoulders back and walk like I'm still the king. Appearances are important and relevant in the clash of kings and would-be kings, half-kings and overmighty subjects.

It's a rare still day outside. I feel the tang of the salty ocean wash my face. I sometimes think I would have made a good Norse warrior. If my kingdom had fallen to another, I'd have been just as happy to make a life on the sea. Perhaps I would have gone with the other settlers to the new land in the far north, although I'll never understand why they called it Iceland. Surely a more hospitable name could have been found? Something that at least promised warmth.

Ildulb's deep in conversation with the priest who tends to the monastery. I raise my arm in welcome, although I'm still not sure whether Ildulb should have allowed Blakari entry. Ildulb returns the gesture, and his eyes flick to Blakari. I assume he knows why he's here. Not that it should come as a great surprise to me. After all, I'm the grandfather to his nephew. However tenuous the link, we're still family. We should work together.

The ground beneath my feet has been worn smooth by the passage of many feet over the few years the monastery has stood. I should speak to the monks and ask them to plant fresh grasses or make a firmer stone footpath. It would make it easier for everyone.

In the bright daylight, I take the time to examine Blakari in more detail. This isn't the first time I've met him, that was before the slaughter field of Brunanburh, but it is the first time I've seen him since his brother's death. In the midday sun's glare, I easily see the similarities and differences. He sounds like his brother and carries a similar build but has a fairer complexion, his eyes a brighter blue. His nephew shares many physical characteristics, especially his eyes. I tease my daughter that he'll be no night-time warrior because all will see the inner glow of his eyes.

Mael Muire laughs at my words, but sadness envelops her. The loss of her husband was hard on her, and I've no one else to offer in his place. None would take the risk after what befell her brother, Alpin. I know she wants more children, but she'll need to beget them however she can. If her brother takes Mael Coluim's place as king, she'll have an opportunity for a good union, but I doubt she'll wait that long.

'Why are you here?' I repeat. My musing has allowed us to walk all the way to the cliff without speaking. Ahead, the sea stretches in an unending vista. Its beauty always astounds me.

Blakari sighs deeply before speaking.

'My lord king, Constantin.'

I don't correct him. Over forty years as a king has made me a 'lord king' no matter what Mael Coluim believes.

'You may have heard I'm now king in Jorvik.'

I hadn't heard that, but I don't admit that. I imagine he's spent the last two years labouring to gain the kingship. His brother died too young, and Anlaf Sihtricson was too conveniently placed for Blakari to take the kingdom for himself.

'Anlaf Sihtricson was weak after his alliance with Edmund, king of the English. The people are pleased to call me king in his place.'

'And you're happy to fill his shoes?' I cackle. I feel uneasy despite my laughter. Blakari might well have affected a political coup similar to Mael Coluim's. As the victim of one such event, I'm not about to endorse a man who thinks it's acceptable behaviour to steal another's kingdom.

My eyes narrow. He must know what I'm thinking.

'You would call on our family affinity?' I ask bluntly.

'I would, my lord king, yes.' His reverence for me is too fervent. I thought he respected me, now I'm unsure whether he names me as such by way of a taunt, or if he finds himself in the unenviable position of coming to seek my assistance, only to discover I have nothing with which to aid him.

'To what end?'

'To attack the bastard English king, Edmund. I'll begin by claiming Bamburgh.'

This is not the welcoming news I hoped for. I've long been a supporter of the independence of Bamburgh. It's a buffer state between the kingdom of the Scots and the English to the south. I was remiss when I didn't support Ealdwulf on his father's death. It's taken him a long time, but he's now king of Bamburgh. I admire him for having such resolve, and luck, against the English. I didn't believe Ealdwulf had it in him. Although, the men and women of Bamburgh are a strange, stubborn breed, more akin to the inhabitants of the Welsh kingdoms. I admire them such independent spirit. I always have. Perhaps then, it was only right that they welcomed Ealdwulf when the English dropped their guard on Bamburgh.

'Bamburgh's an autonomous kingdom. It doesn't belong to Jorvik, and never has.' I can't keep the edge of fury from my voice. I would welcome him attacking the English, but not if it involves Bamburgh as well.

'No it isn't. It belongs to Northumbria. I plan on being king of that land, not just Jorvik.' Blakari's words lack heat, but thrum with conviction.

I gasp at his audacity. Olaf Gothfrithson never held such lofty aspirations. I consider his brother's huge ambitions.

'Why?' I ask before I can stop myself. I'm too curious.

His blue eyes search mine, sparkling aquamarine in the bright light. They're bewitching. 'Why not?' Blakari questions with another shrug of his wide shoulders. I hope it isn't the extent of his reasoning, and it isn't. 'They have a mighty fortress. If I had control of it, I'd never have to fear being ejected from this island again.'

Now that he's condescended to explain further, I grudgingly approve of the reasoning. He has more forethought than the Norse who've ruled Jorvik before him.

He's also correct about Bamburgh. It's survived for so long outside the influence of either the Scots or the Norse of Jorvik because of that fortress. A solid thing built of wood and stone in equal part, with the sea to its rear, and the holy island of Lindisfarne keeping a permanent guard over it. It's a powerful deterrent to all who eye her with hungry eyes. The English were foolish to let it slip from their grasp.

'What do you want from me?' I query, using my arm to indicate the total of my current possessions, the monastery and church. I'm not as weak as Mael Coluim thinks I am, but still, I can be of little help to Olaf's brother.

'Your support and an understanding that when I take the fortress and renew the attack on England, your warriors will not trouble my kingdom.'

'They're no longer my men.' It's impossible to keep the bitterness from my voice. Blakari doesn't placate me.

'We both know differently,' he murmurs, grooming his beard with one hand. He suspects, as I do, that while Mael Coluim might have been consecrated as king, many warriors of the kingdom of the Scots continue to see me as their commander. Few would go against my wishes if I deigned to make them well known. Blakari isn't as blind as I thought.

'In exchange for what?' I ask.

A new light shimmers from Blakari's already blazing eyes. 'I'll help your son, when the time is fortuitous, to claim your kingdom. He'll fight for you, and so will I, and one day, your grandson, my nephew, will be heir to a great swathe of land to rival that the English king claims. One day, your grandson will take the whole of the island of Britain for himself.'

Now I'm licking my lips with anticipation. I've lived a good, long life, but I can't deny Blakari's vision of the future fills my head with excitement. I'd like nothing more than for the royal family of Wessex to be extinguished. The get of Alfred and Edward shouldn't be allowed to control this island. It doesn't belong to them. My people have always been stronger. Hence the ruin of the great wall that runs through the middle of Northumbria, and the other one, even further north. In the far reaches of time, where memory has become swathed in shadows, even the mighty Romans feared my ancestors. We're not a weak people. We're warriors, all of us.

I look toward the church, where Ildulb watches our exchange keenly. I know what he'd say to this.

'Speak with Ildulb. Inform him of your plans,' I offer, reaching out to shake his hand on our agreement.

He grips my arm tightly, his strength assuring me he can fulfil such promises, his eyes burning into my soul as though seeking the truth. It's not uncomfortable because I speak the truth. I'll do all I can for him. If, somehow, I regain my kingdom in the meantime, it'll be good to have Blakari as a bulwark between the kingdom of the Scots and the growing English kingdom. Edmund will not have given up on Jorvik. He'll renew his aggression soon.

I see the tension rise from Blakari's shoulders. His shrugs didn't show insolence but fear and unease that I wouldn't support him because his actions so clearly mirror Mael Coluim's. I hope Mael Coluim struggles as much with discomfort for his actions as Blakari does.

Once more, I hope the usurper's insecurity causes him to make ill-formed decisions, even more terrible than the one that saw me evicted from my palace. The men and women of the Scots kingdom are strong-minded, just as those at Bamburgh. They don't want a weak king, no matter what his pedigree might be. Mael Coluim's father ruled before me, but that was a long time ago. To many, he's only a figure from legend, from stories told around the fires late at night. The men and women of the Scots know me as their king. Not Mael Coluim, and not his father.

Ildulb understands that. He fashions himself into a double image of me.

I'm proud of my son. I'll be even prouder when he returns my kingdom to me or takes it for himself.

'I wish you well,' I offer Blakari, and find I mean it. His arrival here, so unwelcome when we first spoke, has rekindled my love of intrigue, my desire to intrude in the affairs of kingdoms that extend beyond my borders. I find myself standing taller, all thoughts of needing a walking stick to aid me banished. I am the king of the Scots kingdom, no matter that I don't currently sit at Scone.

Mael Coluim has miscalculated badly. I hope Blakari hasn't. All the same, of my brother kings and those who cause conflict upon this island, only Edmund earns my grudging respect. He's a good king, but he need not be for much longer. His brother died young. So might he, especially if Blakari is able to hasten his end. Only time will tell, and God willing, I'll live to see it.

6

943, THE KINGDOM OF THE WELSH

Hywel, king of the Welsh

The scratching of quills over vellum eases my soul. The near silence of the room is a welcome change from the fractious quarrelling that seems to ripple once more through the kingdoms of my conflicted neighbours, both my allies and my enemies.

I know I'm as guilty as others of taking land that doesn't lie within my patrimony, but at least I've done it cleanly and with strength. I hold Idwal's kingdom of Gwynedd firmly in my grasp. These Norse, the men of the Scots, the fragile resurrected kingdom of Bamburgh, it's as though none of them are capable of making great gains and keeping them.

I once thought Athelstan of the English was the wisest and strongest of kings. But in the wake of his death, I've had to reconsider. Perhaps his brother, Edmund, is the greater man. He's reversed the advances claimed by the Norse of York, the men of the family of Ívarr the Boneless, Olaf Gothfrithson and now Anlaf Sihtricson. Although Edmund employs the same tactics as Athelstan, the threat of war and the promulgation of peace treaties, he might be better able to hold on to his gains with the permanence denied Athelstan by his early death.

King Athelstan made significant advances, used marriage alliances to his gain and pressed his claim to York with the thinnest of excuses. Edmund does none of those things. Edmund's young and should benefit from a long life. In that time, he'll build England and make her strong, just as I've done with the various Welsh kingdoms, united now under my rule. Not just the West Welsh, left to me on my father's death, but also Gwynedd, Glywysing and Gwent. I hope that the law I'm labouring to bring forth in written words, to give a tangible and physical form to, will ensure the Welsh kingdom remains strong and united when I die. In such a way, no enemy will ever trouble us. Not the English, the Irish, the Scots or the Norse of Dublin. All will be repelled from our borders. Or so I've convinced myself. Only through law and justice will my kingdom stay as strong as I've made it. That's how the English kings rule. I intend to adopt the same policies.

A cough, a sneeze, and the five monks who write under my directions pass rueful smirks between each other. This room is a sanctuary of silence and industry, but even men must smile sometimes. They're not marble statues. They have needs and wants and basic bodily functions to contend with as well.

I come here often, not to order the monks, but because in the scratching of each feather quill, I feel my united kingdom of the Welsh solidifies. As the ink dries on the vellum, I see a future for the Welsh that will be greater than that of the English kingdom. The English have their laws and codes and taxes. It made them strong enough to withstand the onslaught of the descendants of Ívarr the Boneless in their many numbers.

'My lord king.' A firm but soft voice recalls me to the present. I sigh with irritation. What calamity has befallen us all now? My son, Owain ap Hywel, offers an apologetic glance. He knows my purpose here. He understands I need time with my thoughts away from the work of the court.

I nod and follow him from the room, a remorseful glance over my shoulder that I must leave the monks to their endeavours. The chief scribe observes me. With me gone, I know the monks will slacken their pace. I don't object. I wouldn't wish them to have cramp in their arms or feel the terrible judder of tension working its way along their fingers, making it impossible to continue with the close work.

I want my law code to be beautiful, no matter how long it takes. As long as I accomplish it before my death, I'll have achieved a great thing. I've ruled as king for decades, first with my father when I was a young man, and then alone, after his death. I'm venerable now, into my sixth decade. I thought King Constantin of the Scots an old man, past his prime, when I met him at Eamont, nearly a decade ago. How strange to find I'm now the age he was then. I don't feel old. No doubt, he didn't either.

My son waits patiently for me, knowing he's to be quiet in the hallowed hall of the monastery. The end of the world could come upon us all, and still, he'd be quiet, reverent. I'm building a legacy that will benefit him. I hope he and his brothers appreciate it.

'News, Father,' Owain announces without preamble. It must be important for him to disturb me. Still, I wait. We're within the confines of the monastery. I prefer to discuss politics away from the ears of my God. Our boots echo through the wooden passageway, but soon enough we're outside, the strong wind blowing into our faces.

The view is stunning. I never tire of seeing it. It reveals my kingdom at its best with huge, stark mountains in the distance, sometimes snow-topped even in the depths of the summer. Vast rivers wind through the landscape and the tiny dots and puffs show the cook fires from steadings.

'Well, what news?' I ask, annoyance at being recalled from the shush of the monastery warring with my joy at being outside, feeling the wind on my face, the chill in the air.

'From the north,' he says, his gaze on the view.

I force myself to wait out his silence. He rarely speaks without thought.

'Constantin's no longer king of the Scots?'

It's a curious turn of phrase for him to use if a man is dead. I wait. I know more must be coming.

'Mael Coluim forced him to abdicate during the winter.'

Ah, I think, a sigh escaping my mouth to mingle with the wind. I wonder what my son thinks of this. Is he jealous? Does he wish to do the same? He's been waiting on the sideline for many years less than Mael Coluim, yet it's a long time given the ebb and flow of other kings and kingdoms, in this eddying conflict that infects our island home.

All kingdoms desire the permanence that Constantin and I have brought to our respective domains. It's eluded the English since Edward's death nearly two decades ago.

'Will there be war?' I ask. It's no concern of mine, but upheaval elsewhere causes repercussions in my kingdom. Already, I'm wondering whether I should reinforce the northern borders of Gwynedd, call on half-formed alliances and the unfailing support of my warriors. 'What are the English doing?' I follow up without giving him time to respond. I'm thinking aloud. There's no way Owain will know what our neighbours will do. Not unless the news comes from them.

He turns to look at me. I notice his receding hairline and the worry lines crossing his forehead. It's a constant reminder of my age. My years press on me, stirring me to action and not thought, rushing by with ferocity that only the sanctuary of my writing scribes can absolve. I know my time must be numbered, that more of it lies behind me than before. I know I'll soon be with my God. I still have much to accomplish.

'The news comes from the north,' he informs.

'Dyfnwal of Strathclyde or Mael Coluim himself?' I press.

'Dyfnwal.' Again his terse reply is telling. Dyfnwal's an uneasy neighbour. His relationship with the Scots, or at least with Constantin, is too complicated to unravel. Constantin eased him into the kingship after his father's death at Brunanburh. Since then, Constantin's taken too much interest in Dyfnwal's kingship.

From across his jealously guarded borders, Constantin has done more harm than good throughout his long life. He thinks of only one thing. The Scots. He has no interest in anything else. He doesn't crave land as other men do. No, he's always been happy with what he holds, but he always intended to keep it to himself and give it to no one else. He wouldn't even share it with his son. Now, he's lost it all. Or has he?

My mind flickers over the many possibilities. I keep such thoughts to myself, just as Owain does. We're more similar than either of us care to admit.

In silence, we watch the play of light over the distant woods, standing proudly in the gleaming sunlight, the sound of the river meandering past the only backdrop to our conversation.

'What will you do?' Owain finally asks. I might not like Constantin, but he doesn't deserve to lose his kingship through any means other than his death. Mael Coluim's an unworthy successor to deny him the final years of his kingship.

'Nothing yet. We don't know enough.'

'What would you do?' Owain queries, stressing the 'would'. He means if I knew more. I consider it. What would I do?

I think the Scots need a king such as Constantin. He's a careful, religious man. He's been a good leader and will continue to be one. Surrounded by the Norse to the east and the north in their safe island houses, by the House of Bamburgh to the south and with the strange arrangement in Strathclyde, the Scots aren't in a safe position. They're always open to attack. That's the problem with this island we call our home. No matter where we look, we can see enemies waiting to encroach upon the coastlands, claim the wealth they desire, but have no patience to earn themselves. I've considered building walls and dykes across my borders, just as the old Mercian king once did, his name living on forever in its English naming as 'Offa's Dyke'. But I'm not convinced the effort would be worthwhile. The attacks are usually fragmentary, fading away with the death of a leader.

The ancient Romans built two great walls, neither of which still performs the function for which it was designed. The one that ran through the land of the Scots, much further north, reveals that even the strongest sometimes have to retreat in the face of overwhelming odds. It's little more than ruins now. The other wall, traversing the Northumbrian and Strathclydian lands, is less ruined but is still no impediment to the peoples who live either side of it. It does not define Strathclyde or Northumbria. Despite it all, stone isn't impenetrable.

If such men as those who could erect the grand buildings I've seen in the English kingdoms couldn't secure their borders when they could build roads and move men such vast distances, across oceans, seas and huge land masses, how can I do the same? They didn't attack the land of the Welsh. Folklore has it the mountains were too great for them to traverse, but I also know, because I've been there, that vast mountain ranges litter the huge land mass upon which Rome nestles. I don't believe the excuse. My ancestors were simply too good at fighting. We've always been a bloody-minded lot.

I can't secure our borders. The answer's simple. Instead, I must make my people strong and give them the weapons they need to keep our kingdom safe. I'll allow them to employ the same techniques that kept the Romans from claiming this part of the island for themselves. Resolved, I finally reply to Owain's question.

'If I knew everything, I'd act to return Constantin to his kingship. While he lives, the Scots are manageable. While he lives, I understand each man's motivation. Without him, chaos will reign. There will be conflict.'

Owain nods, the sunlight turning his face to a haze of glowing red. 'Blakari Gothfrithson has taken Jorvik. Anlaf Sihtricson seeks your support to take back his lost kingdom. He requests an alliance, and that you allow easy access for his warriors to reach York.'

Ah, I see my son is feeding me information piecemeal. It's a tactic I've used against him on many occasions. It's good to see how men react to new information when they've already formed opinions based on half the available knowledge. I glare at him. He quirks a smile of apology. He knows what he's doing. I've taught him well.

'Who aided Blakari?' I interrogate. I'm not interested in Anlaf Sihtricson unless there's a good reason to be. The men of Jorvik and Dublin fight and bicker constantly. The family of Ívarr the Boneless is old and dispersed, a curse on his name and heritage, with each man thinking he has the right to rule because of his birthright, no matter how diluted it has become. None of the brood is as powerful as the old man was. Peace amongst his kin never lasts. They thrive on bloodlust, greed and death. The lands across the sea are even more cantankerous than the kingdoms of the English, the Welsh and the Scots combined.

'A holy man,' my son offers. He doesn't need to tell me the name. I know who it'll be. Archbishop Wulfstan of York is a meddling fool. We share a faith, but not an outlook on life. He makes poor decisions all in the name of self-aggrandisement. He wouldn't ensure the laws of his people are written down. I think little of Archbishop Wulfstan. I'm pleased he holds no power within the kingdoms of the Welsh.

'Any other news?' I probe. My son grins at my aggrieved tone. It's one he's used with me often enough.

'The English king will sit and wait to see what happens.'

I laugh, delighting in how well I've taught him. 'When did the messengers arrive?'

He turns away. He's withheld the news, and it should annoy me, but I'm sure he had his reasons.

'The day before yesterday.'

Now I understand, the day before yesterday was fraught with tension and arguments as my councillors argued and fought over elements of my law codes. My son was correct to keep the intelligence from me. My anger that day was immense. I'd have probably marched to war there and then, with whom I don't yet know, but certainly against someone.

'My thanks then,' I offer, and he nods. I see this worried him, this son of mine, a middle-aged man and still frightened of his father on occasion. Or perhaps he was terrified of his king? 'Send word to Edmund of the English that we have no intention of getting involved in the debacle.'

'What of Anlaf Sihtricson?'

'Send his messenger on his way. I've no interest in events beyond my borders. If Anlaf regains his kingdom, there'll be time for reparations then.'

Owain begins to walk away. He knew what my answer would be. 'Is it wise to offend the family of Ívarr the Boneless?' he queries quietly. I understand his worries.

'Both Anlaf Sihtricson and Blakari Gothfrithson count Ívarr the Boneless as their great-grandfather. Let them argue about it amongst themselves. Ívarr never did our kingdom any favours. Neither man should think we owe them anything.'

'Very good, Father,' Owain responds without surprise. He suspected my response. I'm a strong king, a man others can rely on. I don't go looking for confrontation. It's never served me well, and I have other concerns.

I turn and walk back into the monastery, my thoughts returning to my laws and monks. The world beyond my borders could fall to ruin, and I wouldn't care. I want my people to be governed by law and reason, not bloodlust and anarchy.

In the approaching conflict of kings, I'll stay far to the side. The coming clashes will not be mine.

7

LATE 943, WINCHESTER, THE KINGDOM OF THE ENGLISH

Athelstan the ealdorman

Rumours and counter-rumours swirl around the English court, brought on the wind and lacking all foundation. Mael Coluim of the kingdom of the Scots has allied with Dyfnwal of Strathclyde. Dyfnwal is dead. The usurped Constantin has been assassinated by Mael Coluim. Constantin's disaffected son, Ildulb, plots the death of Mael Coluim. Anlaf Sihtricson will reclaim York. Blakari Gothfrithson will cede York back to Anlaf Sihtricson. Dyfnwal of Strathclyde is known to be dying. Blakari's brother, Gothfrith, will help Blakari hold York against any retaliatory strikes from Anlaf Sihtricson who is said to have allied with King Hywel of the Welsh. What part has Archbishop Wulfstan played in all this? My head spins with the implications and the uselessness of sleepless nights spent worrying about the future.

Even now, as we dine in the presence of the king, another tries to earn his unending support by filling his head with more stories and half-hoped-for truths. Edmund listens attentively, as he must, but later, when the man has gone, grovelling his way from the king's audience, his purse heavy with a little English coin, his persona will change.

Edmund hasn't yet mastered the calm exterior that King Athelstan always employed, but he hides his true feelings well enough and shows the right amount of enthusiasm. If this new messenger comes from one of those men, there'll be a report that the English king seemed intrigued and fascinated by the news and might have been convinced to act on whomever's behalf. Edmund can ask for little more as he allows events to develop without taking direct action.

It appears these other kings and would-be kings wait to see what Edmund will do before committing themselves to any cause. Likewise, Edmund's delaying. I wonder who'll make the first move? Whoever sets the next altercations in motion will be unsuccessful.

Later, when a few of his most trusted advisors surround the king, we'll discuss the latest intelligence and see if it changes anything. At some point, Edmund will decide how to exploit these conflicts and divisions. One event will set him on the path to war. It hasn't happened yet. While those north of York toy with their allies, there's little to be done but anticipate the most opportune moment to strike back.

Edmund desires York. Everyone knows it. It's not even an open secret within England but a known fact. Warriors, women and small children alike await the announcement from the king that York is to be taken from the Norse. When it comes is a matter of conjecture, but it will come, and probably sooner than anyone thinks.

This messenger, a respected wool merchant from the Five Boroughs, is full of stories of Mael Coluim in the kingdom of the Scots and Dyfnwal of Strathclyde. It's perhaps best not to enquire how he knows such things. He's convinced of a rift between the two men, he extols loudly enough for all to hear, saying that without

Constantin, Dyfnwal has exerted his independence and decided Strathclyde is no longer subject to the wishes of men who don't even live within her boundaries.

This news thrills Edmund, although he endeavours to hold his spurt of excitement in place. Edmund's predicted that something like this will happen. He wants every kingdom on this island to stand alone. Edmund hopes they'll cause such great ruptures amongst themselves that none will go to the aid of the other. Unlike his brother, who was swayed by the promises of men, Edmund appreciates the dark hatred that can lie within each of these ambitious rulers. He's learned the lessons from his two half-brothers, the one who tried to kill the other, the little-lamented Edwin seeking to kill Athelstan over a decade ago.

If the kingdoms succumb to the tensions between the combatants, Edmund can take them for himself. Or, if he so desires, take them and barter them to the highest bidder in exchange for an oath of loyalty. Edmund plans to quell the unrest within our island, but first, he wants to let the men who would be kings and rulers inflict as much damage to their cause as possible. He need not risk English warriors unnecessarily.

There's an inevitability about it all. Anlaf Sihtricson, Blakari Gothfrithson, Mael Coluim of the kingdom of the Scots, Constantin, Ildulb, Archbishop Wulfstan and Dyfnwal of Strathclyde. They don't realise they're the English king's prey, even if it's only by tearing a small part of the carcass away bite by bite.

When the merchant's finally gone, his constant repetitions fading like dying echoes in the great hall, Edmund grins at me and beckons for his son to be brought to him by one of the servants. He dotes on the boy, Eadwig, little more than two years old and already confident and beguiling. Edmund knows his time with the boy is limited. He must agree for the boy to be fostered by another now that the boy's mother is dead in childbirth. Edmund mourns his lost wife. In unguarded moments, I see the sorrow on his face. It's one thing to command a warrior to die on his behalf. He did not think the woman he loved would perish from the child they'd created together.

Still, it is the way of our people. It's rare for a child to stay with their parents. In this way, alliances will be fostered for the ætheling. One day, Eadwig will have allies outside his own immediate blood family to enable him to become England's king.

One of the powerful families, perhaps mine, maybe not, will find themselves custodians of the young boy. The new child, Edgar, who survived when his mother did not, is too young for such considerations. He needs his wet nurse, not thoughts of the future.

All say the king should remarry. Edmund so far lacks any desire to do so. I understand his feelings, even if they don't make political sense. The family of his dead wife is bound to the future of England. A new wife would bring another such alliance with a noble family.

I'd be honoured to look after Eadwig, but as with all things, politics must come into play first; some recognition of Edmund's dead wife's family must be made. I understand that. It was the same with my sons when I decided on who would foster them. I know how hard it is to choose the most suitable foster parent, who could offer the child the greatest advantage in the future.

The king already holds the future of my oldest son in his hands, Æthelwald, named after my brother. Æthelwald shows great promise and is a favourite of the king's because of his gentle nature with his sons. I'm proud of the boy.

As my king and friend plays with his sleepy son, I see the concentration that mars his face. He's thinking and considering the implications of this new piece of intelligence. I don't think the time is quite right, but he might disagree. He must undo the havoc of the first year of his reign. Already four years have elapsed in which he's not controlled York. He wants it. He needs it to feel like he's a great king, and a worthy successor to his brother. He's also wary of acting only to be seen to be doing something. Grief for his wife has made him unpredictable on occasion. He's endeavouring not to do so with regard to York.

Others took advantage of Edmund's weaknesses when he first became king. Edmund intends to repay the kindness. In that, he's wise beyond his years. Let the enemy make their mistakes and then profit from them. I approve of his policy.

'My lord king,' I say as we discuss the matter later. The night has drawn in cold. The massive hearth flickers and sputters in the stray gusts of wind that blow through the constantly opening and closing door at the front of the hall. It's an excellent building, but the wind is persistent tonight.

'Ealdorman Athelstan,' he murmurs. Although his eyes are closed as though he craves sleep, I know he's deep in thought.

'The time isn't yet fortuitous,' I counsel. It's a statement. Sometimes, I find my thoughts run counter to Edmund's. I prefer to sound him out before I commit myself too thoroughly.

'No, it's not. But soon it will be, and perhaps we should begin to interfere again.'

Edmund's involvement in Anlaf Sihtricson's downfall is a secret to most. I wish the king hadn't involved Archbishop Wulfstan, but there was no one else with the power within York to do what was required.

'You wish to ally with Blakari Gothfrithson more openly?' I ask, my forehead creased.

'No, never. I don't want to support a man who demands lands my brother claimed. No, I need to incite another and have them force Blakari's hand. Blakari has made an implacable enemy now that Anlaf's been driven out of York. Something should be done to solidify the enmity between the two men.'

'But they're cousins, my lord king?' I know about family loyalties. If Blakari were faced with a greater threat, he'd reunite with Anlaf quickly. The men might want to rule independently, but they'd far rather share control than allow the English king to steal York from them.

'Families fight,' Edmund replies, a gleam in his eye. I think he must be recalling the acrimonious relationships of his father's other children. Athelstan and the sons of his father's second marriage were never close. I know Edmund always thought himself lucky that he was too young to be a threat to Athelstan. His brother treated him more like a son than a brother. It made their relationship much easier.

'They do, my lord king. But who will you manipulate?'

'I don't know yet. There are many possibilities. I need to be sure before I do anything. Who would you suggest?'

I've not considered the matter before. I thought the king's meddling in Anlaf's expulsion from York risky enough. This new tactic might prove even more troublesome.

'It can't be anyone else from the House of Ívarr. They all like their power too much. Blakari's brother is the king of Dublin. Anlaf's brother is a Norse warrior of great renown. They'll jealously guard their kingdoms and possessions.'

Edmund's pensive as I speak. It's a conundrum. Relations with the Scots are poor in the wake of Constantin's abdication, while much of the Welsh lands lie calmly under the guidance of Hywel. Hywel isn't likely to be riled into war anytime soon. He loves peace too much.

'We could send support to the ruling house of Bamburgh. Lord Ealdwulf must be keen to prove himself as a better man than his father.'

Bamburgh. It's a name with which to conjure. An ancient family, long in control of their fortress. Ealdred seemed to be a good man, but his death a decade ago left the kingdom in the hands of his ineffectual and young son. Edmund is right. Ealdwulf might welcome some involvement from the English.

'Constantin took too much interest in Bamburgh,' I confirm.

'He did, but only because he wished to maintain the divide. He didn't want the Norse on his doorstep even when his daughter was married to one of them. And, remember, Constantin didn't assist Ealdwulf on his father's death. That will still rankle. And we did help his mother.' Edmund's considered this more than I have.

'I heard that the men of Bamburgh were responsible for Olaf Gothfrithson's death.' I've known this for a while but never discussed it with the king. He eyes me with interest.

'The men of Bamburgh have no love for the Norse kings either?'

I realise what he's thinking. 'So I heard, but it might be another rumour. One of my men brought me the story. He said he'd heard it from someone who carried out the attack.'

Edmund considers the new piece of intelligence. It warrants deliberation. 'Did Ealdwulf orchestrate Olaf Gothfrithson's death?' he muses.

'I don't know that much detail.' There's no point in pretending to something I simply don't know.

'We should reach out to him. Too many years have passed since his father and my brother met at Eamont. Athelstan ruled the kingdom for some years, or rather, Ealdorman Guthrum did. It's only now that we hear Lord Ealdwulf controls it once more.' Edmund's face is immobile as he considers his suggestion. It would be good to hem the men of York in and ensure they have no one to turn to for help. 'Send a messenger to Bamburgh, someone we trust, someone we can rely on for complete discretion, and have him sound out Ealdwulf. See what Ealdwulf's plans are, and find out if he did have anything to do with Olaf's death. If he did, it would mean he's already willing to interfere in the affairs of York, and that would be a good sign. Remind him of our care for his mother.'

'And Strathclyde?' While Edmund moves to isolate York, Strathclyde should also be considered.

'Use your discretion. Find out what you can about Dyfnwal and his relationship with the new king of the Scots. When the time comes, we'll be bold and take decisive action. Whatever that might be.'

I grunt an agreement. 'I know who I'll send to Strathclyde.' I settle back in my chair, festooned with furs and comfortable in the glow from the hearth, thinking the conversation over.

But Edmund hasn't finished with his thoughts of the future.

'Do you remember Hakon?' he asks softly.

'Of course, my lord king. He was your foster brother, and now he's king of Norway, or rather, some parts of Norway. I believe he shares it with his brother or stepbrother; the relationship is complex.'

'He is king, yes. A good Norseman. Perhaps the only one I've ever truly liked.'

My eyes narrow at this. I can't decipher where Edmund's thoughts have taken him. I hold my tongue. I'll have to wait for him to elaborate.

'I hear his older brother, Eirik, causes him some difficulties, saying he should rule the kingdom, not Hakon. He's a vicious man.'

'I've heard the rumours of Eirik. Some call him Bloodaxe. He's a violent bastard, by all accounts.'

'If not for Eirik, I think we could have prevailed upon Hakon to aid us with the problem of York.'

'Perhaps, my lord king,' I murmur. Hakon, I understand, has more than enough to do contending with Eirik. I'm sure he won't be concerned with Edmund's worries.

'Athelstan.' Edmund recalls me to the present, and I realise my eyes are half shut. 'When Edgar is older, you and Lady Ælfwynn will foster him,' he says, sorrow lacing his words.

'My thanks, my lord king.' I stumble over the words. Our complex conversation has muddled my thoughts, but Edmund doesn't notice. Instead, he stares at the fire, considering his future and the fine dynasty he'll bestow upon the English. Men should dream of the future but should be aware of the here and now. I hope his eyes aren't too fixated on what he dreams of accomplishing in the future as opposed to how he'll achieve it. Edmund must face the Norse of York. If he calls in the aid of another of the Norse bastards, York will never truly belong to the English.

8

WINTER 943, SCONE, THE KINGDOM OF THE SCOTS

Mael Coluim, king of the Scots

For years, I've craved the position that should rightfully be mine. I've tormented myself each night with my ineffectual attempts to rally support and conspire against my predecessor, Constantin. Now that I have what I've always wanted, I find it to be far more problematic than I thought possible.

I blame Constantin. He should have died decades ago. Perhaps his son could have followed him soon after. That way, the kingdom would be clear for me to rule as I desire, without men always referring to the still-living man, whom I forced to abdicate.

If the old bastard would only die! It would make my task far, far easier.

Instead, I fear Constantin's grown more powerful, not less, in the wake of his abdication. I hear his following grows at St Andrew's, where he surrounds himself with his powerful family and those who seek his support against me and their rivals in other parts of our island.

By comparison, my court has few visitors. Unlike at my inauguration. Then, men travelled from far and wide to speak with me and pledge their support, including Dyfnwal of Strathclyde, who came despite everything I did to force him not to do so. If he'd absented himself, I could have taken it as defiance. Instead, he smirked all day, assuring me my intentions were too obvious.

I ought to have paid more attention that day and determined those loyal to me. I should have rooted out those merely paying lip service to the abrupt change of power.

Deploying my loyal adherents to speak openly with those in attendance would have ensured I knew the true intentions of all. I foresee Ildulb and Dyfnwal of Strathclyde causing me problems in the future. And Constantin? Well, I ought to have arranged for him to be murdered a long time ago. He's the biggest threat of all.

For now, I have intelligence that Ildulb supports Blakari Gothfrithson in the coming move against the ruling house of Bamburgh and his attempts to claim all of Northumbria for himself. I immediately sent word to Lord Ealdwulf. I'm unsure if the messenger reached him in time. If not, my warning could do more harm than good. Ealdwulf will curse me for not telling him sooner. Not that I could have done. Well, perhaps if I'd paid more attention to Ildulb, rather than exhilarating in my new kingship, it might have been possible.

Even now, I wonder why Constantin chose to help Blakari. I assume Blakari called on their blood ties to bind Constantin to his cause. Even so, it's a risky move.

I brood, sitting in my royal chair. I ought to be doing something, not waiting for the myriad threads in play to fray or come together. But all I ever wanted was to be king of the Scots. Now I have it, I want to hold on to it. I don't desire to pry into others' affairs because I don't want them to pry into mine.

It's a sorry state to be in, to gain what I've always dreamed of and still be unhappy.

Perhaps I should turn my eyes towards Strathclyde. Drive Dyfnwal from his place of power and take the land for my son, despite his alleged loyalty? Or maybe I too could enter the conflict in Jorvik? The bloody progeny of Ívarr. He was a real Norse bastard, but his grandsons and great-grandsons have done little but bicker and argue amongst themselves even while fathering more and more children so that the bickering and fighting and bloodshed goes on, without cease.

Not that my family are peace-loving, but I always thought we were more civilised in our ways, choosing not to kill, kidnap or maim each other. Even now, for all that I wish Constantin were murdered or dead, I know I'll not be the man to give the order.

A gentle murmur runs through the people assembled within my great hall. I turn lazy eyes to meet my steward. He's one of my greatest supporters. He looks worried and excited.

'My lord king, a visitor, from Jorvik,' he offers softly. I know he can't mean it's Blakari for he's already allied with Constantin and his son.

'Who?' I ask because he's not told me this important information.

'Anlaf Sihtricson, my lord king.'

I smirk, hoping this will be an opportunity for me to be triumphant. 'Bring him in,' I order, sitting upright and adjusting my elaborate clothing. I'm glad I dressed formally today. There was no need to, but I thought the people who serve me needed reminding that I'm still the king of the Scots, despite Constantin's survival and the counter-court growing at St Andrew's.

I've met Anlaf Sihtricson before. I joined his attacks in England, which ended in an ignominious treaty with King Edmund and the ultimate loss of his kingdom. I didn't much like the man, but if he provides the opening to interfere and make a name for myself, then I'll leap at it.

Anlaf strides into my hall, entirely unlike a cowed man who's lost his kingdom. I stand to greet him. His drawn face lightens. We meet as friends for all that we didn't part as such. It's funny how the passage of time has reversed our positions. I hold the power now. He has nothing.

I gesture for food and ale. Anlaf, his men meandering amongst my people, reaches thirstily for the gilded cup. He swallows its contents quickly before wiping his hand through his elaborately knotted beard and settles on a stool near my chair. He doesn't notice the disparity in the seating arrangement. That amuses me. Anlaf, once king of Jorvik, brother to kings, and son of a king, is immune to the fact he sits at the knee of another.

'An elegant hall,' he comments agreeably. He's come seeking my support and intends to be amenable.

'Yes, old and well constructed.'

'It suits you,' Anlaf offers with a wry smile. I try to return his gaze but find my attention snagged by the twenty warriors he's brought who are being fed by my servants from the largesse of my kingdom even though it's winter.

'I hear misfortune has struck you,' I begin.

He growls. 'Blakari's a bloody worm, for all he's my cousin. I'm sure you know that feeling only too well,' he suggests, appraising me keenly.

I do. My thoughts turn to Constantin and his son, the two men who are contenders for my position as king.

'What do you intend?' I question. The sooner I know, the sooner I can decide whether today is a good day.

'I seek allies. I will reclaim Jorvik from Blakari, but the pestilent

English king also has his eye on the kingdom. I need reliable men who'll support my kingship and won't baulk at the tactics I'll be using.'

I gasp at the implication. My exploits with Constantin have tarnished my reputation, even with the bloody Norse. I knew I'd suffer, but I didn't imagine it would make me an ally of choice to the great-grandsons of Ívarr the Boneless.

'What would you have me do?' I question, despite being angered by his words. I try not to show it, but my voice is clipped. All warmth is gone. He pretends not to notice. It doesn't make me like him more.

'Men, supplies, and your support for when I'm king.' His demands are reasonable, I grudgingly admit. 'And, of course, a promise you'll never assist Blakari. And you'll do all you can to punish bloody Ildulb and Constantin for supporting him in the first place.'

This part of Anlaf's request gives me pause for thought. I don't wish to make another enemy so quickly. I already have more than enough without adding Blakari. Anlaf senses my hesitation. He fixes me with a stare from his lowly position.

'Sometimes lines need to be drawn; alliances made firm. You'll be rewarded when Jorvik's mine. You'll be comforted by the knowledge your ally watches your borders and prevents the English from crossing them once more.'

Ah, the English. Another problem. I sense Edmund plans great things. His success over Anlaf, of which the man himself has just reminded me, makes Edmund as invincible as his brother, Athelstan.

No, the English will never step foot in the land of the Scots again. If Anlaf can protect the borders with the English, this alliance will be worthwhile. But that 'if' is huge. At the moment, Anlaf doesn't even have Jorvik.

'I've supporters in Dublin, alongside my remaining brother. I might not command Jorvik at this moment, but I will. My brother will ensure I do because he doesn't want me anywhere near his kingdom.'

The image Anlaf presents is appealing. I find myself drawn into the picture of the future he presents. Wouldn't it be worth making an enemy if I could be assured of this future?

'But Blakari has brothers in Dublin. Isn't one of them king? Gothfrith?'

Anlaf's face momentarily clouds. 'It's a fluctuating situation, likely to change on the spin of a coin,' he attempts to soothe.

'How will you maintain your grip on Jorvik?' I question instead. 'You've been king once. You lost the kingship.'

His face darkens. No doubt, he's thinking of the men who ousted him from power, Archbishop Wulfstan and Blakari Gothfrithson, although I suspect the hand of others at play as well.

'Archbishop Wulfstan will be expelled. Blakari, well, if he doesn't die in the attack, I'll have him banished or killed.'

'He's your cousin,' I say incredulously.

A crooked smile touches his lips. 'You seem to have accomplished it.' His retort is more gentle than my goading. The smile on my face freezes. Another slight to rile me and from a man who seeks an alliance. Anlaf knows his worth. The bastard.

'So, in exchange for my support, you'll banish Blakari and keep my borders safe, while getting rid of Archbishop Wulfstan of York?' As I list the promises he's just made in a few short heartbeats, his face clears, as though we've not both been casting words like weapons meant to wound.

'Yes, yes, all those things, and more, if I can and when the possibilities present themselves. And when Jorvik's mine, we could arrange a marriage alliance. You have daughters?' He thinks to have already accomplished what he came here for. But I'm not so keen.

My reservations outweigh the advantages of allying with a man who lacks land, even if he does have the blood of the House of Ívarr in his veins. 'I still have my men and my ships, don't forget that,' Anlaf mutters angrily, sensing my hesitation.

'I'll discuss it with my counsellors,' I offer, but even I know my voice isn't hopeful.

'Do what you must, Mael Coluim, but you need a collaborator, and if it isn't me, I'll have to go elsewhere. I might start with Lord Ealdwulf in Bamburgh. I imagine he'll welcome an alliance. Then we could feed our men by raiding into your kingdom.'

Damn the man. Now he threatens me. While he doesn't hold a kingdom, his warriors are bloody and brutal. Although, why they were overpowered in Jorvik might be worth exploring. As I say, I suspect the involvement of another in Jorvik.

'How many ships?'

Anlaf's eyes narrow. 'Enough to do what needs to be done,' is his less than helpful answer. He's confident Blakari's control of Jorvik is temporary. 'You need to support me, Mael Coluim, particularly since Constantin has allied with Blakari. When Blakari loses, it'll be another blow for the ailing Constantin.'

'Why would Blakari lose?' I question, curious to see if he knows more than he's so far alluded to.

'How can he be triumphant?'

I'm amused by the evasiveness. Anlaf speaks in riddles because he's hoarding secrets. If he hadn't turned to threats already, I'd be warming to him and perhaps prepared to give him what he wants without further thought. But no, he's menaced me, Mael Coluim, king of the Scots, and that pisses me off. I want to inconvenience him by delaying my response.

'Tomorrow,' I assure him. 'Tomorrow I'll speak in council, and seek advice. If they agree, then yes, I'll support you, but in return, there'll be no marriage alliance, not until you're back in Jorvik, and I know you're going to bloody well stay there.'

There's no malice in his gaze as he weighs up my answer. I mean it. He can bloody well wait for a decision. After all, other than Ealdwulf of Bamburgh, who else could he turn to for support? No one. I know, as he doesn't seem to realise, that Hywel of the Welsh has already refused him.

9

EARLY 944, BAMBURGH, THE KINGDOM OF BAMBURGH

Blakari Gothfrithson, king of Jorvik

The fortress of Bamburgh stretches out before me, its domination over the surrounding landscape takes my breath away.

This is what I call a bloody fortress. It's proud, unmoving and menacing in the low winter sunlight. Any man would be honoured to call this his home. Jealousy stirs within me. I've ridden past the fortress more times than I care to recall, both on horse and ship. I've always hungered for it. Now, I need it to show the remaining supporters of Anlaf Sihtricson that I rule Jorvik. I will reunite Bamburgh with the once mighty kingdom of Northumbria, and make my claim unassailable.

I suspect those within must be responsible for the murder of my brother, Olaf Gothfrithson, two summers ago. I should punish the inhabitants of Bamburgh for that. I will, in due time, but for now, my need is different. Taking Bamburgh will mark me as a true king, on an equal footing with my great-grandfather, Ívarr the Boneless. Once I'm inside, I need never leave. When it's mine, no one can pull me from its haven. But first I must get inside, and for now, that exercises my thoughts and those of my men.

We've ridden to Bamburgh from Jorvik, taking horses and iron. I decided to travel with stealth, using the hills and peaks that stretch away behind me to mask my warriors and our numbers. We've ridden through every weather imaginable, from blazing, if cold, sun to dripping rain to mizzling sleet. It's winter. Not a good time to make war, but for that reason, my advance will be unexpected. From afar, much further than I thought possible, I could see Bamburgh growing on the horizon, the so-called holy island of Lindisfarne stretching out behind it when the clouds allowed, the dotted islands of the Farnes blazing in the weak sunlight, or shrouded in fog and mist in the rain.

This is a wild land, not unlike the stories I've heard of the fjords in the far north of Norway, a place I've never visited, for I was born on this island.

Amongst the high hills of Northumbria, where the wind screeches and teases a man's clothes and unsettles his horse, it's possible to believe that destructive spirits wander, waiting to prey on men and beast alike.

I'm pleased to be away from the enclosing hills, with the fortress of Bamburgh firmly before me. By now, my force must have been sighted. Still, I linger. Ildulb of the Scots is joining my endeavours. I must wait for him. He'll bring more men to swell my force. Between us, and the small fleet of ships I've sent along the coast from Jorvik, I'll take Bamburgh. Partly in revenge for my brother's murder, but mostly because I bloody want it.

Men might think me a fool for staking my future on stealing an impregnable fortress from the House of Bamburgh, and aligning myself with the usurped House of Constantin, but bold action is required. I must reveal myself as a king without question. A mightier man than even my brother, Olaf, was.

If I fail, I've little chance of uniting Northumbria beneath my rule. If I fail, Anlaf Sihtricson will sneak his way inside Jorvik. Even now, he could be grovelling at Archbishop Wulfstan's feet. He might be begging for his support. And bloody Wulfstan could change allegiance once more. For a man of God, a man of peace, he thrives on war and controversy. The fat little duck takes pleasure in interfering.

I believe Archbishop Wulfstan to be ungodly, a man of the Christians' devil, come to cause rifts and ructions wherever he can, to line his coffer and give him the most power. If he had his way, he'd rule Jorvik in more ways than just in the eyes of his greedy God.

The smell of roasting meat assaults my nostrils. My stomach growls loudly. We've eaten well from the animals that dot the hilly landscape behind us, taking the stragglers separated from their herds when taken in from summer pasture. But this morning, I was keen to be away. I ordered the men to their horses before we'd broken our fast. I'm rueing that decision now.

I look towards the north. Ildulb will come from that direction, but I see no sign of him. A flicker of unease worms its way down my spine, settling in my growling belly. I'm relying on Ildulb to assist me. If he doesn't come, I'll have failed even to retain an ally. I won't countenance it. Instead, I eat the hunk of meat given to me by one of my men. Hungrily, I tear into the bloody flesh, allowing the juices to dribble into my beard before I lick them away. I'm keen to begin my assault on the fortress. I'm anxious to be inside it. I wish to enact my retribution for Olaf's murder and start my life as the king of Northumbria, not just the king of Jorvik.

On the journey here, I forced the local guide to show me the former stronghold of the ancient Northumbrian kings, destroyed by fire many winters ago and yet still visible in the burn marks and few pieces of remaining wood etched into the plain beside the gurgling river swelled by winter rain. The early kings of Northumbria, the men who built Bamburgh and enlarged Ad Gefrin, had huge ambitions. They thought to temper the nature of this land and tame it to their ways. Only at Ad Gefrin did their desires fail. Fire licked through the buildings, destroying them all. Few make the place their home now. It's the residence of whispers to the past, and a few hardy goats.

At Bamburgh, however, their forward-thinking has sheltered the men and women of their long line almost ever since Ad Gefrin burned, other than when Ealdwulf's father died nearly a decade ago. Then, the English king took control of Bamburgh. His hold on it didn't outlast the death of the ealdorman he ordered to keep it safe.

It's a stunning place, I admit. It might well be buffered by the wind whenever I visit, and the sun might shine only rarely, but Bamburgh is a name from which to conjure ancient tales. I plan on it being where my future begins. My horse shares my excitement, stirring beneath me.

Soon, very soon, I'll give the command to march, once Ildulb arrives. I hope his father hasn't thought better of involving himself in this assault.

But, first, I've ordered my men to light a chain of fires along the ridge upon which I stand. I want the people of Bamburgh to know we're coming and to fear our numbers. Then, when their attention's focused on my mounted men, and hopefully Ildulb's when he eventually arrives, those from the ships will begin the attack.

The man who leads the shipmen, Egil, assures me he knows the coastline. He boasts of how he'll force his way into the fortress. He better be bloody right. Losing now will cause untold damage to my reputation.

My scout from the north arrives then, face flushed from the strong wind. His grin tells me all I need to know. Ildulb's coming and bringing with him men, as he promised, with his father's tacit acceptance. He's late, but at least he's here in time to begin the offensive.

Seeing the former king, Constantin, in his monastery was a sobering experience and one that taught me something essential. The man in power isn't always the man in authority. Mael Coluim believes he rules the Scots. But he doesn't. He only thinks he does. The majority of people support him because they cling to the hope that Constantin will be returned to his rightful position when the opportunity arises.

I hope to control Jorvik in a different way. Anlaf Sihtricson is gone. I hear rumours he's in discussions with all and sundry, even the peace-loving Hywel of the Welsh people. How Hywel keeps order in his land and amongst the always rebellious Welsh is a wonder to me. He acts more like a monk than a king. Yet the kingdoms of the Welsh are serene beneath his rule. He spends his time making laws and praying to God. He must be bored by the tediousness of his life. A man always needs an enemy to feel alive.

As I sit and muse, Ildulb and his men ride into camp. I wasn't sure how many warriors he'd bring. We never discussed numbers. I'm surprised it's a good-sized force, perhaps as many as four hundred strong. Once more, it reveals to me that the man who rules in name isn't necessarily the man who wields the most influence.

Ildulb brings greater strength than when he joined Anlaf Sihtricson. I smirk with pleasure. Last time, Ildulb came south with his king's blessing, no matter that he was also his father. Now he rides with his father's approval and not his king's. I consider if Ildulb fears repercussions for aiding me. Mael Coluim has made a messy start to his reign. I'll fare better than he has once I'm king of Northumbria.

'Blakari Gothfrithson,' Ildulb calls. His thick accent mangles my name but I know what he means. I ride to meet him, admiring his strong horse. The beast isn't a thing of beauty, but I know it can be ridden all day and never tire of its burden. I'd rather that than a pretty prancing thing.

Ildulb's horse has teeth to match a boar's, and as it reaches to nip my more temperate beast, I swing him away from Ildulb. Ildulb's grin isn't lost on me. He delights in his horse's nature.

'Ildulb, son of Constantin,' I respond, my voice steady despite fighting with my horse.

'Have you been here long?' he questions, as though we've met for ale and wine. I imagine he knows the answer to that.

'Only this morning. We built fires to scare the men and women of Bamburgh.'

He grins once more, but it's tinged with malice. 'The warriors of Bamburgh will need more than a few scattered fires to concern them.' His words bite deep, and momentarily I feel foolish for taking such pride in my feats. Ildulb knows these lands and people better than I do.

'You brought archers?' I ask, deflecting.

'Thirty, all I could tempt away from their homes. Most of them are from the troubled borderlands, and by God, they hate the kingdom of Bamburgh.' He speaks with spite. These lands are riddled with communities who detest one another. I've set myself a steep task in trying to unite them.

'My thanks,' I reply. Men who hate each other don't always make the best enemies. It's better to hold aloft from the work that needs doing in battle than become too embroiled in the honour of the thing. I'd rather kill men I've never met than face my neighbour behind the shield wall.

'They'll fight like bastards,' Ildulb reassures with relish and turns to face Bamburgh, assessing it, as I've just been doing. 'Your ships are coming?' he queries. We talked at length at St Andrew's about how to accomplish the attack on Bamburgh. It was his idea to bring ships, a suggestion that even now makes me smirk because the Scots are no fans of ships and seafaring, unlike my ancestors. I should have been the one to suggest ships.

'Egil will be here soon,' I confirm. 'I've a scout following him along the coast. Last night, the ships were still to the south, but if the horseman can return in a day, then so can my ships.'

'So we have what? A thousand men?'

'Yes, Bamburgh has far fewer than that.'

'So we hope,' he mutters darkly. 'Not that it matters if we don't make it inside the fortress.'

Again, I hold my tongue. Ildulb's reservations about my plan have been voiced. I don't need to hear them today, on the cusp of our attempt to overwhelm Bamburgh. I want Northumbria. Bamburgh is the key to it.

'We'll get inside,' I resolve. What he doesn't know, and neither do the majority of my men, is that I've spies inside Bamburgh. They went on a trading vessel a few weeks ago but will work from inside to enable our entry. We'll attack by sea, land and from the inside. Our defeat should be impossible, but I know better than to be overconfident. Overconfidence is a killer; exactly what happened to Olaf when he met his death not far from here.

Olaf believed he was safe, emboldened by his reputation and warriors. He forgot that men who know the terrain are a more tangible enemy. I wish I'd been with him when he was attacked, I suspect by the people of Bamburgh. Perhaps I could have saved him, but then, my brother was never one to exercise much caution. He never took kindly to having his methods questioned.

If he hadn't been my brother, I wouldn't have liked him, let alone served him. But my brother's dead. I seek vengeance for that killing even while accomplishing something for myself.

'Do we attack today?' Ildulb questions, eyes narrowing as he watches the fortress. Men litter the earth bank surrounding it.

They're visible as small dots. They've seen me. They need to be looking this way so that Egil can take the sea gate, and my men inside Bamburgh can force their way through to us.

'We do, yes.' I left it to the men inside to determine the best course of action. They can open the main gate that slopes along the sandy dunes to the south, or if they deem it safer, help the men through the more difficult sea gate to the north. Either way will work for me. I know they're safe because one of them placed a message at the ruined site of Ad Gefrin, as planned. It was a simple alignment of stones, as though a grave marker, but my man left it to show no one within Bamburgh suspected him. He should be free to move about when the attack starts. No one will question his position and that of his handful of men near the sea gate or on the landward approach.

I'm confident as I watch Ildulb's men ride into position. I have the numbers. When we launch our assault, we'll be a formidable force.

I allow some time for the Scots to recover from their journey, to eat, drink and piss. I'm assuming they've been travelling for a few days.

'Should we advance?' I question Ildulb, being courteous in the face of my certain victory. If he has any fear that Mael Coluim will punish him for involving himself in this fight, he doesn't reveal it.

Ildulb nods once decisively, short hair falling into his eyes. He's a talented man, like his father. I can tell from the way he thinks before committing. I thought grief for his son might have made him impetuous, but I'm wrong. Instead, the time and distance from the event has made him a cold, hard killer, one keen to take his vengeance on anyone who steps in his way. When he becomes the king of the Scots, he'll be a great man. I see it in his future already.

I order the men to ride on, not exactly fast, but not slowly, either. We've been seen. There's no point in hiding our intention. I hope the warriors of Bamburgh don't prevail on the new king to seek a treaty with me. I'm in no mood for talking. I have vengeance to seek against the warriors I suspect killed my brother.

The terrain fluctuates between hill and trough. I never take my eyes from the fortress. Soon, I hope to have an indication that all is going as planned within. As of yet, there's nothing, merely a host of warriors coming into clearer sight the closer we ride. My men inside need to be quick. Soon I'll no longer be able to see the fortress in its entirety. I need to know which way to direct my force.

There must be two hundred men outside the fortress on its sloping approach. I'm surprised. I didn't expect so many to be battle-ready. I didn't imagine that Ealdwulf's Bamburgh had so many warriors to call upon to protect him. I consider calling to Ildulb, but he's veered away, riding with his men.

Ildulb's warriors are well-armed with spears and swords. Their horses are sturdy and step well over the uneven ground. I have an image of them riding for days without pausing for breath or rest. Perhaps some of the horses should be added to my herd.

Ildulb doesn't look as magnificent in battle garb as I do, I admit. I wear my brother's byrnie, not because it's finer than mine, but because I must carry some part of him into the battle when I avenge his killing. My sword's a family heirloom. Legend has it that it was brought all the way from the lands in the far north where snow and ice rarely leave the ground. I'm not sure I believe it. The pattern-wielded blade looks similar to others I've seen forged within Dublin. My helm's shining brightly. It lacks any decoration because I don't understand why any helm used for war and bloodshed should be elaborate.

I've seen men with animals etched onto the metal and strange shapes leaping down the faceplate. They look acceptable on other men. But weapons should be functional. Jewels are beautiful on the neck of my women or mounted onto clothing.

Quickly, we ride toward the enemy because there is still no sign as to which gate my warriors have opened from within. Then I curse, for I can see the outer rampart of the fortress and the limp bodies of men hanging from stakes set into it.

'Bollocks.' Disappointment crushes me. My men have betrayed me or betrayed themselves. Bamburgh knew to expect me and for longer than a day or two.

'Was this your big secret?' Ildulb calls, coming next to me again. His words thrum with anger. I rein my animal in, looking closely at the bloated bodies of the men who came garbed as traders. I swallow against nausea as I gaze at the purpling faces swinging gently in the breeze. It wasn't a good death.

'Yes, they were my secret,' I mutter angrily. How did the people of Bamburgh even know to look for spies in their midst? Surely not one of my men? Surely not Ildulb? I glare at him. His eyes sparkle with sudden amusement at so easily deciphering my thoughts.

'It wasn't me, you bloody fool, or my father. He mightn't have wanted to attack Bamburgh, but he saw the undeniable logic of it. Who else did you tell of your plans?'

I want to think about it, decide where the blame lies, but instead, a collection of ten horsemen ride toward me from inside the fortress. This must be the king of Bamburgh, Ealdwulf.

'Blakari Gothfrithson and Ildulb, of the House of Constantin?' The voice is thick with malice. Immediately, my anger flares. He knows my name? What more did these fools tell him?

At my side, Ildulb chuckles darkly. I flash him a furious stare.

'You look like your brother,' Ealdwulf offers. 'And you, Ildulb, look like your father.'

'Ealdwulf of Bamburgh?' I utter through tight lips. He comes dressed for war. His byrnie shimmers beneath the winter sun. His horse steps high. On his head, he wears a helm decorated with emblems I don't recognise but which seem to move over the iron.

That he references my brother reinforces my belief that he was responsible for Olaf's murder.

'The same,' he replies curtly, lips curled with delight. 'Your feeble efforts to take my kingdom have failed before starting. You've an enemy you don't even know about,' he mocks. I can't stop glancing to where the bodies of my dead allies swing on creaking ropes. They were good men. I will mourn them, when my fury fades at their failure.

'Who told you?' Ildulb demands, overly keen to have his name cleared of any wrongdoing. I don't miss his sword is once more sheathed. He's readying himself for a nice chat on a sunny day, not a battle to decide who rules here.

'A friendly messenger from the south.'

Ildulb groans in response. The English king, or one of his ealdormen, conspires against me. That angers me, for it was the English king and his Mercian ealdorman that lent their weight to Archbishop Wulfstan, enabling me to take the kingdom from Anlaf Sihtricson. Are the English determined to interfere in every action that takes place within this island? I thought King Edmund incapable of such double deceit. I was evidently wrong.

'I take it you don't mean to hand Bamburgh over to me?' I ask, curiously. Do I want to know how arrogant this man is? Will he take affront at my words, or will he brush them off?

Annoyingly, he smirks. He's younger than me, and yet he has Bamburgh as his stronghold. Jealously stirs within me once more.

'Bamburgh has always had friends in the south. I rule here now. I might not have done so when my father first died, but I wasn't a man then, and looked towards the wrong allies for aid. Now I am a man. I'm a ruler, and a king. Ildulb, of the House of Constantin, tell your father, he should have assisted me when I was young and foolish if he wanted to win my support. Tell him I hope he enjoys his "retirement".'

'You'll bow your knee to the English?' I jibe, while Ildulb growls angrily. Ildulb's told me how unhappy Ealdwulf's father, Ealdred, was to be a signatory to Athelstan's great treaty agreed in 927 at Eamont. He wouldn't welcome his son's alliances now, would he?

Ealdwulf, a pleasant-enough-looking man with bright blue eyes and long dirty-coloured hair, grins at my attempts to rile him. 'The men of Bamburgh do what must be done. It's a pity your kind never have, nor yours, Ildulb.'

Ildulb's silent at the words, neither agreeing nor disagreeing, just accepting them as Ealdwulf's due, while he fights his anger. I should never have come here. Now, unless some miracle occurs, I'll appear even weaker than bloody Anlaf Sihtricson. There'll be no battle today and Bamburgh won't be mine.

'You should look to your lands, not mine,' Ealdwulf calls mockingly. He turns his horse and rides away, taking his men with him. I'm left with a thousand hungry and enraged men who won't be fighting for treasure and women today. Their anger burbles around me.

'Well, that's you bloody told,' Ildulb mutters, turning his horse to face the north. 'And what did he mean by looking to your lands?' Ildulb's reminder of those words worries me.

I peer towards Jorvik as though the distance were only short and not at least four days' travel at a gallop. Surely Anlaf Sihtricson isn't reclaiming Jorvik in my absence?

'He wouldn't,' I mutter angrily, my gaze switching between the impregnable fortress of Bamburgh and south, where I know Jorvik lies.

'He might,' Ildulb taunts over his shoulder. It's evident he's not going to stay any longer.

'Arse,' I exclaim, and a few other choice words as well.

I need to get back to Jorvik. Yesterday.

10

944, ST ANDREW'S, THE KINGDOM OF THE SCOTS

Ildulb, prince of the Scots

My father seems to have grown in stature during my brief absence. He's still an old man, and yet he commands a small court now. He might have gambled on supporting Blakari Gothfrithson and lost on this occasion, but it's had little impact on his influence within the land of the Scots. Mael Coluim must be cursing the day he usurped my father's kingship.

Blakari didn't take Bamburgh but rushed back to Jorvik to prevent Anlaf Sihtricson's suspected action to reclaim it. Only, or so rumour has it from one of the traders I met returning to St Andrew's, he was too late. Now Anlaf Sihtricson has Jorvik once more while Blakari besieges him, not Bamburgh. Blakari has gone from wishing to be king of Northumbria, to being king of absolutely nothing.

My father greets me with a smile of welcome, and yet I can tell he knows something he needs to share with me. Quickly, he walks through the throng of men and women who've come to watch him pray, shuffling over the stone floor. He leads me outside into the bitter wind and icy chill. It's cold, the tang of sea salt hanging heavy in the air. My father huddles into his cloak as we approach the cliff edges.

'It's good to see you, Father,' I say. I mean it. He hugs me warmly, his ageing body frail against mine.

'And you, son. I hear the battle was short-lived.'

'Non-existent, not short-lived. Blakari believes Anlaf had set his sights on Jorvik.'

'I hear the same. And with the support of Mael Coluim this time.' So this is my father's news. It interests me, for Ealdwulf implied the English king was the cause of Blakari's problems. He lied. Or maybe, both Mael Coluim and Edmund vie for influence with Bamburgh. Ealdwulf perhaps relishes being pulled back into events between the English, the Scots and the Norse of Jorvik and Dublin. 'As long as Blakari ultimately prevails, it doesn't matter that he's so far failed. This will be Mael Coluim's first mistake of many.'

Curiously, I watch my father. Before, he was prepared to sit quietly and wait for Mael Coluim's errors; now, he hungers for them. While Blakari might have failed, he has reinvigorated my father by demanding his assistance. My father has enjoyed interfering. He's revelled in it a great deal. He's a man of his God. He lives to pray, even while thriving on intrigue and misdirection. How else would he have remained king for four decades if the politicking wasn't so enjoyable?

I shrug. I don't know if Blakari will retain his kingship. He's a Norseman. I suspect he will know how to fight. Not that I've seen it yet. For all that, his men seemed loyal. The name of his brother, or his father, perhaps keeps his warriors faithful despite his drinking and whoring. His brother, Olaf, was a king. Of the many brothers, all sons of Gothfrith, two are dead long before their time. Yet

Blakari has so far failed to prove himself as anything more than a man to be manipulated by events outside Jorvik. He might be dead soon as well.

I wish Anlaf Sihtricson had sought me first. I predict he'll endure for longer than Blakari, although he has three dead brothers to Blakari's two. Even Haraldr Sihtricson who once claimed Limerick in exchange for returning my sister to her husband is long dead. Perhaps, after all, Blakari was the right man.

I rub my forehead as I consider the possibilities. I have many brothers and one sister. I have sons and daughters as well, but already one of my sons is dead at the hands of Edmund. Of all my enemies and allies, it's Edmund who must suffer. I'll need to rely on my father for that. I'm pleased to see him reanimated.

Mael Coluim is a temporary setback, nothing more, I'm sure of that. I wouldn't be surprised to find Dyfnwal of Strathclyde at my father's court shortly. Nothing would shock me.

'Ealdwulf plays Anlaf Sihtricson and Blakari Gothfrithson off against each other, with no desire to see either succeed. Mael Coluim has come too late to the intrigue that infects the kingdoms. I've heard rumours that Anlaf wooed Mael Coluim. I suspect Mael Coluim is too scared of losing his kingdom to intrude elsewhere,' I inform my father. 'I imagine that Hywel, in his Welsh kingdoms, keeps himself aloof and independent. He thinks to survive and keep his hastily amalgamated country together by seeking no outside assistance. I believe he's a fool and an idiot. Look at England. More than fifty years after Alfred tried to keep the Norse out through unity of purpose, England is still not complete. Too much of it remains in the hands of Anlaf and Blakari,' I conclude.

'The English king's marching north,' my father announces. Despite my thoughts, this does surprise me. Perhaps Ealdwulf didn't lie after all. Maybe it was the English king who appraised Ealdwulf of Blakari's intentions.

'What do we do?' I question.

'You should support Blakari. Put the failure at Bamburgh behind you and sail to Jorvik.'

At my father's brusque tone, my mouth falls open. I'm not used to him treating me as though I'm simply one of the members of his political faction, to be directed as he sees fit. I hear the command in his voice. I'd not have expected such from my father unless he thought it was urgent and necessary.

'You shouldn't have left him,' he adds, all the apology I'm going to get for riding to Bamburgh and back again, and now being ordered to travel south once more to Jorvik.

'Very good, my lord king.' I bow my head. If he wants to act as king, I'll do him the honour of responding to him as my king. I might have wanted to come home, but I'll ride back to war.

'Take our ship army,' my father advises. Only then do I truly appreciate the strength of his resolve. He wants Blakari to succeed. In the past, we've pledged our help but prevaricated, often trying not to get too involved. This time, everything is different. He means for me to take the ship army which belongs to the kingdom of the Scots. It seems he's won the support of the commanders. He has been very busy in my absence.

'I'll leave tomorrow, my lord king.' He nods and reaches out to grasp my strong arm, his weaker fingers only just snaking their way around my strength.

'My thanks,' he murmurs. In those two words, I hear many things he doesn't say.

'You've had many visitors?' I question him, turning the conversation away from war.

'I think more than Mael Coluim. Your sister manages them well and ensures no one waits too long.'

My sister, Olaf's wife, the murderer of my brother Alpin. If Mael

Coluim had any stones, he'd have married her, despite her tendency to kill men.

'Does she have a new husband yet?' I question. My father shakes his head.

'It won't be long. She doesn't ask for one, but I see the longing in her eyes. She wants more children. A noble marriage will come soon.' It's interesting that my father makes no mention of Alpin. That is his way. How quickly he rewrites the past in his mind to suit him.

'Doesn't Mael Coluim send spies?' I worry.

'Of course he does. We let them see what they must and try to keep the rest hidden. He's not blind to what happens here, but if he has no proof, there's little he can do.'

'And you ensure he has no proof?'

'Only what he can see with his eyes. He knows you went south, naturally, but other than that, he doesn't realise we work actively against him.'

'And allying with Blakari isn't acting against him?' I taunt because, suddenly, I worry my father isn't quite as sly as he thinks.

'If he doesn't know you've returned home, he'll never know you've left again.'

His argument is good, but I imagine some of the riders I passed on the way here will report back to Mael Coluim. I sigh. I could go after them and ensure they never see Mael Coluim, but there's no time, not if I'm to sail tomorrow.

'And if he already knows?'

'Then he can think what he will. You'll be gone. I can always pretend to be the senile old man he wants me to be and deny all knowledge.'

My mouth turns down at my father's words. It's my future he's imperilling, not his. As I gaze out at the ocean before me, black and foreboding, I decide I've little choice in my immediate prospects. I'll allow myself to go where the storm-tossed waves take me.

'Tomorrow then,' I confirm, and walk back to where a host of men and women wait to speak to my father, the man who is the king of the Scots in all but name.

11

EARLY 944, WINCHESTER, THE KINGDOM OF THE ENGLISH

Eadred, prince and ætheling of the English

The court's in uproar. Men and women rush from one end of the vast hall to the other and sometimes back again. Still, they don't seem to have accomplished what needs to be done to enable them to ride to war tomorrow.

Edmund's amongst the furore, orders crisply given, and his intentions clear. He discusses the finer details with Ealdorman Athelstan and his brothers. Between the great men of the witan, the decision has been made that York's now open for an attack. Edmund's mustering quickly. I watch them with a sense of longing and also great relief. My brother, my half-brother, my father, my aunt and my grandfather before them were all warriors who fought for our land. I'm no great warrior, and neither do I hope to be one. Not yet. Perhaps never.

My mother, Lady Eadgifu, watches me carefully. Even though I think she's old, she remains an exceptional woman to look upon. Men comment on her beauty and wisdom in the same breath. She perceives my thoughts well. She's proud of her oldest son and doesn't want anything to detract from what she's already calling his moment of glory.

Athelstan, my half-brother, claimed York through a marriage alliance between our half-sister and Sihtric Ívarrson. When he died, York became a part of England. But, with Athelstan's death, Olaf Gothfrithson took York for himself. Now the descendants of the House of Ívarr bicker and argue over York. Edmund has set each side against one another with the readily given help of the interfering Wulfstan, archbishop of York.

It's a dizzying array of people and family connections. I'm pleased my brother's a young man with two sons, two æthelings, who will grow to manhood in the coming years and will follow in his footsteps. He has also remarried, so I hope more children will arrive in good time. I need do little but pay scant attention to affairs that affect the kingdom. My mother despairs of me. Yet, I don't see why I should be aware of everything that happens. I'll never be the king of England, and for that, I'm pleased. I'll be only the second of my father's sons not to be proclaimed as king. I try not to consider what would happen if something befell my brother before his sons were men. Until such time, I am, I admit grudgingly, his heir.

'Brother,' Edmund calls to me from his place near the hearth. I walk towards him. I imagine he'll leave me in control of the kingdom while he fights for York. I won't be ruling alone, however, which pleases me.

'My lord brother,' I respond, bowing my head respectfully.

'The ealdormen will accompany me to York, all apart from Athelstan, our cousin. I've tasked him with supporting you in my absence. I know you'll listen to him. In turn, he'll respect your decisions. I don't envisage either Anlaf Sihtricson or Blakari Gothfrithson threatening to invade Wessex. They're too busy arguing, but if any attack does come, Ealdorman Athelstan will lead the Wessex fyrd against them until such time as my warriors and I can return.'

Fear temporarily grips me. I don't welcome the threat of war, here, in the heartland of Wessex. 'Excellent, my lord king,' I reply, voice quivering.

'Nothing will happen, brother, fear not.' Edmund relaxes his tense posture, and leans over to grip my shoulders. He's taller than me. My mother thinks I might grow taller yet. I'm not convinced. 'Keep the æthelings safe, and my new wife. Ensure mother is informed of everything while I'm on campaign. Ealdorman Athelstan will help with anything else.'

I appreciate his confidence. He slaps my shoulders reassuringly. Edmund's a strong man. I'll miss him when he's gone, but I don't envy him. He fought in Cait, with Athelstan, and took the life of the Scots king's grandson, and earned for himself the regard of England's warriors. He fought at Brunanburh, bloodied his blades and made a name for himself, and he's welcome to that victory. I've not been allowed to take up arms against our enemy. As the final remaining son of King Edward, I am too precious. All the same, I sometimes think the warrior blood that runs through the House of Wessex is absent in me. I hope it never becomes a problem. I wish never to rule, but even so, I practise with shield and blade for when I might have to stand in my first shield wall.

Ealdorman Athelstan smiles with confident reassurance. He's almost as much a brother to me as Edmund. But Ealdorman Athelstan treats me with more respect than my brother.

'You leave tomorrow?' I ask. My brother grunts an affirmative.

'The men are enemies. Everyone knows it. While Anlaf Sihtricson tries to retake York from Blakari Gothfrithson, who must fend off his enemies, both to the north and the south, I plan to attack the rear of Anlaf's forces. I'll drive them into the shields and swords of Blakari's troops. I'll kill as many enemies as possible without risking more of my warriors than necessary.'

Ealdorman Athelstan nods as he listens to Edmund's words. He approves of his plan, but for all I like him, and I do like him, I fear his ambitions. He might be my cousin, and I love his wife, Lady Ælfwynn, as though she were my sister, but if something happens to Edmund, Ealdorman Athelstan will be more powerful than me. He'll have the reputation of a warrior as well as having married into the ruling line of the House of Wessex, albeit through the Mercian link.

My mother suspects the same. As the king's brother, I should have a power base of my own, but there's been no time to build one since Edmund became king. It's been enough to ensure the ealdormen stayed true to the king, without worrying about the king's brother.

My mother has spent her time ensuring Edmund was supported, and there were none to dispute the kingship. Edmund's a father to small boys, but Ealdorman Athelstan has four sons and two brothers who could support any declaration for the kingship. I've no one but Edmund's young sons and my mother. Perhaps I shouldn't underestimate my mother. She's survived at the English court for decades. I imagine she would have no problem moving against Ealdorman Athelstan and Lady Ælfwynn if it were ever necessary to do so.

All the same, despite Edmund's preparation for war, he has failed to consider the future if he doesn't return.

'Send word of your victory,' I offer with a smile of confidence I don't feel. Fear rides me today. I don't know why. I trust my brother, I trust his warriors, and yet. I swallow thickly; trusting my brother doesn't mean he and his men won't all meet their deaths against the Norse. Allies and enemies are too easily interchangeable for my comfort. Even as young as I am, I know that.

Edmund's face splits with delight to hear my confidence. Although Ealdorman Athelstan watches me carefully, I hope he sees no sign of my worries.

'I will, Eadred. Keep England safe and whole for me,' he announces, but it's a flippant comment. The Norse menace has faded away to almost nothing. The men and women of the Five Boroughs are content with my brother's rule. No other Norse leader has yet laid claim to England. She stands at her calmest for over fifty winters. Old men of Wessex might just die in their beds for the first time in generations. Young men, well, they might die of boredom if Edmund's plan is a success.

'Go with God,' I offer. His face turns serious.

'I will, Eadred, my thanks for reminding me.' Abruptly, he's gone in a swirl of his cloak and a trail of men who wish to ask him questions. I watch him go, then I feel the eyes of someone on me. I turn to meet the gaze of my mother. She's watching as carefully as Ealdorman Athelstan. I hope I meet her expectations. Her eyebrows rise slightly. I consider what she sees, but then Ealdorman Athelstan's talking to me, unaware of my inattention.

'The king will fight well,' he reassures.

But, as England grows calm beneath my brother, I already see problems in the future. Peace will be the making of men who are bored, men who are great, and men who decide to cause problems and strife amongst each other instead of using their skills against the Norse. I consider what damage they'll cause. Will they resent my family for holding power when they don't?

'He always does,' I acknowledge with a smile. Pretending I have urgent business elsewhere, I walk away. Now I feel two pairs of eyes on me. I don't like the scrutiny.

I'm not a king, nor ever likely to be a king, yet I'm watched as though I were one. I resent it but have no power to stop it.

I shake my head irritably. In the wake of my family's final

victory over the Norse, I should be excited, not nervous and worried. It all sounds too easy when my brother discusses tactics, which concerns me the most.

I think the coming battle will be difficult. I fear for my brother's life and my future.

12

944, THE KINGDOM OF JORVIK

Ildulb, prince of the Scots

I've always liked being on board a ship, but Olaf Gothfrithson taught me to love the feel of the waves beneath my feet and the wind in the sail. He might have wanted to hold Jorvik and Dublin, but he should have been a hero from a scop song, seeking out new places to plunder and forever sailing onwards into the infinite horizon.

Now, although the weather is dark and bleak, the days too short to travel far, I find I don't want the voyage to end. My men have been seasick and fearful and can't wait to reach Jorvik, but I want to stay right where I am. I feel free and have nothing to be concerned with but where we'll anchor for the night and where we might sleep, sheltered from the wind in a cove along the shoreline. It's a life devoid of responsibility. It's perhaps the first time in my life I've felt like this.

Eventually, the days bring the ship within sight of land near the great Humber Estuary, which will take us to the tidal River Ouse running to Jorvik. I know my freedom's at an end. If I'm not already too late, I must seek Blakari Gothfrithson and reinforce him against the imminent English attack. I hope he's made his way inside Jorvik. I pray Anlaf doesn't retain his hold on the settlement. That will make things very difficult.

Not that the foray inland is quick. We've a long way to travel along the Humber. As we go, I notice the surroundings. To the south is territory the English king claims. To the north is territory claimed by the king of Jorvik, whoever that might be right now. The journey takes much longer than I anticipated. I always believed Jorvik was close to the sea, but I'm wrong. I've only ever travelled to Jorvik via the land before, making my entrance into Jorvik through the ancient walls which do more to protect Archbishop Wulfstan and his church and monks than the rest of the population.

My ship's captain, Drostan, knows the route well. He calls to me, pointing out local landmarks, and eventually turns the ships north along the River Ouse. And still we travel. Perhaps, after all, I needn't fear the endeavour coming to an end, because it seems we have much further to go.

Only then, in the distance, I do detect a haze of smoke on the horizon. Immediately, I fear I might be too late. Moving with the motions of the tidal river, my ship glides past another craft listing to the side. I've been warned about this. It's not a new trick, to scuttle ships to prevent others using the river to reach Jorvik. It doesn't entirely block the wide River Ouse, though, and we can still navigate around it, or rather, my captain can. Perhaps it's one of the ships that went to Bamburgh with Blakari, and Anlaf has submerged it to stop his cousin reclaiming Jorvik.

A little further ahead, the river splits, but Drostan, knows the way.

'The Foss,' he indicates with his chin, 'but we stick with the Ouse. The river's easier to navigate because it's so much wider,' he reassures me. To either side of us, the riverbanks steepen, but the haze of smoke doesn't lessen, instead becoming intermingled with low-hanging clouds and a sullen wetness that has everything damp before we even realise it. I'm grateful I wear my sealskin cloak to keep me as dry as possible. I thought it was to prevent the sea and river water from drenching me, but instead, it's from the mizzle that descends from above.

'Stop here,' I urge Drostan, deciding to go no further until I find out what's happened. He hurries to obey, his men carrying out instructions to remove the sail and bring in almost all of the oars. I consider what I should do now that I've arrived close to Jorvik with my few ships. Where am I likely to find Blakari? Is he within Jorvik itself? Are the fires sending smoke high into the sky those of the English or the Norse? There's no sign of anyone to question. I can see the settlement of Jorvik ahead, and of course, I've been here before, but other than allowing me to know where the ruler of Jorvik should be, I don't know what to do to find Blakari. I don't want to come upon Anlaf unexpectedly. I'm here to support Blakari, not Anlaf. I need more information.

'Where should I go?' I question Drostan. He's been to Jorvik many more times than me.

He shrugs, eyes alert to everything around him. 'I'd suggest the quayside, but perhaps not. I suspect they've fouled the river channel with more ships than the one we've just seen.' There are quaysides and docklands up ahead on the northern banks, but the ships have been brought up high either against the tidal surges of the river, or to prevent them being damaged by whatever's been sunk beneath the water. Or, perhaps because it's likely to flood with so much rain falling from the sky. There are no signs of activity other than the smoking fires and the incessant rain. It's not a day for men and women to be taking their ease. It provides me with no intelligence upon which to base my next decision.

'We go ashore,' I decide. I must find out more.

I need to know if the English king and his warriors are here. I must also determine if Anlaf or Blakari claims the king's hall within Jorvik. I know where the building is, but the riverbanks are too steep to climb closer to Jorvik. I must come ashore before the banks are so sharp it's impossible to crest them.

Jorvik has many natural barriers, as well as the remains of the enclosing walls, which are so unusual to my eyes. Of course, I've seen the ancient wall that runs across the kingdom of Northumbria from west coast to east, and there are some remnants of something else similar within the kingdom of the Scots. But it's strange to see the remains of the ancient walls being put to such use. Within Jorvik itself, I know the walls stretch far above a person's head. There are even towers that can serve as lookout points, but these are to the north of the River Ouse. We must come ashore to the south, where the rest of the settlement lies. Only from there will I be able to see the English force, if it's there, and, hopefully, determine where Blakari might be. If he's in control of Jorvik, the bridge over the River Ouse from the southern to the northern settlement will allow me to reach him quickly.

If Blakari lives, and I hope he does, I can do some good for him. If he's in command of Jorvik, and the English are here, I can join his warriors and assist him in overpowering our enemy. Despite the dankness, a grin touches my lips.

'Stay with the ships,' I order Drostan. We've struck up a good friendship on the journey here. It seems a man who loves his ship is always keen to speak with someone else who shares the same enthusiasm. His loyalty to my father is without doubt. All the same, I place a shimmering ring of silver into his hands, which I remove from my money pouch. I don't want another to offer him silver and riches to abandon us. Drostan opens his mouth to deny the treasure. 'Take it. If the worst happens, hurry back to the Humber and the open sea with the rest of the ships, but stay as long as you can.' I grip his shoulder, and hold his gaze. He nods, eyes conflicted. Perhaps he wishes to join the fight. Maybe he's happy not to be called upon to do so.

My warriors and I stealthily approach the southern settlement, slipping on the muddy riverbank. We're all on our guard. The smell of defeat is as tangible as the sodden vegetation, limping beneath the deluge. Abruptly, I find we're on some recognised trackway. It's not wide. Perhaps it's used by those taking their animals to pasture in the summer. Ahead, I see the familiar outline of a wooden church, grey and forbidding in the gloom. I listen for the sound of prayers, but there's nothing.

'This way,' I urge my warriors, using the church to obscure our passage. I venture to the rear of the building, mindful of the thick mud and the rumble of the river behind us. I sense eyes everywhere, but I can see no one. Not here, and not on the other side of the River Ouse. It's as though everyone has disappeared beneath the low-lying clouds.

I peer around the side of the church, eyes squinting against the gloom. It takes me some time to decipher what's happening.

Here, we're distant from the southern settlement of Jorvik. In the far distance, I can see the walls built there. They're nowhere near as solid as the ancient ones. For some reason I've never been able to determine, the people who built the walls around both sides of the settlement, separated by the River Ouse, never thought to fully enclose the western-facing walls of the southern settlement. Instead, those who've ruled Jorvik have produced something of a shoddy replacement. The mud walls and banked turf perform almost the same function as the other walls.

'We need to go there,' I order my warriors. I can see an encampment stretching away, grey and damp, but I don't know whose it is. It's just too far.

With boots filling with mud, and on legs that slip and slide, we work our way to the replacement turf banks. There's a ditch here, filled with all sorts of vileness. I decide I don't want to fall in it. Creeping forward, I can finally see around the wall, to the landscape that opens up before me, sodden and damp, as rain drips into my eyes.

There's not one but two encampments, and my heart sinks. Close to the gate that would allow access into the southern half of Jorvik, one of the camps is smaller and more compact than the other. I see Blakari's emblem of a raven hoisted high into the air, the banner hanging limp and uninspiring. It seems evident to me that Anlaf has taken Jorvik from him. Now Blakari besieges his former kingdom.

But the other encampment is more threatening. I look to the banners flapping in the damp air, lips curling at the sight of the wyvern of Wessex depicted in red, yellow and black. For now, King Edmund of the English has been held at bay by Blakari. I don't know how long that will last.

I don't know what to do for the best. The wisest action could be to return to the ship and travel home, turning my back on this fight for Jorvik. But King Edmund is close. I can smell the bastard. I came here to assist Blakari, which I intend to do. If I also get to kill King Edmund, so much the better.

With Blakari restored to Jorvik, my father should be able to reclaim his kingship from Mael Coluim whose feeble support for Anlaf will be ineffective.

But first, I need to gain access to Blakari's camp, unseen by the enemy. It's not as simple as walking there. While Blakari surrounds the southern gate, he is, in turn, encircled by the English. If we're not careful, or if the clouds suddenly part, we'll be seen by our enemy.

'We should retreat,' my warrior, Giric, urges me, eyes wild with unease.

'Half of you, go back to the ship.' I point to those who'll withdraw. 'Keep it safe from attack and inform Drostan of what we've discovered. If it's imperative for your survival, allow Drostan to move further east along the River Ouse, but come back tomorrow at dawn. The rest of you, we'll watch and learn.'

The warriors don't favour the idea. I can understand why. This isn't a fight for the kingdom of the Scots, or for my father's restoration. Men such as these will not understand the complexities of this situation. They think our intention was merely to assist Blakari. With uneasy glances, half of the men retrace our steps. The others look to me. I ignore the disquiet in their eyes.

'We need to keep watch.'

I stay low to the ground, retreating back towards the turf bank. I've never felt so exposed. I can hear voices but quickly realise they come from those behind the walls. They speak the language of the Norse, but I don't know to whom they owe their loyalty.

A sudden shower of crap has me and my men running from the side of the wall. I look up and see the glower of angry faces. Whoever they are – and I don't shout for their attention, because we'd risk being seen by the English – they're making their intentions clear. Now I can see how the ditch has filled with such filth.

With the remaining daylight, I eagerly watch events before me. Instead of concentrating on reinforcing defensive ditches dug between Blakari and Edmund's forces, the English harass Blakari's camp with intermittent attacks, and the occasional twang of an arrow can be heard. I can't imagine they stand any chance of reaching their target in the damp.

The Norse stand out of reach and show the English their naked arses, or cheer when each arrow goes awry. I almost smile at the familiar sight of such tactics.

I consider the implications of finding Blakari here, on the southern side of Jorvik. Why has he not used his ships to retake

Jorvik from the inside? Like me, was he prevented because of the steep sides of the riverbank? Or have he and Anlaf already fought one battle? Whatever's happened, Anlaf has the work of defending Jorvik from the English done for him by Blakari, and his warriors.

The day draws to a close, and I'm no further forward in deciding what needs to be done. My stomach rumbles loudly. My men have been grumbling for some time. We've no food with us. The most important thing is that we've not been discovered. With the coming night, perhaps we can do more when the cloud cover and lack of a moon will enable me to move more easily.

I send the men and myself back to the church. It's safer to spend the night behind its walls. But I'm shaken awake in the middle of the night.

Giric speaks quickly and urgently, his words tumbling through the air, so I have to turn my head to catch them. He gesticulates, and eventually I realise what he's trying to tell me.

'There's one spot on the English line where the fires have died. No one guards it.' He speaks so quickly that his words almost run into one another.

I turn and look to where he's pointing, even though it's too dark to see, and the church walls obscure my view. I move aside, hurrying where he leads me, back to the turf wall of Jorvik's southern settlement. Immediately, I realise he's correct. Small fires dot the English line. There's one genuine gap. My breath catches. It could be a trap, but it might be my only chance to reach Blakari.

There's no choice.

'I need to go now. I'll go alone. You stay here and meet up with the ships tomorrow. If I'm successful in getting inside Blakari's camp, I'll come back and get you.' My words are as rushed as Giric's. I'm half out of my concealment when he hisses at me.

'My lord, you can't go alone. I'll come with you. Only some of the men need to meet with Drostan.'

'No, stay here,' I whisper urgently. I bend and emerge from the protection of the walls, crawling across the muddy grassland before me. My eyes focus on the space in the campfires. Quickly, I detect the sound of another following me. I stop and wait for Giric to catch me.

His eyes flash dangerously when he draws level with me. We can't speak for risk of being discovered by one of the English. I content myself with shoving him angrily. He rolls his eyes at me and pushes on, determined to lead. He wants to put himself in danger should anything befall us. It's his quick thinking that found the space in the English defences. Should it prove false, he wants to be there.

The grasses are long and muddy. They tickle my nose as I crawl through the English encampment, and it takes too much effort not to sneeze. Here, the camp doesn't quite meet Jorvik's walls. Instead, there's a slim passage. Perhaps the English mean to avoid the crap the Norse intend to throw at them. It certainly smells bad enough; I think I might be crawling through horse shit and excrement.

The night passes slowly. With each unwelcome sound, I stop, my breath freezing until I'm assured one of the English hasn't discovered me and Giric. The grey of dawn is beginning to streak the sky as we finally slide through the break in the English line into the Norse encampment. We remain low to the ground. Only when a pair of filthy boots enters our view do either of us even stop to look up.

'Who are you then?' a deep voice questions, in the language of the Norse.

I look into the eyes of a man I met on Blakari's ill-favoured endeavour to take Bamburgh.

'My lord Ildulb?' he startles, voice high on recognising me. 'Get up, my lord. Come, I'll get you to Blakari. He won't believe it,' he burbles with delight.

It takes me a while to stagger upright. My clothes are caked in mud. I don't miss the grimace of disgust on the Norse warrior's face.

'You crawled your way in,' he acknowledges, surveying the English force while stroking his long black beard with interest. 'Well, I never,' he mutters as he waits for Giric and me to right ourselves and wipe as much muck and filth from our bodies as possible. 'The English didn't see you?' he muses in surprise.

No one notices us or asks him his business as we're led through the camp. Neither does he speak. I look up and note the walls of Jorvik. I've seen them before, of course, but from the outside, the walls are imposing, and the only entrance, directly in front of the camp, is a daunting wooden door.

Not until he stands before a tent does the man who found us speak again, and this time only to shout inside.

'My lord, I've a surprise for you.'

Blakari's familiar grumble filters through the canvas. 'I don't want another of your bloody surprises.'

But the man laughs and pokes his head inside the tent. 'You'll like this one. A lot.'

Blakari stumbles from his canvas, eyes glowering at his warrior, only for them to clear when he sees me. A huge grin touches his whiskered face.

'Ildulb? Bloody hell, how did you get here?' As the guard who found us, his eyes sweep over the English encampment. He's pleased but suspicious despite the grin on his face. I'm insulted and only the thought of going back through the tall, muddy grasses holds me in place.

'I flew,' I offer acidly. Blakari's grin widens, gesturing to my mud-stained clothes.

'Apologies, Ildulb. I can't believe you've made it through the English defence without being seen. How's my nephew?'

'No idea. I didn't see him in the single night I spent at St

Andrew's. I'm here now though, with the support of my father. More of my shipmen will come this evening.'

'How many?' he asks greedily.

'Four ships, provided they all make it past the scuttled ship in the River Ouse.'

'Two hundred?' he clarifies, even while appearing pained at the memory of the sunken ship. I expect him to complain that I took a larger force to Bamburgh, but he doesn't. 'The bastard attacked us. We swam ashore. Some of my warriors weren't as lucky. There's no honour in being killed by your fellow Norse,' he complains.

He hands me his mead cup, even so early in the morning. I drink deeply. Crawling is a thirsty business.

'Mind, the other ships escaped unscathed, but the captains sent my men ashore and then turned tail back to the River Humber. They didn't want to endure the same.'

'How big is your force then?'

He gestures around him, indicating his camp. 'Six hundred, give or take a few.'

'And in Jorvik, how many does Anlaf have?'

Blakari's face darkens at the mention of his cousin. 'More. He's staying locked up behind Jorvik's many defences. He's made no appearance, even when the bloody English arrived.'

'So who's your enemy?' I can't imagine he means to renew his attack on Jorvik, but he's a Norse warrior. They never take no for an answer.

'Who isn't?' he responds with a flash of humour.

'What will you do?' I persist, but he shrugs again.

'Stay here until we starve, the English attack, or perhaps you'll show us how to escape.'

I shake my head at that. I haven't come all the way here to retreat. 'How long has it been?' I question.

'Two weeks. Our ships' attack was foiled. I ordered my warriors to set a camp here, meaning to take at least the southern half of Jorvik from Anlaf. It's impossible to the north. The ancient walls are much firmer, and there are no means of gaining entry – the riverbank's also too steep between the two settlements. We'd never have made it up without being set upon by Anlaf and his bloody warriors. Only, then the English came, and settled themselves around us, trapping us between Anlaf and them. We have food, for now, and the people of southern Jorvik, or at least some of them, have made it clear they'll feed us even if Anlaf doesn't condescend to do so. They know we're an extra line of defence against the English.'

'But the English king will attack?' I question.

He nods quickly. 'Yes. He'll be a little more patient, but it'll happen. My warriors will feel the full force of it. My scouts say the English have more men than I do, but I don't know if they have more men than Anlaf and I combined.'

'Have you sent a delegation into Jorvik to treat with Anlaf?' It seems foolish to me. These two must have the resources to overwhelm the English king. After all, they've managed in the past.

'No. I won't be the one to capitulate and seek an alliance first. He stole my kingdom.' Blakari's response is stubborn.

'After you stole his,' I remind him sharply. 'Should I seek an audience with Anlaf?' Jorvik will survive if Blakari and Anlaf unite to fight off the enemy, and I can join them and defeat the English at the same time, and then kill King Edmund.

'You?' Blakari chuckles, suspicion flashing in his eyes once more. 'Why would Anlaf speak with you when you support me?'

'He might see me as neutral. I could ensure you return to your role as sub-king if you work together. He might think that a fair bargain.'

'Anlaf will use me and hope the English kill my men. He knows we're trapped. He need only wait, and I'll be dead, and he'll have done nothing to bring it about.' His voice is sour.

'Is that what you want?' I demand. 'After all, I've made my way to you. I can show you how to retreat if that's what you wish to do.' He has few options.

'Of course I bloody don't,' he replies angrily. His frustration is evident. His words are almost shouted. 'I didn't bring my men here to bloody well die. We came to fight for a kingdom we thought was already ours.' Bitterness drips from him. I empathise with him. Kingdoms are fickle creatures, perhaps more so than women and enemies. Enemies are the least changeable of the lot. An enemy is an enemy and rarely changes from being so, unlike an ally.

'So let me speak with Anlaf. The people of Jorvik support your men, or so you say.'

'The people of Jorvik are more intelligent than Anlaf. They see us for what we are. I've almost convinced some guards to let us inside the southern settlement without Anlaf knowing. That way, I can surprise the bastard and, hopefully, kill him. Then I'll defeat the English.'

I see Blakari has a plan, but it will likely fail. He needs to focus less on gaining Jorvik and more on defeating the English.

'Anlaf won't just roll over and die,' I mutter. Blakari's rage and infuriation are starting to infect me. My mood's souring.

'I know he won't,' he mutters again, gesturing I should follow him into the tent. I indicate my soiled clothing. He shrugs. 'It's filthy in here. It's not stopped bloody raining since we arrived.'

He holds the canvas door open. He's lying. His clothing and bedding are neatly arranged above the muddy surface. He points to a small camp stool. I sit on it and my clothing creaks. The mud's drying. I might be stuck standing up or lying down forever if I don't get it off.

'You should remove them,' he comments, standing once more.

'Here, put these on.' He throws some of his clothes at me and steps from the tent to give me some privacy.

With difficulty, I manage to work my legs and chest free from the confines of the horrible muddy clothes, great clumps falling to the floor as I struggle. Although I doubt I'll be clean anytime soon, I feel less bedraggled in the drier, more decent clothes.

'Blakari,' I shout through the doorway. He quickly calls for one of his men to come and take my clothes away.

'Give them a good bash,' he offers with a wrinkled nose. I don't envy him. 'And see the other one has clean clothes as well. They'll bloody stick in position, the amount of mud on them.' Blakari cracks a grin as he speaks. His defeatist mood has disappeared. We need to plan and decide what to do because being the dividing target between Anlaf and the English isn't an ideal location. 'What a bloody mess,' Blakari announces. He's slumped to his bed, a rueful grin on his face. 'I couldn't have arsed this up any more if I'd planned it.'

'You could escape. Go back the way I got in.'

'I could, yes, but I don't want to. Neither do my men. Well, not all of them. Jorvik's ours. We won it.'

'Well, you won it by driving Anlaf out. It wasn't exactly a fair fight.'

'It's a Norse thing,' he offers, waving his hands dismissively. 'Honour amongst thieves and all that.'

'So you're going to sneak into Jorvik, murder Anlaf and then face the English?'

'Bloody hell, you make it sound so simple,' he says contemptuously.

I grin. 'Nothing ever worth having is easy.'

'No, it's not.'

'The English are the worse of the two evils,' I say.

He nods. 'I know, but I came for Jorvik, not to kill English scum.'

'Well, you've got to decide to face one of your enemies first, and to me, it makes more sense to turn one of your enemies into an ally. That way, you only have one enemy, not two.'

'I don't like it.'

'Then sit here and bloody bitch about it until the English attack and crush you on Anlaf's walls. He'll laugh because you'll be dead, and he'll still be holed up and in possession of Jorvik.'

'I know, I know,' Blakari announces with resignation, running his hand through his ragged beard and long hair. 'Would you go into Jorvik and treat with Anlaf on my behalf?'

At last, some progress.

'Of course. I'm the son of a king. I've power in my right. When my other men arrive, I'll have my warriors to support me. I don't need to take a single one of your warriors with me. Anlaf doesn't need to see you other than from Jorvik's ramparts.'

'He doesn't need to see me. He knows who I am,' Blakari mutters.

'I know that,' I explain patiently. Blakari's infuriating me with his belligerence. 'But it would be better for him if he didn't have to see you in person. Then he might, oh, I don't know, forget what a two-faced bastard you truly are.'

'It's part of our heritage,' Blakari explains again, 'he's the same. After all, we share a great-grandfather. The same blood runs through both of us.'

'And, still you won't reach an accord with him? That says more about you than it should.'

'Oh bugger off, Ildulb,' he mutters darkly. 'I blame sodding Archbishop Wulfstan. He told me to take Jorvik from Anlaf after his failures against the English at Lincoln. I should have known he was working for the good of himself, not me.'

I laugh, long and clear. I can't believe it's taken Blakari so long to realise that about Archbishop Wulfstan.

'Perhaps he agreed to hand Jorvik back to Edmund, and you and Anlaf and your bickering have cocked it up for him.'

'I don't think so. Why would Edmund have brought his warriors if he didn't expect resistance? No, Archbishop Wulfstan plays his own game. I don't know what the hell it is. I'll banish the little weasel when I next look at him.'

'You should kill him, not Anlaf. You kill Wulfstan and take his body to Anlaf as a sign of your acceptance of his leadership.'

Blakari gives a delighted bark of laughter at the suggestion. 'If I knew where the turd was, I might just do that. I don't think he's even within Jorvik. Not at the moment.'

'I'm not surprised.' And I'm not. Churchmen have a dizzying ability to cause problems only to distance themselves from the consequences. Some might call it divine intervention. I think it's just a matter of understanding men and knowing how far they can be pushed before they snap.

'So it's agreed then. You'll bring your men here tonight. Tomorrow, you'll approach the gate and demand admittance to arrange a truce with Anlaf.'

'I'd be honoured,' I offer with a gleam in my eye that Blakari doesn't miss.

'It's a pity Mael Coluim stole your father's kingdom,' he muses. I stiffen at his words. 'You've a sound head for politics.'

I think that's a compliment, but I'm not sure. Exhausted from my night crawling through the mud, I feel my eyes close as Blakari offers the use of his bed. Immediately, I fall asleep. Battle could rage all around me, and I doubt I'd even notice.

Tomorrow, I need to effect a reconciliation, and then I'll get another chance to fight the English. My sights are firmly set on killing Edmund. I'll have my revenge against him, even if it's taken ten years too long.

13

944, OUTSIDE YORK, THE KINGDOM OF JORVIK

Edmund, king of the English

I'm beginning to question why I feel the need to reclaim this rugged land with its many rivers and quagmire of mud. Rain's been falling non-stop since we arrived, the nearby river is swelling with the deluge. Our campsite's thick with mud. As the ground slopes towards the southern walls of York, our path involves more muck and filth.

I'd prefer to fight in dry conditions. I'm not to have my wish. It's going to be mud, filth and blood all the way.

Admittedly, I'm pleased that the bad weather delayed our journey. It's allowed Blakari Gothfrithson to arrive before us. I suspect he was to the north, perhaps at Bamburgh. His small force sits between mine and Anlaf Sihtricson's, precariously balanced just this side of the ancient standing wall that would allow entry into the southern half of York. I'm surprised to find him to the south, which does make me question if he has been to Bamburgh. Surely, I consider, he'd be to the north if that were the case.

Regardless, we'll have to attack Blakari first, which will delay our recapture of York. But then my triumph will be complete. Both Norsemen will be dead, and the Norse menace will finally be banished from England.

Admittedly, on the advice of Ealdorman Æthelmund, I considered making peace with Blakari and uniting with him to attack Anlaf within York. But I don't trust Blakari. If I aided him in overpowering Anlaf, he'd quickly show himself to be a traitor, as soon as my back was turned when I returned to Wessex. The only Norse man I'd ever ally with is Hakon, my brother's foster-son and now king of Norway.

Ealdorman Ealhhelm supports my preference for an all-out battle. Not that Ealdorman Uhtred's far behind him. I agree with them, yet I still delay. I hope a day will come when the rain stops. Not that I believe I'll get my wish anytime soon. I can't allow our supplies to run too low. We have the means to reprovision the warriors, but it feels like a waste when I know the numbers are to my advantage. Blakari's force is small enough to count easily, no more than a few hundred.

Anlaf's force is even smaller than Blakari's, I'm advised. In dividing, the two men have weakened the Norse hold on York and perhaps given the power to Archbishop Wulfstan. Not that I trust him either. I thought he'd aid our entry. It seems not.

However, I need to manipulate this strange situation to my advantage. I should perhaps have brought my ship army, but I was warned about the precarious nature of the rivers that run close to and through the settlement of York, and the length of the voyage from the open sea, along the Humber estuary to York itself. The rivers are tidal, the journey treacherous, and that's without allies of Blakari and Anlaf trying to defeat my brave shipmen.

No, I'll not rush into battle. Choosing the most advantageous time to attack is important. Blakari and his small number of men must feel there's no hope of prevailing against my greater numbers.

Then, they'll make an ill-conceived attack on York's walls or my forces. Either way, Blakari and his few warriors will be crushed by the might of the English warriors.

The only way we'll lose the coming fight is if Blakari's reinforced by thousands of warriors battling my force from the south. But Blakari doesn't have that sort of support, and my burhs which stretch from Kexburh to Coningsburh will prevent a counterstrike. The only weakness is that, because Blakari holds the ground closest to York, it's possible ships might come to his aid. I doubt it, but Ealdorman Uhtred assures me I should be wary. He says that while we've not taken the risk, the Norse are extreme and might do so.

Anlaf also needs more support to achieve success against us. He believes Mael Coluim's his ally, but Mael Coluim's unlikely to send his warriors to battle on Anlaf's behalf. The warriors from the kingdom of the Scots could gain entry to York through the northern gate, but I'm reliably informed Mael Coluim's more intent on trying to crush Constantin's resurgence than helping Anlaf. The kingdom of Bamburgh will not ally with the Norse leaders either. Ealdwulf didn't welcome Blakari's threat. He certainly won't countenance an alliance with Anlaf.

Anlaf's as alone as Blakari. Both men have allowed Archbishop Wulfstan to drive a wedge between them. I appreciate it's not been done to aid the English. Archbishop Wulfstan thinks only of Archbishop Wulfstan. He means to come out of this as the man who has control of York. He's an ambitious bastard. I've learned to trust none of these men, not even Archbishop Wulfstan. It's the only reliable aspect of their personalities.

My ally, Hywel of the Welsh, is a man of his word. He reinforces it with action, or inaction. He stays neutral on the outer edges of the ongoing war between the English and the remnants of the Norse, where they cling to York. Hywel has nothing to gain from involving himself. His focus is elsewhere. If he won't stand with me in the shield wall, then I'm grateful he won't support my enemies either.

Despite the obvious advantages that my warriors hold, Ealdorman Eadric's uneasy. He has the overall command of the English warriors in the encampment. Eadric wears his unhappiness like the black clouds that have obscured the sun since our arrival ten days ago. I almost wish I'd left him behind to guard my brother, Eadred, and my two young sons rather than Ealdorman Athelstan. Eadric prowls the earthen bank we've thrown up between our encampment and Blakari's like a wolf hunting sheep. He growls, bear-like, at all who talk to him. This morning, his mood is even bleaker.

'Some bastard's entered Blakari's camp. Or escaped from it,' Eadric announces without preamble, flinging the tent door wide open and glaring at me where I sit on my bed, bringing with him a thud of heavy raindrops.

His face is pale with cold or fear, probably both.

'Show me,' I command, sliding from my makeshift bed and pulling my boots on after a struggle to free them from the oozing mud. Not even my shelter is immune to the deluge from the heavens.

His cloak hangs limply on his massive frame; not even the treatment with grease can stop it from absorbing moisture. His hair and beard are streaked with water. He's beginning to take on the appearance of a drowned rat.

Outside, the noise of the rain on my canvas roof materialises into a sea of deep, dank puddles and the hammer of heavy raindrops falling on cloth and clothes. I scowl at Eadric, huddling into my cloak. I could be inside my muddy tent where the rain can't hit my face and cloud my vision. Eadric doesn't notice. His gaze is on the steps he must take to avoid his boots being inundated with cold, stinking water.

Before we set off for the north, the scent of warmer weather had infected Wessex. It's as though time has marched backwards here, in the north. Had I known, I'd have delayed our arrival even further.

My household troops scramble to their feet to follow me from where they've been sheltering beneath awnings and canvases. They wear unhappy faces at being dragged across the morass. We might have had more luck if we'd brought the damn ship army with us after all, and countered the threat from the rivers. We could have used ships to slide our way into York. They'd certainly have been more helpful than the herd of bad-tempered horses that don't like being away from their fields and warm stables in the south. They'd potentially have been drier as well.

I call greetings to my warriors as I walk with care through the sludge of rain and muck. I don't want to fall on my arse. Not here. Muted words return my greetings through the torrential rains, but none of them are happy. No matter how terrible the weather, the men would rather be doing the work of war than sitting, cold and miserable, in their little canvas tents. They don't want to watch our enemy in their camp, or further away, those parading along the standing walls that ring the southern section of York, guarding the gate. I will have to call for the attack soon. To delay much longer will impact the morale of my warriors.

My warriors and I slip and slide through the mud to where Eadric stops, just this side of our line of defences, to the east of the encampment.

'There,' he glowers. The ground's far more disturbed than elsewhere along the border with Blakari's camp. I look quizzically at Eadric.

'What the hell's happened here?'

'You agree?' he asks. I nod vigorously. I can feel the heat of his anger. It's about as warm as I've been for ten days. 'Halfdene assures me his men were watching this area last night. I know the bastard's lying. I'm going to gut him,' Eadric roars. I knew he had a temper, but it's not like him to threaten to kill men on the production of such evidence.

'Calm down, Eadric,' I try to placate. He turns his candescent glare on me.

'Blakari might be behind us. All of his men could have escaped last night. It was too dark to see your hand in front of your face because of this damn persistent rain, and you tell me to calm down! Halfdene could have undone all of our efforts here because he doesn't want to get his sodding hair wet.'

Eadric makes an excellent point. Yet I find myself laughing at the image he presents.

'We would have heard them,' I sober, trying to take the sting from my humour. But Eadric's beyond hearing.

'Bring me Halfdene,' he bellows at the two men standing behind me, holding shields and spears, while rain drips over helms to thud onto their already wet shoulders. They jump smartly to attention and stride out as best they can in the slick mud to where this Halfdene's tent must be. 'And I don't care if the bastard's asleep. Bring him here in whatever state he's in.'

I don't think I know this Halfdene, but from Eadric's response, I assume he does.

'Bloody waste of space,' he mutters while I bend to examine the churned ground. The rain might have obscured signs of passage, but there are still some distinctive marks where, I suspect, hands and toes have pulled men through the dividing line between the two encampments.

'They didn't walk,' I comment. Eadric makes no reply. He's still facing towards the campsite, waiting for Halfdene to appear.

My focus is on the tracks.

'I can't see they crawled all this way,' I murmur to myself, head down so that water pools down the back of my cloak, chilling me immediately. I step to one side, watching the ground intently, and then I see the signs of footsteps. Whoever came this way has only been clever enough to mask their passage through some of our line.

While Eadric glowers and hollers for Halfdene, I follow the signs of boot steps. After all, Eadric might be correct to be so worried. The path leads to the eastern side of our encampment. I squint into the low-lying cloud. There's a church there. I know the riverbank is not far behind it. I grimace. The bloody river. That must be where these people came from.

'Assemble the men,' I call. One of my warriors rushes off to rouse more of my warriors from their tented homes. I must conduct a thorough search of the area to discover if my fears are right.

Battling the sucking mud, I stride towards the church, mindful that I'm being observed by those within York. Eyes watch my every action, but no one thinks to throw more than rotten vegetables my way. Despite my gloves, my grip is slick with rain. I hold it firmly on the hilt of my seax. My warriors lead. It's easy to see that people have sheltered here. The ground's disturbed with heel marks as I peer unhappily at the pathway that leads off into the gloaming towards the River Ouse. I can hear its thundering roar from here.

Ordhelm, my household commander, glares at the obvious sight of enemy movement. With a swift bow, he steps out smartly, ordering six men to accompany him to follow the footsteps. I stand and listen. Even from here, I can hear Eadric offering his thoughts to the man who's allowed others to slip through his guard post. I might have to punish Halfdene for such a dereliction of his duties, especially if this proves catastrophic for my ambitions towards York.

'My lord king.' Ordhelm's voice drifts to me, distorted by distance. 'It leads to the River Ouse.'

It seems that someone with a ship army might well have braved the river to get close enough to York to aid Blakari. I consider why they didn't continue to seek entry from Anlaf. Why have they risked such a journey just to come ashore and walk this way?

'A ship's been here,' Ordhelm continues. 'Maybe more, but I think only one. The wet grasses have been knocked at a strange angle by the passage of men but not by hundreds of them. I can see no ship, but there are the ruins of another craft in the middle of the Ouse. Whoever came here risked a great deal, but I don't believe their ship sank.'

None of this makes sense to me. I feel my forehead furrow, rain slipping down my nose with the movement. What good would one ship be? Has it transported someone here or someone away? Has Blakari decided to leave and travel to Dublin, after all? I look at the damp encampment. I can see few people moving around, but it does still stand. The fitful, dank fires are being tended to by someone.

Has another Norse leader come to reinforce him? His brother, perhaps? Although what good one shipload of men could do, I can't guess. My force numbers thousands, Blakari's far fewer and Anlaf's fewer still. I was assured the river routes were all but inaccessible, ships scuttled to block easy passage in the light of the war between the two men who claim York. Why then has someone come this way?

'What good would one ship be?' I mutter aloud.

Frustrated and now sharing Eadric's anger, I stomp my way back to him and the unfortunate Halfdene. Halfdene's been dragged from his bed half dressed and made to kneel in a muddy pool to answer Eadric's questions. His face is bleached of colour, his auburn beard the brightest thing on this grim day. I could almost pity him if his oversight weren't potentially so damaging.

'Who lit the fires here?' I question.

'I did, my lord king,' Halfdene answers in a small voice. If I blinked, I swear I'd see my son kneeling there, not a great warrior. Regret fills Halfdene's voice. He won't raise his head to meet my eyes.

'Why was there such a huge gap between the two fires?'

'The ground dips, my lord king. It makes it hard to see anything in the hollow. I didn't think there was a need for a fire that I couldn't see at night. It would have been difficult to keep lit in the rain.'

His argument's sound. Still, I'm angry he's made the decision without asking Eadric or Ordhelm.

'Go and get dressed,' I order, ignoring Eadric's howl of rage. 'And then come back here.'

Halfdene slips to his feet, his footing unsteady as he slides onto his arse. No one smiles at the sight he makes, floundering around in the mud.

'What do you think?' I question Eadric, but reason may be beyond him. He can't even form a coherent sentence. Only when Ordhelm returns momentarily do I begin to understand what's happened.

'I found this.' Ordhelm holds an arrow high above his head. It's bedraggled and wet. Yet I'd recognise an arrow of the Scots anywhere.

'Ildulb,' I breathe, everything suddenly falling into place. 'Just the one ship?' I check.

Ordhelm nods smartly. 'I believe so, my lord king. There was just the one. The ground's churned, but the passage of many feet would be difficult to ignore. I didn't go far along the River Ouse. It's possible that there are more ships waiting, but if they are, we'll now guard against it.' As he speaks, I realise men are already fulfilling his orders, moving to the campsite to summon other warriors to watch the River Ouse.

'What?' Eadric asks, finally realising that we've discovered something else. I'm looking at Blakari's camp with a new understanding.

'We had intelligence that Constantin and Ildulb had allied with Blakari, Gothfrith's brother. It seems, Eadric, that Ildulb, the bloody fool, has come to help Blakari overpower Anlaf. Finding him wedged between the might of England, and the walls of York, he's taken his men through our encampment and pledged his support to Blakari. Inform the men that we attack Blakari in the morning. Ensure they know to be well-armed. There are Scots amongst our enemy now, and they have archers.'

Eadric and I gaze out into the sea of muddy puddles and disturbed land that greets our view. Blakari's camp is small, but it will still need to be countered before we can get to York's gate. The coming battle is no longer one between the Norse and the English. There'll also be a contingent of the Scots to counter as well. I don't miss that if I capture or kill Ildulb, I'll be assisting the new king of the kingdom of the Scots. I would rather not do that but Ildulb has perhaps engineered his own downfall.

'Bollocks,' Eadric mutters before stamping away. I watch him go, sharing his anger and frustration, and, frankly, I am amazed. Why would Ildulb be so damn stupid? Does his rage against me drive him onwards to such an inexorable death?

14

944, THE KINGDOM OF JORVIK

Anlaf Sihtricson, king of Jorvik

My triumph has been distressingly short-lived. I took Jorvik back when Blakari Gothfrithson tried unsuccessfully to take Bamburgh from Lord Ealdwulf, bribing the guards on the northern gate to allow me entry and then taking control of the king's hall and all the gates. But Blakari's return was too quick and unexpected, as though he had a premonition I was taking advantage of his ambitions while leaving Jorvik almost undefended, other than by men too old and weak to truly stop me. I hoped Mael Coluim might waylay him on his journey back to Jorvik, but Mael Coluim is the sort of man who offers much but produces little, as I'm beginning to understand.

Now, I find myself within Jorvik while Blakari besieges the southern settlement. He failed to gain entry with his mounted warriors through the northern gate and then tried to slip through my defences with the use of his ship army, that he rode to meet, coming along the River Ouse. When that was also unsuccessful, he erected an encampment at the southern gate, no doubt thinking to bribe his way through the guards there. I've had them replaced with men I know are more loyal.

But now, the English under King Edmund encircle him outside the southern gate. Now I have not one, but two enemies who mean to deprive me of Jorvik. Blakari will meet his death before the English can reach me. Blakari has no way to flee from the English. If necessary, I can escape via the northern gate. But I have no intention of abandoning Jorvik. I've no plans ever to leave it again.

Blakari will meet his end outside Jorvik's imposing southern walls, to the south of the River Ouse. Provided I hold Jorvik, I won't. Edmund's aggression will remove a contender for my kingdom. I could almost be grateful. Only, I can't be.

Angrily, I listen to the gate guard who's run from the southern gate, along Micklegata, and then over the bridge crossing the River Ouse, to Ousegata to find me within the king's hall. Now, allowed before me, he bends low. I don't order him to stand, and so his words are muffled.

'My lord king. Ildulb, prince of the Scots, demands admittance.'

I snarl in reply to such unexpected news.

Where has Ildulb materialised from? I have men on guard duty on every gate and along the standing walls. How has he made it to the southern gate without being seen? Blakari must have provided Ildulb with safe passage through his camp, it can be the only way. Although, how he reached Blakari's encampment, I don't know. I can't imagine that the English have stood back and allowed Ildulb to stroll through their forces. All know of the long-standing enmity between Ildulb and Edmund.

Do Ildulb and Blakari work together? Mael Coluim made no mention of this development. No doubt, he's unaware of it. Mael Coluim will not hold his kingdom for long. I'm sure of that.

'Allow him within. Bring him to me.'

The man stands, but keeps his head pressed low.

'Oh, show me your face,' I urge him. He does so, and I realise he's a loyal warrior. I've fought with him many times. 'Escort Ildulb to me,' I order him.

He turns, and rushes from the building. I amuse myself in the interim by striding to the tallest standing tower within Jorvik, to peer at the southern half of Jorvik, behind which the English force is constrained. As is Blakari.

Eventually, I'm aware of warriors walking over the Ouse Bridge. They don't quite wear the same clothing as my fellow Norse. This then is Ildulb, the prince of the Scots. I return to my hall. I won't greet him here. I have, however, assured myself, that there is no danger of imminent attack, either from the two rivers, or from the English. Ildulb comes at the head of a very small force.

As I enter my hall, I'm not at all surprised to find Archbishop Wulfstan already there. I'm grateful no one told him where I was. I despise the man. He's tried to make amends for supporting Blakari, but his shock when I overwhelmed the guards he'd set over the northern gate assures me he doesn't really welcome me here. We're wary of one another. I'll never forgive him for conspiring against me.

Now, he stands with his crows behind him, or so I think of the black-robed monks who follow their master everywhere he goes. Archbishop Wulfstan half bows towards me. He shows me enough respect not to be ejected from Jorvik, but nothing above that. It helps that he has ancient walls that protect where he lives and the church he ministers within. I haven't missed that he's encouraging men to join his swelling ranks of guards. He means to protect himself from whoever is king of Jorvik.

Archbishop Wulfstan settles on one of the benches, his fat little hand availing itself of the food waiting for me. Of course, he eats my food quite happily, even while distancing himself from my kingship.

Ildulb's flanked by a small contingent of warriors, no more than seven of them, as my gate guards escort them into the hall. The men of the Scots are dirty. They smell so badly of that special Jorvik mud aroma that I almost expel them again. It's warm inside my hall. Too warm for the stench they carry.

Only two are clean and reasonably tidy. One of those numbers is Ildulb himself. I recognise him, particularly the scar marking the right side of his face. He eyes my hall with interest. He has such a way about him that already I feel my shoulders tensing. His eyes sweep over where Archbishop Wulfstan perches. Ildulb shows no surprise to find him here.

'My lord,' I greet, stepping towards him, fixing a smile to my face that feels as though cold wind has scourged it. I agreed to this meeting, but it'll be far from private. Everyone will know I welcomed Ildulb into my hall to hear him speak.

'My lord king, Anlaf,' he replies, offering me an insolent bow. He watches everything, counting my men, determining who's armed and who isn't. He stinks of the sea and Jorvik mud. I'm sure the clothes he wears aren't his. A man such as Ildulb would ensure his tunic fitted him, his trews as well. Perhaps the boots are his. They're covered in mud. I wish he'd thought to clean those before entering my hall. The marks of his passage are clearly depicted over the wooden boards. The servants and slaves will not enjoy cleaning up when he's left. Not that it's an isolated occurrence. The riverbanks of the Foss and Ouse are covered in the stuff, and as Jorvik is so reliant on trade to survive, there are few who ever benefit from having clean boots.

'How did you get here?' I question.

'You're not strong enough to drive the English back from your walls?' Ildulb's reply isn't what I was expecting. He stands arrogantly, as though he's the lord of this hall, and not me. My eyes swivel from him to Archbishop Wulfstan, but Wulfstan's as surprised by his tone as I am.

'I have many loyal men,' I'm stung into replying instead of pursuing my initial query. What right does he have to come here and question the strength of my force? It isn't large enough to attack the English. Undoubtedly, he's been counting my guards as he's been escorted to my hall along Micklegata and Ousegata, filled with dwellings and workshops. I'm already regretting my decision to summon him here. I should have travelled to the gate and spoken to him there.

'You'd have more if you and Blakari countered the threat together.' My loyal warriors hiss at his words. I caution them to peace as hands reach for weapons belts, and also to stop Archbishop Wulfstan from hustling his way into our discussion.

A smirk touches my cheeks, as I begin to piece together why Ildulb is involving himself in this. Somehow, Blakari's convinced a prince of the Scots to come and speak on his behalf. I'm astounded. Perhaps I shouldn't be. I allied with Mael Coluim. It makes sense that Blakari went to Constantin.

'Blakari isn't to be trusted,' I denounce, unable to stop myself or the snarl on my lips.

Ildulb's burbling laughter unnerves me. 'And any of you bastards are?' he growls, all humour fled from his face. 'No man in power can trust those who want to be in power. I know, believe me. But, you'd be stronger if you were together. The English king has his ealdormen and warriors. You won't prevail against them with the small numbers at your command. You'll lose Jorvik.'

'Blakari and his men provide a bulwark. While he lingers, the English won't risk an altercation.' I speak dismissively, not enjoying having my fears spoken aloud by Ildulb. He's a haughty bastard.

'Perhaps, but the English king and his men will attack. If your force has instructions to prevent Blakari and his men from entering these walls, as those I've already spoken to assure me you've ordered, your fellow Norse will die. Then you'll have to fight the English yourself. You don't have the numbers. That much is obvious from my brief visit.'

Ildulb's argument is logical, which frustrates me. I'm honest enough to admit that without Blakari, I won't prevail against the English. I was aghast when, only days after Blakari returned from Bamburgh, the English force was sighted. Of course, I knew the burh forts had been reinforced recently. I didn't realise it was only the first step in a movement to take Jorvik from me.

Alone, Blakari and I will face huge losses. Together, we might manage to hold Jorvik against the aggression of the English king, and the hundreds if not thousands of warriors he has at his disposal. Even Archbishop Wulfstan has been arguing to start a dialogue with the English, offering me his advice even when I don't wish to hear it. Archbishop Wulfstan knew better than to suggest an alliance with Blakari, however. But Ildulb sees how success could be accomplished. I find I prefer Ildulb's suggestion to that of the slippery Archbishop Wulfstan.

'Why does this even concern you?' I query.

'My sister was married to Blakari's brother. We share a nephew. We have a family bond that can't be ignored.' Ildulb arches his eyebrows as he speaks, stepping to the table where Archbishop Wulfstan sits, and pouring ale into a jug without invitation. His arrogance once more astonishes me.

'It's more likely that with your father bereft of a kingdom, he's thinking of one for his grandson,' I counter aggressively. The idea might be a good one, but I'm not about to immediately agree to it.

Ildulb doesn't deny my outburst. 'The boy remains a member of your family,' he offers with a shrug. 'He shares ancestry with Ívarr the Boneless, no matter how diluted. Norse men and women will do anything for Ívarr's descendants. After all, they're here, with you now, even though not one but two enemies surround you, and your numbers are so small that you can barely guard the northern and southern gates.' His knowledge of affairs within Jorvik frustrates me. How does he know so much when he's just arrived? I suspect the men at the southern gate are being freer with their support of Blakari and their fellow warriors than I've ordered. I will have to replace them again. If Archbishop Wulfstan hadn't taken all of the finest fighters for his own walls, it would be much easier to accomplish.

'I've my sons to consider before this boy who's vaguely related to me. Blakari does as well.' I sense the scrutiny of my sons from where they sit close to the hearth. Rognavaldr and Gluniarann are the oldest. I've ensured they know of their descent from the mighty Norse king, Ívarr the Boneless. They're as proud of their ancestry as I am. It saddens me to think that, one day, they'll probably hate one another when they realise they can't both be king of Jorvik.

'Everyone has children to consider,' Ildulb dismisses, waving his ale cup around so that liquid sloshes onto the ground. One of the hounds hurries to lick it. 'We need to consider a scenario where any of your sons has even a small chance of keeping Jorvik against the might of the English. At the moment, divided as you are, I see nothing but disaster in your future. Edmund will win. You'll all be dead. My nephew will have no kingdom to rule when he's older. The descendants of Ívarr the Boneless will become nothing but a legend with no true claim to rule anywhere.'

The vision of the future Ildulb presents is bleak. It's potentially not far from the truth. My desire to punish Blakari for his deviousness in taking Jorvik from me shouldn't blind me to this. With our forces split, and loyalties divided, we're much weaker than when united. United, we could counter the threat the English pose, and Archbishop Wulfstan.

'What does Blakari say?' I realise Ildulb's intention is to force us to work together. He must already have Blakari's support. That means Blakari's the weaker of us. I can work with that.

'Honestly, he's about as happy as you about the whole thing. But then, you're both bloody fools.' Ildulb beckons a servant to bring him a stool. He sits, even though I don't. He's a conceited bastard. Archbishop Wulfstan watches our discussion with his piggy eyes in his rotund little face. He opens and shuts his mouth, desperate to speak and yet wise enough to allow us to argue about the finer points. Once more, my fury at the man's duplicitous nature cautions me to accept a man of Norse blood over his. And knowing Blakari doesn't wish to be my ally makes the whole distasteful business easier to accept.

'He'll become my sub-king?' I demand, watching Archbishop Wulfstan to see how he'll react to reinstating the status quo from before Blakari stole my kingship.

'He will, yes. You can pretend you haven't both tried to kill the other to gain the upper hand in this shit tip, and that Archbishop Wulfstan is an ally to you both.'

Despite myself, I find a smile on my lips. I decide I like Ildulb, after all. I never did before.

'Archbishop Wulfstan, do you agree it's better for the future of Jorvik if Blakari and I work together?' I ask him, but within, I'm realising that with Blakari back as my ally, we could counter any threat from the archbishop. He is, after all, an uneasy ally who is much too close to home for my liking.

A condescending smile plays on Wulfstan's lips. 'My lord, it has always been in the best interests of York for the descendants of Ívarr the Boneless to collaborate.' I scowl at his unctuous words. After all, it's his damn fault that we don't. Wulfstan watches me as though daring me to state this. I will work with Blakari to eject Wulfstan from Jorvik. I have no problem with his God, and the people here who are Christian, not worshippers of the old gods, but I truly hate him.

I incline my head and call for mead to seal the bargain that we've struck.

'How should we proceed?' Ildulb questions when we're seated before the great hearth. I've positioned myself so that Archbishop Wulfstan's the one to bear the brunt of the smell of Jorvik mud which pervades Ildulb more strongly than the foulest stink from the tanneries.

'We continue to fool the English for as long as possible. We won't simply open the gates and welcome Blakari and his warriors. That will allow the English to attack the southern walls. Blakari's camp prevents them from taking any direct action,' I decide.

'You should send reinforcements to Blakari. That way you could attack the English on open ground. The English won't be prepared for such an unexpected development. All know of the discord between you and Blakari. They'll be caught with their arses hanging out.'

I see Archbishop Wulfstan smirk at the delightful image. He's wisely holding his tongue. How we proceed in the arena of war is not his concern. Although, if he knows everything, he could find a way to inform the English king. Would he do that?

'It's worth considering,' I admit. 'But Blakari should attend a council of war. We'll discuss our next actions then.'

Ildulb nods in agreement, only to offer a caution. 'The English will notice any fanfare. They can't know you've decided to reunite.' He glowers at Archbishop Wulfstan. I share his concerns. We'll need to ensure none of the archbishop's men are able to get word to the English. He's about as loyal as a bitch in heat.

'Shadows and mirrors,' I mutter softly. Ildulb doesn't appear to hear my words.

'Can I have a bath?' Ildulb asks abruptly. 'I stink of mud from crawling through the English lines.' At last, I know how he made his way here. That knowledge, so belatedly given, assures me that I've done the correct thing. If Ildulb can evade detection by the English, then hopefully, we can do the same, and sneak amongst their encampment, once Blakari and I are formally reunited.

'I'll arrange it.' I glance at the rest of his men. 'Do they need one as well?'

Ildulb grins, showing me his surprisingly straight teeth. How does a man like him have all his teeth when he's fought so many battles? 'Well, we all stink,' he mutters. 'Can't you smell us?'

'My hall smells like the pigsty. Of course I bloody can. Go,' I beckon, 'find baths for your men and then return. I'll consider our plans for the future while you groom your beard.'

We part as allies, not friends, a handclasp sealing the agreement, witnessed by everyone including Archbishop Wulfstan. I must turn my attention to winning the approaching battle. I've been too content to simply hold the walls. My men and I will need to do something other than sit within Jorvik and extol our good luck on being so far distant from the English force.

Edmund will not have Jorvik. This kingdom's mine. All mine. Well, apart from the parts that will become Blakari's, and the elements which Archbishop Wulfstan claims. The thought isn't as unpleasant as it once was. I'm astounded it's taken someone like Ildulb to show me the error of my ways. I cast a sly glance at the archbishop. If not for him, I'd never have become separated from Blakari. I must close my ears to his lies, and hope Blakari does the same.

Archbishop Wulfstan is friend to no one but his ambitions. Not the Norse, and hopefully not the English. I'm pleased to have finally realised that.

15

944, OUTSIDE YORK, THE KINGDOM OF JORVIK

Edmund, king of the English

The damp day passes quickly, the men eager now they have a goal in mind as preparations for the coming battle finally take shape. Although I try to sleep, the night passes slowly, with rain continuing to hammer against my canvas roof.

I replay my memories of the eve before Brunanburh, my last great battle against the Norse and the Scots combined. Since then, I've fought little more than skirmishes. I find the images strangely hazy. I can't even recall how it felt to face such a huge force. How did Athelstan feel knowing he was leading so many men into a battle from which they might never walk away?

I remember him praying on the morning before the battle. I smile sorrowfully at that. I miss my brother, even now, so many years since his death. I wish we'd had more time together.

I think of my new wife and my sons. I've mourned the boys' mother and wed once more. But what will happen to my children should I meet my end in battle? I know my mother will care for them and that there's yet a spare son of my father who lives. Eadred. What sort of king might he be? I dismiss the worry. Knowing I have others to continue the family line is strangely consoling.

When the grey of dawn nearly illuminates the sky to the east, and the rain falls in a continuous stream, I stir from my bed, unrested. I almost offer a prayer that Anlaf and Blakari remain enemies and that Ildulb hasn't meddled, but I think God probably has more important prayers to listen to now. I content myself with thinking about it.

After all, how much damage can Ildulb have done in one day and two nights?

From outside, I hear men moving fervently in the gloom. I want my attack against Blakari to be unexpected, but I don't know how realistic a hope that is. I've many men under my command. Their preparations could have been seen, and news may have reached Ildulb and Blakari that we've discovered Ildulb's presence. After all, we spent much of yesterday seeking the source of the line of footprints.

Last night, I went to the small, smoking campfires to encourage my warriors for today's battle. My enemy would surely see a big speech before our attack. With their high walls, they can see long distances. But I sought to ensure my men know the importance of the coming fight and how much I value them. I wanted them to have the comfort that, should they die here, they'll be mourned and never forgotten.

I've slept in my clothes. It's too cold to undress. I need only add my byrnie, weapons belt and gloves to be battle-ready. I offer a prayer to God to keep me safe. I don't pray for victory; to do so would be to presume my God cares either way. I carry my shield, with its emblems of Wessex and Mercia, or rather England, depicted on its front, the twisting symbols of the red, yellow and black Wessex wyvern and the gold and red of Mercia's double-headed eagle.

I hold a beautiful helm in my hands, consideringly. It was once Athelstan's. I've not yet decided whether I'll wear it to fight. It's elaborate and polished to a high shine, but it'll mark me as Edmund, king of the English. It would be better to wear a more functional item, although my men expect me to be visible and to allow them the opportunity to fight in my name. For England.

I hum and haw, and then Ealdorman Eadric, all impatience again, sticks his wet head inside my tent.

'Put the damn thing on, or take it off, but stop delaying. We're ready. It's bloody slippery,' he cautions as I toss the helm onto my bed and grab the one I wore at Brunanburh and Cait. It'll bring me battle luck. It's resplendent with a wyvern embellished on its crown in silver.

Eadric nods his approval at my choice. I step outside to my men's ragged but muted cheers in the half-light of dawn. The clouds have barely lifted. It's as though they drag the moisture from the ground, only to be forced to redeposit it.

I raise my sword above my head and hold it there. I offer no other words. They knew to expect this. Instead, my ealdormen quickly construct our predetermined battle configuration. I find myself beside Eadric. I miss his brother, Æthelwald, but he's not here. These two men have shielded me in almost every battle I've fought. Today, I no longer need their protection, but I welcome Eadric's, all the same.

The ground's slick underfoot, and the beacon lights burn smokily to light our path. Those on guard duty at the edges of the camp don't caution us. Blakari's men, it appears, remain unaware of our movements.

Or I could be too late. Blakari could be reconciled to Anlaf, and under cover of darkness, might have slipped inside York. I'll find out either way in a few moments.

As I peer into the gloom, I can't tell whether my enemy is forming up to meet the warriors I have with me or if they're sleeping in their beds. I hope for the latter but fear it might be the former. Despite his failure to take Bamburgh, I've been assured that Blakari isn't the useless warrior he's always portrayed as being. Neither is he always drunk.

The dark of night wins the battle against the weak sunlight. I hear the rain hitting my battle gear with soft metallic pings as we wait for the daylight to grow. It takes forever for enough light to enable us to see. I almost wish I'd ordered the attack to start later. I could have spent longer not sleeping in my bed.

Men whisper to each other, some pray, but most stand as glum and silent as I do. It's not pleasant to stand in battle gear in the rain. I move my body to ensure it stays limber enough to lift my shield and weapons when I order the attack.

Ealdorman Eadric grumbles under his breath, the words too soft for me to hear. We don't speak of our past glories or our fears for this fight.

Finally, the thin grey streak of light thickens to the east. I wipe my damp glove on my wet clothes to dry it enough to ensure my grip will be good and firm. It accomplishes little.

Abruptly, daylight pools before me. I see everything and grin. Whatever Ildulb's been doing, he's not been quick enough. Blakari's men rise sleepily from their tents, the men on guard duty dashing between the still tents, finally shouting the alarm as the weak sunlight illuminates the might of England arrayed before the southern gates of York, with only Blakari's encampment in the way. My warriors are ready and keen.

'Shield wall,' I cry. In one swift movement, the English shield wall forms up to the far side of the ditch, which until now has demarcated the two camps, and through which Ildulb was able to gain access to Blakari. The crash of wood on wood is dulled by dampness, but the actions of my warriors are sharp.

I watch as Blakari's warriors dash through the camp, some heading toward the southern gateway. I acknowledge that some sort of alliance may have been made between the three men as I see that, but it's incomplete. If the alliance had been formalised, these men would be inside York and not abandoned on the muddy ground outside.

The first arrows fall amongst my men, confirming our suspicions – Ildulb and his warriors are with Blakari. I might have the chance to kill a Norse bastard and a prince of the Scots on this day.

'Advance,' I bellow, the cry taken up first by Ealdorman Eadric, and then all of my ealdormen and battle commanders.

A wave of self-belief sweeps through me, such that I've never experienced before. I'm going to win this battle. Such confidence must have guided Athelstan's steps all those years ago. I'll overwhelm the Norse and the Scots, just as he did, and win my acclaim as the second king of the united English.

16

944, OUTSIDE YORK, THE KINGDOM OF JORVIK

Blakari Gothfrithson, once king of Jorvik

'My lord.' The words are filled with urgency as I rise from my bed. Today, Anlaf and I will reach a formal reconciliation. I'll be restored to Jorvik, even if only in a subordinate position. We'll rule together, and in that way we'll defeat Edmund's ambition to claim Jorvik for himself. He'll be shown as weak, and we'll be strong.

I smile at the memory of the arrival of Ildulb, prince of the Scots. He's a brave man. I admire him afresh.

'My lord.' The words are more urgent this time.

'What is it?' I hiss with a snarl. The damn weather has made everything wet. My clothes. My boots. My weapons. And worse of all, my damn bed.

'The enemy, my lord.'

'What enemy?' But now I hear the rumble of warriors on the move.

Hastily, I stand, thrust my feet into my sodden boots, kick Ildulb awake where he lies asleep, and step outside. Ildulb's sleepy response follows me out the damp door of the tent. I peer towards the south, and my heart sinks.

'Bollocks,' I glower. 'The English are attacking,' I shout, mindful that, last night, I might have drunk too much ale to celebrate Ildulb's success. I should have waited to be inside York's walls before doing so. 'Ildulb.' I duck my head back inside the tent. He's rolled back over in sleep. 'Ildulb, we're under attack.' This has him awake far more quickly.

'What?' he glowers, rubbing his head as though checking it's still attached.

'The English.' I hasten to find byrnie and weapons belt, even as I shout instructions through the tent door. 'Have the men form up. Inform my commanders they're to meet the advance.' And then I look at Ildulb. 'Hurry to the gate and order the Norse within to open it.'

I hear his growl. I know exactly what he'd rather do. I hold his gaze as he finds his boots and stuffs his feet within.

'We don't have the numbers. Anlaf knows that, but he's a stubborn fool. Ensure he knows the English will overwhelm him without us, and without your men.'

'I will,' Ildulb growls threateningly. He's unhappy about it.

I leave my tent again. The English shield wall's locked in place. I can see it even beneath the low-hanging clouds, and across the overfilled puddles that mar the landscape, turning everything slick and sodden.

I swallow heavily.

Behind me, Ildulb emerges from the tent, his shipmen awaiting his instructions.

'Go,' I urge him, licking my lips, and deciding how I can best make use of my warriors.

'What?' Ildulb responds.

I sigh softly. 'Go,' I plead with him again.

He turns to move, and then pauses, and crosses to me, gripping my forearm. 'Stay alive,' he exhorts me. 'When we live through this, we'll plot our nephew's future.' He offers me a grin but his eyes are sullen with lack of sleep and too much ale. I swallow and grip his arm as well.

'It'll be my pleasure.'

Without further thought, I turn and stride towards the shield wall, my shield to hand, forcing my helm over my wet hair.

'This weather is shit,' I growl, already slipping on the muddy surface. My warriors follow me.

I call to those still preparing for war.

'Hurry, hurry. Ildulb will have the gate opened in no time. We need only endure.' But even as I speak, I sense the English force advancing quickly.

I peer into the gloom, seeking who leads the force. I imagine King Edmund is arrogant enough to be amongst the men in the shield wall. If only I had the numbers, I'd kill him here and now. My brother humiliated him, and how I wish to do the same. But I don't have the numbers without Anlaf's men.

Cursing my ill luck, I turn and glance where Ildulb's gone, hurrying towards the foreboding gate of Jorvik. I can't see the gate's opened yet. The banners of Jorvik, the black raven on a white linen, stand limp in the dull day. I can hardly tell what mighty creature is depicted there.

'Bollocks,' I exclaim, slipping in the mud, landing on my arse, while my shield falls from my hand.

I look down. The mud has almost covered my gloves. My arse is cold, my legs trembling. Another shout and I hear the English progressing more quickly, the terrified cries of my brave warriors ringing in the air.

I stand and swallow.

I eye the way I've come towards the shield wall, which is only ten horse lengths ahead. I'll never reach it in time to stop it from overwhelming my small force.

'The gate,' I murmur. 'We go to the gate, and hold it for our courageous warriors.' I don't want to countenance retreat, but it's the only way. 'Shout the order,' I inform my warriors. 'Shout it,' I demand, and turn, gathering up my legs to run the short distance. Even the roadway is covered in mud. I see the gate opening, and a grin touches my taut lips. Ildulb's been worth his weight in silver. His actions will save my warriors and me.

'Come,' I urge those close to me. 'Come, we'll hold the gate until we're all inside, and then we'll slam it shut in the face of the bastard enemy.' I smirk at that. King Edmund will think he has the victory, but he won't. If I'm to take any joy from today, it'll be that.

A few grumble at my decision, but most look relieved. We're a small force. I thought to take Bamburgh with only my most loyal men, leaving the might of Jorvik to hold firm against the English. A pity they switched their loyalty to bloody Anlaf. Still, Anlaf will save us today. I find I can be much more forgiving of his actions now. Together, I hope, we'll cast out the snivelling Archbishop Wulfstan. How I despise the man.

I don't return to my tent, despite the riches I'll lose. Instead, I hurry, mindful of the slick mud stuck to my boots and legs. It's so cold; it feels like the slap of a corpse every time I take a step.

Ahead, Ildulb appears from within Jorvik, beckoning me to hurry. Beside him wait men I recognise, the warriors of Jorvik, who patrol the decaying walls and hold tight against any invasion that comes from the south. I could weep to see them standing aside, allowing warriors who are closer than me to slip inside the inviting gate. I've never appreciated how reassuring it can be when that gate slams shut behind my warriors.

'My thanks,' I speak quickly to the commander of the Jorvik

warriors, where he watches the advancing English. He grimaces, but it's almost a smile.

'I hear the accord between you and Lord Anlaf will be reached today. Seems damn foolish to die before then.'

I grip his forearm, welcoming the heat from his skin on my cold, mud-splattered glove.

'Where do you want us?' I question. Somehow, I've lost sight of Ildulb and his warriors. I wanted to thank him for ensuring I lived through this. I'll have to do so later.

'Hold the gate. We'll close it when your men are within. Order them to hurry.' His low grumble ends on a high. I turn to gaze back at the crumbling shield wall. One man holds out against an English warrior, but mostly, it's entirely collapsed. In a rush of panic, my warriors slip and slide through the mud to reach safety.

'Shields,' I order my warriors. The gate commander's busy ordering men to the walkways overhead. I can hear the sharp slap of boots over what must be dry stone. I watch my warriors outside Jorvik.

Their progress is slow, but so is that of the English warriors.

I urge them onwards. 'Come on, come on, come on.' Only then I realise that some of the fools are stopping, redirecting their steps, heading for where they've left their treasures. If I can forsake mine, they can bloody abandon theirs. 'Leave them,' I bellow. 'Leave them. To me,' I call, licking my lips, tasting the raindrop that's just fallen there. The day's dank and grey. The only colour to be seen is that of blood and guts. And still, my men bend to collect their wealth. 'Leave it,' I bellow. Only four horse lengths away now, the English shield wall's getting too near. We must close the gate soon, and my warriors are still not safe.

The gate commander's behind me.

'My lord Blakari, we can't risk it,' he shouts, fear lending his words too much force.

'We hold,' I counter. I can see good men out there, men I've known all my life. I'll not abandon them. 'Get Prince Ildulb. His men will assist me,' I order the gate commander as though he's one of my warriors, and not one of Jorvik's.

'My lord.' And I sense the unease in his voice. 'My lord, Prince Ildulb is nowhere to be found. He's gone. Some say they saw him escaping towards the River Ouse.' I open my mouth at that terrible news, unsure what to say or what to think.

'He can't have bloody abandoned us,' I howl, earning myself worried looks from the men in my shield wall.

'The English are getting too close,' the gate commander remonstrates again. 'Shut the gate,' he calls to those waiting to force it across the open gap.

'Waylay that order,' I shout, but the gate's already closing. If I don't move, I'll be struck down by it.

I eye my warriors. They're so close, so very close, but some of them dip to collect others who've fallen, and the English are even nearer. I can see the eyes of the English warriors who think to hunt us down and end our lives.

'Shut the gate.' I echo the gate commander's cry, but as I step back inside Jorvik, allowing the gate to close in front of me, despite the frightened and anguished cries of my warriors, a line of English shields, daubed with their too bright colours and muddled depiction of a wyvern and some other winged creature, blocks the gate. 'Bollocks,' I exclaim, even as the gate commander growls in my ear.

'You'll answer for this, Lord Blakari, to Lord Anlaf. If you're bloody lucky enough to live.'

17

944, OUTSIDE YORK, THE KINGDOM OF JORVIK

Edmund, king of the English

I take a moment to look for Blakari Gothfrithson amongst the sea of men rushing to counter the English shield wall. I want to see him. I want to find him and Ildulb so I know where to direct my assault, but it's impossible. In the chaos of our attack, the enemy all look the same in their byrnies hidden behind helms and shields. I'll find him, but not now.

Our attack begins long before Blakari's men have formed against our shield wall. My warriors have been commanded not to rush. By keeping our pace slow and measured, we can ensure our enemies are all killed. Our lines will not break with the ease of the coming victory. If too many men rush forward while the rest are left behind, it'll be a catastrophic failure. We move at a steady step, Ealdorman Eadric echoing my commands.

Norse voices rise in outrage. I listen for Blakari's orders. But the rumble of noise is too loud. I can't decipher a single distinctive voice. Finally, the Norse shield wall knocks against ours. We can smell the spluttering campfires of our enemy. I could almost help myself to their pottage. My feet sink into the mud. It's damn slippery.

I feel a shield above my head. My brother fought with his men but also directed from the rear. An attack as dirty and filthy as this one demands I suffer as much as my warriors. I need to be here. I need to kill the Norse kings to know it's finally accomplished. I'll not fight Blakari and Anlaf again. I'll not allow these bastards to overwhelm my kingdom once more.

Our tactics aren't those of civilised men.

My war axe is in my hand, my shield in the other. I lower my shield, sight the man before me and strike. I use my axe, not to slash across his well-made shield, but to pull it down, force it away from the protection he's gaining from it so that the warrior behind me can hack through his exposed neck.

My foeman's strong, his grip tight. It takes longer than I'd like to overwhelm him. I consider if I face the most solid of men or whether I've grown weak from camping in terrible weather. Then the shield finally gives. I see a little of my enemy's face that his helm doesn't cover. His eyes are wild with shock, his breath stinking of last night's ale.

'Duck,' Ordhelm, the warrior behind me, bellows, leaning over to slice our enemy's neck. My foeman stumbles, his blood mixing with the mud, the shield he held falling lifelessly to the ground. He might have been strong, but no strength can defend against such a blow. I kick him aside, lifting my shield to protect me from the next enemy.

The new Norse foeman is covered from head to toe in byrnie and leather. He holds his shield loosely before him. He might be a good warrior, but he's also a cocky one. I'll enjoy battling him to the death: his, not mine. I remain in formation. The men beside me and Ordhelm, to the rear, protecting me.

My foeman grins. I return his smirk, feeling my eyebrows rise, although he won't see that. He won't know I'm the king of the English. He's ignorant of the fact that the king of the English is about to kill him.

He holds the seax as loosely as his shield. I grip my war axe. I could use the same tactic as before, but my enemy's derogatory hold on his shield speaks of overconfidence.

I raise my war axe as though to pull down his shield but instead turn it to the side. I direct my strike towards his upper body, left undefended because he's lowered his shield to counter my attack. The war axe rebounds off his metalled byrnie. His laughter is feral, his lips bloodied from an earlier encounter. While he smirks and laughs, the man to my left slices his axe down my enemy's exposed side. The blow's a good one. My opponent's smile fades, replaced by a grunt of pain. He didn't expect to be attacked by more than one man.

'Bastard,' he mutters through his beard, tied with trinkets of his gods. I aim at the right side of his body. My blade scrapes the surface, working to wrench aside the padded material of his byrnie and rip apart his flesh.

Abruptly, he's on the defensive, shield tight before him. Now he looks to his fellow warriors for support, but everyone's focused on their own attacks. My enemy raises his seax to strike my head. The shield protecting my helm, held aloft by Ordhelm, blunts the blow, but only momentarily. A swirl of air rushes over me as Ordhelm batters the seax aside. With his far heavier war axe, Ordhelm hammers it firmly onto our foeman's head, axe striking against the helm and head of my enemy. Our foeman stops, stunned, his arm half raised, as his helm tumbles free, the straps giving way under the onslaught. Blood seeps down his neck, the deep red a shock in the grey dawn.

I use the head of my axe against his chest. He drops quickly, eyes unseeing. I kick him aside, focusing on the next Norse bastard who needs to die.

I can't see much more than the enemy before me, but the sounds of battle assure me we're winning. The cries of the injured are in Norse. Any moment now, Blakari's warriors will realise the peril they're in. They can attempt to retreat within York or face certain death. Perhaps dying on an English blade will be a better option than on a Norse one.

My next foeman's a wiry older man, white flecks of beard showing beneath his chin guard. He's been the victor in many battles to live to such an old age and still be fighting. Behind his helm, his eyes are flinted with grey. He has no plans on dying today.

My war axe crashes against his shield; the paint faded in places, and the shield boss blackened with age. Abruptly, the shield wall lurches forward around me while my opponent remains staunch in meeting my attack. I crash against his shield again with my war axe, hoping to force him backwards, but he meets my assault with as much strength. My warriors rush on, voices wild with the promise of victory. I lift my foot to kick below his shield, but nothing happens. The muck and mud hold me in place. My enemy fares no better. I see a flicker of fear in his cold eyes. The mud has him. His allies are retreating under the English advance, stranding him. Swinging my war axe, aware Ordhelm remains at my back, I hack at our enemy's exposed leg.

He attempts to wrench his feet free from the sucking mud, focusing more on that than my attack. My axe sweeps low, severing his ankle above his boot, blood gushing forth. His foot's finally free, but he's not. He wobbles, unable to move with only one working foot, still wedged in the mud. I lift my shield and smash it into his face. His shriek of pain rings too loudly. I wince. He falls. I rush into him, felling him like a tree, desperate to rejoin the advance at least ten paces in front.

The Norse retreat descends into chaos and confusion. I glance up and see the routed warriors aiming for the single gateway into York that might protect them. I hear voices raised in fury. No doubt, they demand their former allies open the gate to allow them inside. I hurry to run faster and faster, legs pumping beneath me, battling the terrible slippery mud.

I hear the unmistakable creak of the wooden gate being swung open. I must reach it before my enemy is gone, and the English are left stranded outside York's imposing walls. Anlaf and Blakari must have reconciled. No doubt, a rampaging force will make two enemies become allies. I growl angrily.

Quickly, I realise those led by Ealdorman Eadric should reach the gateway before it closes.

Abruptly, I fall, tripping over the tents' snaking ropes, my hand landing in the discarded bedding of one of my enemies. The shock of such recently abandoned warmth and shelter has me scrabbling from the tent, consternation and fury on my face.

Ordhelm offers me his hand, and I regain my feet with fumbling boots. The daylight remains weak, filtered by the falling rain. I squint, catching my breath to see my warriors winning through to the gate.

The enemy warriors hamper their retreat by bending to pull others upright and to grab what they can of their belongings. While they delay, the gate remains open. Led by Ealdorman Eadric, I watch some of my men gain entry. I try and hurry, reinvigorated by how easy this is, adding speed to my movements. But my progress could be faster. The strewn debris of the camp and the sheer number of dead warriors slows me.

Ahead, the last of the Norse warriors struggle inside the safety of York, fighting all the way. The ring of iron and wood's muted in the damp. I grin with battle joy, the mud and blood caking my face, making the movement feel too tight. No doubt, on the northern side of York, men consider escaping into the wilderness of Northumbria now that York's close to falling to the English. If I'm lucky, Ealdwulf of Bamburgh will be waiting for them.

Any who can escape to the few ships within York have my blessing to leave with their lives, provided they don't return or foul the water source with their rotting corpses. They must navigate past the scuttled ship that blocks the River Ouse. I wish them luck with that. With all the rain, the river's running high, the current too fast. The ships within York aren't in the best condition. Traders are always the first to sense coming strife. I've been assured all the best ships left York as soon as they heard of the arrival of the English, well, those few who were left after Blakari and Anlaf's altercation.

York's walls are finally huge before me. They're old and tired yet in a good state of repair. They kept York safe from the Norse when my brother was king here. They'll do the same when it's mine. But I must concentrate on securing York for the English first. Once I hold the gate and the wall to the south of the River Ouse, I'll have to take the bridge to the northern half of the settlement. There are ancient walls there as well, which mostly protect the archbishop and his church, but which the kings of York can also use to hide behind.

I plan on overawing both the Norse and the archbishop. York will not have two masters. It might have aided my brother to make Archbishop Wulfstan so powerful, but Wulfstan has proven to be a tricky individual. With the church under my command, I'll ensure Archbishop Wulfstan remains loyal to the English. If not, I'll have him driven from York. I'll even invoke the aid of the pope to accomplish it.

'Well, my lord king, we're inside,' Ealdorman Eadric crows from his position inside the open gate as I finally arrive. Beneath his feet lie the lifeless bodies of our enemy. Those who opened the gate for their allies have paid the ultimate price. 'They're running for the bridge,' he informs me. 'Our men follow while others will secure the wall and gate to this side of the River Ouse.' His byrnie's dark, saturated with the blood of our enemies. His forearm shimmers with the stuff. His nose guard's streaked with the maroon of those he's killed.

'We've reclaimed the south of York,' I call triumphantly while my fellow warriors raise their voices in acclaim as we spill into the street within York. There's still much to do. We've only completed half of the task. But for now, I luxuriate in the ease with which we've overawed Blakari and Anlaf's warriors.

Ahead, I'm greeted by a broad thoroughfare, wooden dwellings to either side of it. The Norse warriors who live flee along it, their voices raised in fear and fury. From within the dwellings, with doors barred, I hear the cries of disturbed residents, their voices a mixture of English and Norse. They're not in danger. The warriors who owe allegiance to Anlaf or Blakari are.

'The bridge,' I shout. We must take command of it to secure the whole of York. I rush onwards, Ordhelm staying close, not caring that the mud inside York is almost as thick as it is outside. It's a prosperous place but a busy one too.

At the slim wooden bridge that crosses the wide River Ouse, I stop to catch my breath once more. From amongst the tightly backed dwellings, the voices of my men echo back to me as they hunt for any Norse warriors who might be hiding. I stare across the River Ouse to where the lords of York have always lived. The walls are daunting. There are a number of ruined towers, only one of them remains largely intact. I glare at it, hoping to see the fearful faces of Anlaf and Blakari from here.

The river water's turgid and brown beneath my feet from the near-constant rainfall of the last few weeks. It's also loud, a river threatening to burst its banks. On the river's far side, I see some ships being lowered into the water despite the risk of capsizing. Men and women intend to escape from my kingship. Even though we still only hold the southern side of York, these people realise I'll triumph. I grin at that, wiping water from my sodden face.

My helm's slick with moisture, and my clothes are heavy. It's an effort to move my arms. The grip on my shield is fleeting, even with my gloved hand. My boots are brown with mud. They squelch with every step. My war axe remains sharp despite the slivers of flesh and blood stuck to it.

I force my way to the front of the bridge with the aid of Ordhelm and his warriors, eyeing the steep drop and rushing water warily. My warriors growl to be released into the northern reaches of York, but they were instructed to wait while the southern part of the settlement was secured. There's not any need for me to head them. They'll overwhelm the area for me. Then, I'll walk unmolested to claim the seat of York's power in her king's hall.

Yet, I want to lead my men, no matter how dangerous it might be. I want to strike the final blows against the Norse pretensions of Anlaf Sihtricson and Blakari Gothfrithson. I appreciate that neither man has the stones to stand against me. I pity their warriors fighting for such pathetic lords.

I eye the gurgling river once more and the overfilled ships balancing precariously on its rumbling flow. I should let my men rush across first. I must heed the lessons my brother taught me, when he stood back, allowed others to fight for him until the battle was all but won.

Ealdorman Eadric's suddenly beside me, his breathing even.

'We've got all the fighters, my lord king,' he announces quickly. His eyes flash to the north. A handful of my men hold the northern bank of the bridge. There are some Norse warriors who menace them, but no one has yet made a move.

'Go,' I command. Ealdorman Eadric bows swiftly, eyes gleaming with battle joy.

'With me,' Ealdorman Eadric bellows. A roar greets his words. The English warriors surge onwards, parting around me.

The bridge is slick in the rain, yet its foundations are massive stone struts beneath the water, only the very tops visible. They'll withstand the storm, but if my men slip, they risk plunging into the brown water to never be seen again. They're weighed down with armour and weapons. I almost can't watch as they run steadily across the vast wooden expanse.

It sounds as though a herd of horses careers over the wooden bridge. Above the growl of the surging water, those struggling to board ships look up fearfully before redoubling their efforts to make it to safety. Some tumble into the river. I close my eyes in dismay. It's one thing to allow men to die on the battlefield and when a kingdom is at stake, but these people are dying from fear of my kingship.

Unable to remain passive, I launch myself across the bridge, Ordhelm and his warriors staying with me. The bridge sways beneath my feet, its wooden surface greasy under my mud-stained boots. I keep my eyes focused on the far side, not daring to look at the bulging river.

My orders are simple. Some will secure the northern and eastern gates under the command of Ealdorman Ealhhelm. Others will hold the eastern commercial district with Ealdorman Wulfgar. More are to take command of the king's hall and the church-owned walls and land which Archbishop Wulfstan claims under Ealdorman Eadric's instructions. Ideally, they'll bring me the cowardly Blakari, Anlaf and perhaps even Ildulb, either dead or alive. Dead would be best. They're to allow Archbishop Wulfstan his freedom, but he's to be brought to me. He will answer for his actions.

To the north of the Ouse Bridge, the settlement of York slopes down towards the River Foss. It's filled with dwellings and workshops, almost all in square shapes, no bigger than the length of three horses, standing nose to tail. The smell of cooking and metalwork is ripe in the air. Here, shopfronts are closed. The men and women who own them hide behind barred doors or rush to the quayside, or perhaps, to the northern gates, hoping to escape.

Ealdorman Eadric orders warriors left, toward the king's hall, and others inside the standing walls that protect Archbishop Wulfstan's church. No doubt, the archbishop will be found, praying within his church, pretending to have no control over the actions of Anlaf and Blakari. I will see through those lies.

Resolutely, I follow my warriors and Ealdorman Eadric towards the king's hall. I need to be there. I must witness Blakari and Anlaf meeting their death or being taken prisoner. I encounter few living enemies as I stride along Ousegata. The Norse warriors might have given up, but they're undoubtedly reinforcing the king's hall, inside which, I hope, Anlaf and Blakari await me.

The smell of burning reaches my nostrils. I growl low.

'I said no burning,' I shout, turning in the hope those who set the fires will hear me. The York dwellings are built too close to one another. Each house touches its neighbour. If one burns, they all will, even with the heavy rain. Yet the burning isn't coming from behind me, but from the west.

I curse. Bloody Anlaf's setting the town on fire. I watch flames lick the sodden roofs of the homes nearest the king's hall. I hope too little of the roof is dry, and the flames fail to take root. If they do, I'll have to divert men away from the attack to ensure that there's still some of it standing when I win the northern part of York.

Ealdorman Ealhhelm rushes toward me, his warriors trailing behind him. His face streams with water, his clothing sticking to his body, but his seax is to hand, and he holds his shield ready to crash it against an enemy.

'They're escaping through one of the northern gates, my lord king. Should we pursue them?' he asks breathlessly. I've not seen him cross the bridge, but he's been following the enemy more closely than I have. My focus has been on the king's hall, and on securing Archbishop Wulfstan. It shouldn't have been.

'Are Anlaf or Blakari amongst them?' I demand.

He bends over, hands on his knees to catch his breath as Commander Ordhelm guards my back and head. When Ealdorman Ealhhelm looks at me again, surprise shows on his familiar face.

'The messenger didn't reach you? Blakari died in the first wave of attack. He was fighting to close the southern gate.'

My mouth drops in disbelief. I turn to my closest warriors. They shake their heads. This is news to us all.

'A good death?' I ask.

'Oh yes, an excellent death. On my blade, my lord king.' Ealdorman Ealhhelm licks his lips as he speaks, showing me his seax and the skin and hair that adheres to it.

'And Anlaf?'

'He lives and was within his hall. I've seen many escaping through the northern gate in the archbishop's enclosure. The burning's a means of distracting us so we don't follow. He could be amongst them.'

'Take your men, follow and engage them if you can.'

Ealdorman Ealhhelm nods and sheers away as I redouble my efforts to get to the king's hall. If the bastard's run off, I want it.

Sodden ash falls from the sky to join the heavy, thundering rain. Somehow, flames leap along the rooftops, adding much-needed warmth to the day while burning the homes of men and women I want to rule. I hear screams from inside. I spare a thought for them. I don't have the numbers to help them. Not yet. Not until I know Anlaf's dead or fled.

I resume running only for the street I'm rushing down to open out, the king's hall to the western side. In the open space, Ealdorman Eadric's organising men to take the hall, his words short and easy to understand even above the thunder of the rain and the roar of blood-crazed warriors. He sends men within to check every nook and cranny and ensure no one's hiding inside, waiting to take their vengeance.

'You there, douse the flames, if you can,' Ealdorman Eadric instructs, when he sees men doing nothing but cleaning their blades. Warriors bend to the task. It's not hard to find buckets filled with water. The rain's been relentless. The fact the fire battles against the elements astounds me.

The most difficult part of our attack was getting through York's southern gate. Once inside, Anlaf seems to have simply run away. Did he know Blakari was dead? Now, all I need to do is find Archbishop Wulfstan.

'Empty, my lord king,' Ealdorman Eadric informs me with a sharp bow, 'apart from the servants. They speak English.' As he states this, servants and slaves are led outside the hall. Eadric isn't a trusting man, even if they speak English.

Ealdorman Eadric harangues the servants and slaves as I make my way to the open doorway, Ordhelm striding ahead. I follow him inside the king's hall in York for the first time in my life. A fire rages at its centre, with weapons strewn along the floor as though dropped by a small child too tired to play any more.

I inhale sharply, ensuring the tang of whatever hangs in the air is nothing noxious. Then my eyes look toward the hearth where a wizened old tree trunk crackles with blue flames. No doubt the source of the strange smell. Perhaps some old magic left behind by my Norse predecessor. Pity, its meaning is lost on me. Anlaf would have done better to leave behind a stinking pile of bloody corpses. At least I'd have known he sought revenge against me.

The hall's well built, watertight despite the constant rain. Its wooden floorboards are slick with the mud of many men but the fire burns bright. With my warriors standing guard at the two entrances, I take my time to walk around, surprised that this is what the Norse descendants of Ívarr the Boneless have been fighting over for so long.

It's little more than a fine hall, nothing as spectacular as my palaces, some of which extends over two floors. As I turn to seat myself on the ceremonial wooden chair, the view I glimpse out of the door surprises me. Suddenly, I know why the hall was built here.

From here, the Norse kings of York could survey the source of their wealth. The view stretches down towards the River Foss and the bustling quayside that serves York.

It seems that Blakari is dead and Anlaf is fled. Where are Ildulb and Archbishop Wulfstan?

A soft shuffle over the dirty floorboards, and I see Archbishop Wulfstan coming towards me. He has his head held low, eyes downcast, and his monks follow him. Behind him, Ealdorman Eadric watches with his lips curled down.

'My lord king, welcome home,' Archbishop Wulfstan mutters, the words only just audible. 'Long live the king,' he intones, and his monks join the cries of acclamation. I feel my lips curve at the sight of him, the archbishop of York, pretending to be my subservient. I imagine he's already plotting the means of ejecting me from York.

I force a benign look to my face. 'Rise, Archbishop Wulfstan,' I order, and he does so, revealing relief on his fat little face. He's not dressed for war. He had no intention of protecting his kingdom. 'Where's Anlaf Sihtricson?' I question.

'Anlaf?' Archbishop Wulfstan replies as though he's never met the man.

'Yes, your previous king. Where is he?'

Archbishop Wulfstan turns to look at his monks. They all shake their heads, some wailing with fear. 'We don't know, my lord king. Isn't he here, fighting you?'

'No,' I muse. Seeing him is diluting the joy of my victory. 'And Ildulb, prince of the Scots, where is he?'

'Ildulb, of the Scots?' Archbishop Wulfstan parrots. I find my patience wearing thin.

'We know he was here. Where is he now?'

'With Blakari, my lord king.' Archbishop Wulfstan lowers his head once more, perhaps realising that he's admitted too much former knowledge by speaking as he does.

I close my eyes, seeking some measure of calm. The battle rage is still upon me. I could happily sweep the archbishop's head from his neck, but I must not do so. It would undo the good of my victory.

'Blakari Gothfrithson is dead,' I intone. Archbishop Wulfstan startles, as though wounded. 'He died protecting his kingdom, which is more than Anlaf did.' I don't add *or you*, but I think it loud enough for Wulfstan to wince once more.

'I will pray for his soul,' the archbishop informs me, already turning away.

I look to Ealdorman Eadric. 'Escort Archbishop Wulfstan to his church. I would be assured of his safety while panic still rumbles in the streets.'

Eadric bows his head low, even as Archbishop Wulfstan's head bobs high.

'We'll speak more, on the morrow,' I inform the errant archbishop. He simpers and leaves in a rustle of wet cloth and damp boots. When he's gone, I take a deep breath and look at the king's hall, allowing myself to enjoy this triumph.

Blakari's dead, Anlaf has fled and Ildulb's elsewhere. But for now, I can be happy knowing that England is whole once more.

My brother would be proud of me, my father and my grandfather too.

A short while later, Ealdorman Eadric stamps inside the hall carrying with him the bloodied remains of a man's head. The hair's long and bloodstained, the familiar blue eyes forever staring, the lips curled in a snarl. Ealdorman Eadric's grin of triumph matches mine.

'Some decoration,' he offers, unheeding of the blood dripping from Blakari's head onto the dirty floorboards.

'My thanks,' I retort. 'Perhaps that should be displayed outside the hall?' I suggest. Our grins stretch wider, and we begin to laugh, the sound joining the echoing thunder of the rain and the sounds of men cheering within York.

York has been restored to England.

The Norse kingdom of Jorvik is as dead as Blakari Gothfrithson.

My triumph would be complete if Ildulb and Anlaf had also perished, but I'll console myself with York and the death of Blakari, for now.

18

944, DUMBARTON ROCK

Dyfnwal, king of Strathclyde

The struggle of exiles trailing into my hall infuriates as much as it honours. These men and women think I can help them regain what they've lost; that's the honour. The aggravation is that, despite what they think, I've neither the numbers nor the desire to assist them in reclaiming Jorvik. In fact, I harbour the thought that King Edmund of the English has done our island a huge service by taking it from the Norse.

With no home to call their own, Anlaf Sihtricson and his men have nowhere to go. I've no wish to aid them. Mael Coluim prowls on my borders like a mountain cat, keen to strike as soon as a weakness is sensed. In light of that, I must prove my strength, not my weakness. I need to banish these men and women, Anlaf in particular.

Once more, I question why he's sought my help and not Mael Coluim's. Mael Coluim is, or was supposed to be, his ally. What game is he playing by coming here? Has Mael Coluim ordered him to do so?

A sullen air infects these exiles. They know they'll not be returning home to Jorvik anytime soon. They won it back from Blakari, only to lose it a few weeks later. Yet they plague me with their demands and haunted eyes. I'm no great warrior and never have been. My battles are fought only with Mael Coluim and, even then, through words and belligerence, never sword and shield.

Still, I've flattered Anlaf with a place at my table. He eats and drinks with me, eyes gloomy, demeanour sunken. I hear many of his warriors were in the ships trying to escape Jorvik. The weather was terrible when Edmund attacked. Many perished in those ships, coming foul of their own defences that blocked the river to prevent Blakari's ships from reaching the settlement. While King Edmund sits and demands the loyalty of those who remained in Jorvik, the rest of the former inhabitants brood over their losses and blame either Anlaf Sihtricson or Edmund of the English, and sometimes Blakari Gothfrithson as well.

The bloody Norse. I wish they'd all sod off.

'What are your plans?' I question the almost-sleeping Anlaf roughly. He's been within my court for three days now. All he's done in that time is grunt answers at me and eat. He wears his defeat poorly and the rushed escape from Jorvik even more badly. Why didn't the man simply go overland to the battle site of Brunanburh and take a ship to Dublin? I'm sure he'd have received a far warmer welcome there. He must have allies within Dublin. All of the bastards claim descent from Ívarr the Boneless. Does his brother not hold Dublin? Or is that Blakari's brother? I find it impossible to keep track of them all.

'I need time to consider,' Anlaf grunts, head lolling. I'm pleased he feels safe enough to sleep his days away, but as he does so, his people eat the food stores mine have so carefully hoarded and carried up the steep sides of my high stronghold to last until the next harvest. I wish he'd bugger off to Mael Coluim or Dublin. I don't want him here.

'And in the meantime?' I probe. I can't just let this man, his warriors and exiles consume all my food. It's been a long and cold winter. The crops need time to regrow. He's eating my supplies, and he'll not pay for them.

His eyes open abruptly at my brusque tone. 'Are we unwelcome?' he asks hotly. He's desperately trying to keep his temper in check, but my words have riled him. Good. Perhaps I can anger him so that he'll leave.

'Of course not, Anlaf,' I smooth, although the words sound false to my ears. 'But I can't feed this many people after the winter. We don't have the supplies,' I explain instead.

'We'll buy more,' he counters. Questioning him isn't going to bring about the desired response. I sigh quietly. I must better understand his situation and think how I'd feel if I were in the same predicament.

'What happened to Ildulb, Constantin's son?' I query. I know he went south to support Blakari. Rumour is that Blakari is dead, but where Ildulb is, I don't know.

'Mael Coluim sent no one,' Anlaf says instead, his fury grown cold and no longer hot and filled with rage. I'm beginning to understand why he's here. He genuinely has nowhere else to go. Mael Coluim has reneged on their alliance, and Anlaf has no kingdom and no one to assist him in winning it back upon this island. He lacks the support of all.

'Mael Coluim's a stuck-up turd,' I offer with sympathy, half an eye to where his warriors watch me with fiery resolve. If I upset their oath-sworn lord, I might be in trouble.

Dumbarton Rock is my stronghold, and a place of great security, almost impossible to attack because its sides are so steep and littered with rocks, not grasses. Defences encircle it. Guards at every level. I don't often descend from its peak. It takes too much effort to climb back up. But it could just as easily be a prison. Men could be thrown from its summit and crash heavily to their deaths on the ground far beneath it. Or they could be captured and drowned in the gushing river that almost surrounds it.

Perhaps I should have left Anlaf at its base?

Only the fact Anlaf doesn't understand the customs of my people stops me from worrying that they would, in turn, support him. No, for all that the scops speak of a shared and ancient heritage with the men and women of Ireland, I can't see it amongst my people. We've no love for outsiders, none at all. We live in small communities, isolated by air and sea. We look on all who come into our lands with suspicion and unease. It takes a cunning and devious man to hold the disparate kingdom together. Anyone not born to our people stands no chance.

That's one of the reasons Constantin wanted my father and me as his puppet kings. He knew he couldn't rule my people, yet he wanted their strength to stand as a bastion against the Norse and the English incursions.

Bloody Constantin. I hate him, even though, and I barely believe it myself, he was a greater friend to Strathclyde than Mael Coluim has been. Perhaps I should support him more and offer him the use of my men to regain his kingship. The idea warrants consideration. I could make myself a strong king if I were shown to help others hold their domains. Both Anlaf and Constantin? I could be the sort of king Edmund of the English has become. A man that others admire and send their sons to for protection. A king who allows no one to rule for him.

'Apologies, my lord.' I'm suddenly aware that Anlaf looks at me as though he's asked a question. His face hardens with anger.

'If you don't wish to speak with me, you only have to say.'

I wish I could tell him to sod off and that his tetchy behaviour has no place in my court. After all, he came here to seek shelter; I didn't invite him.

'No, no, I was just considering the future,' I say, calming the atmosphere. Have I resolved to help the man? I haven't decided yet.

'I asked you if you'd assist me in taking Jorvik from that bastard, Edmund of the English?'

I wonder if I could, but I don't honestly think I can. It would involve taking on England, and the country is fertile and well cultivated, its coin honoured by everyone without recourse to argument.

'Must it be Jorvik?' I complain. We've had this argument before.

'No, it mustn't be Jorvik,' Anlaf admits with half a sigh. I feel his anguish. What must it be like to lose a kingdom to an overmighty warrior, who's impossible to beat? Edmund has tasked himself with driving Anlaf and Blakari and all the Norse from our fair island. He's almost accomplished that.

Perhaps I could win favour with Edmund against Mael Coluim if I helped him dispose of Anlaf. Maybe I could arrange Anlaf's murder? Perhaps I could just loan him ships to get to Dublin? That, I think, would be the best answer to the problem of this landless Norse warrior and his entourage.

'Would not the isle of Manx or one of the Outer Isles be a better target?' I cajole. My brother wed a women from one of the Outer Isles. Perhaps Anlaf could steal his kingdom.

'No, neither will do. My people are proud. If we can't be restored to Jorvik, and I think you're correct to baulk at such a bold move, it must be Dublin, the other half of my heritage.' Now that he can eye a future where he has land once more, he seems to have cheered up considerably. Damn. I liked him as a sad little man. Now, he seems reinflated and imbued with a purpose once more. I wonder if this was always his intention.

'How?'

'My warriors would storm Dublin,' he announces blandly. 'We know the place. It's been our home.'

'Are the rumours that it's impregnable incorrect?' I jibe. The Dublin Norse are proud of their strong fortress. Anlaf might have forgotten that.

'There are ways,' he comments. Now it's his turn to gaze off into the distance, seeing things I can only imagine. I've never been to Dublin. It's not the way of the kings of my land to leave it to the whims of the Scots or the English or even bloody Ealdwulf of Bamburgh.

'Doesn't Blakari's brother rule Dublin?'

'What if he does? My claim is just as good.'

I absorb that. By supporting Anlaf I'll be making an enemy of Gothfrith Gothfrithson. Of all the brothers, Gothfrith actually seems to know what he's doing.

'What would you need?' I don't want to seem too keen to have him leave my shores. Neither do I want to expend too much of my wealth on him.

'Ships, warriors, and food.' It's a simple reply and nothing that seems outrageous. Yet there's more, hovering on the periphery. I see it in the gleam in his eye. He means to involve me in this far more than I want to be. 'An assurance of your support when Dublin's mine and restored to the rightful ruling line,' he concludes.

I could curse him. Giving my tacit acceptance, even providing him with men and ships, is one thing. To outright side with him before he's even stepped foot in Dublin is a dangerous endeavour likely to have me surrounded by Gothfrith Gothfrithson's Dublin Norse ships before Anlaf crosses the sea, should word seep out of what I've done.

And yet? And yet, if I back the winner in this attempt, I might also benefit from it. It might win me the favour of Constantin. I consider where Ildulb is once more. Anlaf didn't answer my question, and hasn't answered my question whenever I've asked him. Could Constantin's son be dead? Would that change my decision if he is? I don't think it would.

Supporting Anlaf would annoy Mael Coluim. It would reveal him as weaker than me. I like that idea. The kingdom of the Scots has always thought itself better than Strathclyde. Now is the time to prove that belief wrong.

'I'll give you an answer tomorrow,' I reply. He grunts as his head nods backwards. I thought him abruptly restored to his former vigour, but until I give him what he wants, he's going to sit and brood. I wish I'd agreed to do what he asks, but I must have the support of my son and my nobles. After all, they'll be the ones who have to fight for him while I sit here and wait anxiously for news.

The thought fills me with fear. I don't wish to be left denuded of warriors when Mael Coluim's on the warpath and Edmund of the English presents an ever-greater threat now that he has his kingdom of York back.

Anlaf grunts in his sleep. I feel the eyes of his hundred warriors within the hall on my face. There are another four hundred who sleep wherever they can find room, in the beds of the men and women of my kingdom, or within the animal barns. I want them gone from Dumbarton Rock.

Supporting Anlaf's ambitions will be a small price to pay for the possibility of a high reward. I like that my name is linked with the word 'kingmaker'.

I probably like it too much.

19

944, ST ANDREW'S, THE KINGDOM OF THE SCOTS

Constantin, deposed king of the Scots

News of events in Jorvik reaches me long before I know my son is safe. My daughter grieves for her son's lost patrimony, not that it's easy to tell. Her mind has been mangled by the birth of her son, the death of my son, Alpin, and the loss of her husband, Olaf. Anger fills my days.

That Edmund has reclaimed Jorvik is a bitter tonic. His brother, Athelstan, was king there. Athelstan's success in Jorvik led to the peace terms of Eamont, then to the attack on Cait, and inexorably to my failure at Brunanburh. While Athelstan started with peace and ended with war, Edmund finds his sword and shield to be better at enforcing his will than Athelstan ever did.

All too soon Mael Coluim will be paying Edmund homage for my kingdom. The Scots people will be as fettered as Athelstan tried to make them. I doubt Mael Coluim has the stamina to ignore Edmund's demands, for they will come. Even now, I imagine Mael Coluim running to Edmund's court and bowing low for the privilege and speaking the oath of loyalty Edmund demands from his allies.

For me, the burn of that humiliation a decade ago is far from banished.

Mael Coluim waited too long to become king of the Scots to allow another to take it from him when all he needs do is pay lip service. Neither is Mael Coluim a great warrior surrounded by greater warriors. No, he's a politician, the leader of a strong faction. That will make him loath to make an enemy of Edmund, king of the English, and murderer of my grandson.

I must do something to ensure Edmund's wings are clipped before he gets too comfortable in his new position of strength. I already know he has an alliance with Bamburgh. Lord Ealdwulf, locked in his fortress apart from when he determines to raid the borderlands, is in the most defensible position possible. No one can take Bamburgh, as Blakari discovered to his detriment, not with guile and not with an outright attack.

I appreciate now that Lord Ealdwulf would be a better ally than an enemy, but Edmund has him firmly within his circle of influence. I'd berate myself for such a bad decision in the past, but Ealdwulf was useless and weak when his father died. Who knew he'd ever show such stones?

I fear for Ildulb. Does he still live? If he does, will he never have the opportunity to seek his revenge against Edmund? Will he always be a man with a blood vendetta against the English king?

I wait impatiently for news, for if Ildulb is gone, I'll be forced to pledge my full support to another of my remaining sons or perhaps one of Ildulb's many sons. My family line must endure. There will be someone to continue battling against Mael Coluim. Ildulb remains as Mael Coluim's heir. That is the way of our people. The ruling lines must alternate between those of my family and that of Mael Coluim's.

Yet, worry and anger conflict with my need for contemplation and desire to spend the days praying to my God. I shy away from asking or begging my Lord God to tell me if Ildulb still lives. With my long life, I fear asking for more. I've had so much already.

* * *

On a blustery day, not that many are ever any different in my isolation, a ragged ship finally beaches far down on the small pebble foreshore that runs close to my monastery home, quickly followed by three others. I stumble to the cliff side to see and reassure myself that Ildulb is on board.

The ships are weathered and tatty. I almost dread to think what state the inhabitants will be in if the ship looks so terrible. My oldest son strides towards me, his face filled with emotions as he makes his way higher and higher, curling up the steep embankment. I can scarcely believe my eyes, but almost all my men are returned to me despite the terrible calamity that befell Jorvik.

My son lives. Jorvik is lost, but really, I don't much care. Jorvik was never mine, but my son always will be.

The men are filthy and grimy, the muck of the ship and their excursion to Jorvik worn like a piece of armour.

'Father,' Ildulb calls as soon as he crests the cliff side. He's out of breath and puffing hard, but he shows such vigour I know he's not injured.

'Ildulb,' I acknowledge, my hand raised high in greeting.

He races toward me like a small child. I engulf him. I feel his strength. He can sense my weakness as I shake in relief, but he grins as I raise my hand to bat away his stench.

'It was a bloody battle,' he acknowledges. 'Our brave shipmen fought well, but once Blakari fell beneath the onslaught of the English, it was wiser to escape. It was a close-run thing. Thankfully, the English were more concerned with taking Jorvik than capturing me.'

'Blakari's dead?' my daughter asks, disappointment clear in her voice, as she seeks confirmation of what we've been told. She's made no secret of wanting to become Blakari's wife once he became king of Jorvik. If she couldn't have his brother, then she was determined to content herself with the younger brother. I have no idea what Blakari thought of that.

'Sadly, yes,' Ildulb confirms, with the right amount of contrition. 'He fell defending Jorvik's southern gate.'

My daughter emits a small sob and turns to bury her head in my shoulder. The girl will have to begin her ruminations all over again about whom she wishes to marry. I think she'll remain unmarried and with one son to her name. She's too unstable for any man other than a Norse warrior to wed her.

The rest of the men flow up the cliff face behind Ildulb, calling to him as they do so.

'Jorvik is a mud-filled mess. I don't think it stopped raining for weeks,' Ildulb recounts as we turn to walk toward my home.

'Did you see Edmund of the English?' I ask. I want to know if he fought with his men.

'I did, Father, yes. He had the greater numbers. Divided, Anlaf and Blakari had no chance of countering the threat.'

'What of Anlaf Sihtricson?' I'm curious. 'I've heard that Mael Coluim supported Anlaf.'

Ildulb turns to watch his men. 'The pair made a pact to fight together, one that Archbishop Wulfstan also pledged to support. Whatever Mael Coluim offered, he reneged on it. Anlaf had no help from Mael Coluim. Blakari would have upheld his end of the bargain, but the English were too quick. They attacked before it was formalised.'

'They were reconciled though?' I press.

'They were to be, yes, and all at my insistence.' Ildulb smirks, despite himself. I can see he's proud of what he accomplished, even if it amounts to nothing now. 'That Archbishop Wulfstan's a tricky fellow, but even he realised playing the Norse cousins off against one another wasn't the way to overwhelm the English. Now we must accept that the English king comes ever nearer and has allied with Lord Ealdwulf of Bamburgh.'

Ildulb's words are bitter. He fears another incursion by the English. I imagine he's also angered by Mael Coluim. If Mael Coluim had aided Anlaf then Jorvik would still be in Norse hands. Mael Coluim is an arse. How I hate him.

But the bloody English are also our enemy. Their power comes because the rest of us on this island can't stop bloody arguing amongst ourselves. I admit that. Perhaps I should reconcile with Mael Coluim? Working alone isn't effective. Indeed, Jorvik fell because two powerful men thought to fight over it. I can't allow the same to happen to the kingdom of the Scots, even though I hate Mael Coluim.

The future looks bleak. For now.

But my years of experience have taught me a great deal. Somewhere, something will happen. The English king will become too comfortable within Jorvik, and someone, whether it be Anlaf or another descendant of Ívarr the Boneless, will think to evict him.

I'll need to determine who that might be.

I'll certainly promise my support to them.

PART II

Here King Edmund brought all Northumbria into his domain.

— ANGLO-SAXON CHRONICLE, A TEXT, FOR 944

Mael Coluim son of Domnall reigned...

— CHRONICLE OF THE KINGS OF ALBA

20

EARLY 945, ST ANDREW'S, THE KINGDOM OF THE SCOTS

Ildulb, prince of the Scots

I watch my father with interest as he speaks to the stranger. I don't know the man, but he comes with the stance and clothing of a bishop, and my father's always pleased to speak to men who share his love of God.

The man's well dressed, his face devoid of beard or moustache, his tonsure that of the Irish monks. The men of the Christian God always seem better dressed than the religion they sprout warrants, almost as though they have more money and are far less frugal than their religion dictates. The tonsure is merely a means of pretending to the ideal. This man reminds me of Archbishop Wulfstan of York. I sneer to see it. I thought my father might share my disdain, but his face is animated. Whatever the man's saying, my father's enamoured of it. I can't imagine anything he speaks about justifies the rapt expression, but then, my father's not asked me to join their conversation.

I watch this unknown bishop with interest. Why would the people of the Scots need someone to walk amongst them and preach the faith they already follow? The men and women of this kingdom have more than enough bishops of their own. If that's his intention, why speak with my father first and not the king of the Scots people? Mael Coluim, the bastard, is still king in my father's place. How I hate him. In not punishing me for our involvement in the loss of Jorvik from the Norse kings' control, he's revealed himself to be even weaker than I imagined.

Mael Coluim began his reign with the support of many. It's withering, but still, he clings to the kingship with more tenacity than a barnacle to the underside of a ship.

Bishop Cathroe's older than me but many winters younger than my father. On seeking an audience with us, he announced he was beholden to no one other than the pope. He originates from a monastery on the continent but now moves amongst those of the faith. But, from his tonsure, he must be from Ireland originally. His intentions, he states, are to bring peace to our troubled lands. He's here 'to quiet the beasts within men's breasts that cause them to make war on others'. I don't believe him. His words are like the air he breathes: vaporous. Or so I suspect.

I wish I knew what the pair spoke about in confidence now the bishop's stopped preaching to those within my father's church. I'd like to know why my father excluded me from their conversation. He shares so much with me this banishment stings. And makes me uneasy. My father and I have been close in the near-enough year since my return from Jorvik. This feels like a betrayal.

Still, I watch, hoping to determine something, but instead they kneel and, with heads bowed, pray together. I don't foresee them discussing politics in such a position. But it's all I can think about. Bloody Edmund of the English has become the greatest threat to the people of the Scots now his reach stretches into the north. With the failure of both Blakari Gothfrithson and Anlaf Sihtricson to hold tight to Jorvik, only Lord Ealdwulf in his fortress at Bamburgh stands between our two peoples. I know Lord Ealdwulf has no love for the people of the Scots, or the Norse. I suspect he's not much enamoured of the English either, but the English did care for his mother on his father's death. Perhaps then he felt impelled to ally with Edmund.

All this is bad news for my father and our desire to restore him to the kingship of the Scots. If the Scots feel threatened by the might of the English and Lord Ealdwulf of Bamburgh, they'll rally around King Mael Coluim. My father knows this.

Despite their praying, I suspect Bishop Cathroe has come here to tempt my father back into the political arena of this island, and it is as complicated as ever.

In the wake of King Edmund's success at Jorvik, King Mael Coluim endeavours to exert his authority over King Dyfnwal of Strathclyde. Dyfnwal, aggravated at Mael Coluim's heavy-handed attempts to drag him under his control, has reached out to his allies, my father and Anlaf Sihtricson, who is now king of Dublin. I fear Dyfnwal might also seek an alliance with the English king. My father, equally frustrated with Mael Coluim, toys with Dyfnwal, just as he did with his father, Owain, who met his death on the slaughter field of Brunanburh. It should have happened by my hand, but Owain stepped into the fighting and allowed himself to be killed by the English.

I urge my father to coerce Dyfnwal. Strathclyde must remain weak so that when I become king of the Scots, or my father returns to his position, Dyfnwal can be brought back under our control. Strathclyde's a kingdom with a limited lifespan. Only my father's current predicament and Mael Coluim's uselessness stop it from being entirely controlled by the Scots. Dyfnwal's ineffective and always will be. I pray the English king doesn't fully understand Dyfnwal's weakness. If Edmund did, he could manipulate events to control Dyfnwal's lands. Then he'd be more than a neighbour. He'd almost be sleeping in my bed. Her enemies would surround the kingdom of the Scots.

Equally, I hope Anlaf Sihtricson, who sought Dyfnwal's aid to reclaim Dublin, doesn't grow powerful enough to consider replacing the loss of Jorvik by taking Strathclyde. The Viking raiders held Strathclyde many summers ago. It could happen again. It wouldn't be the first time an ally became an enemy, biting the hand that once fed it.

All of these problems I can blame on Mael Coluim. He should never have taken my father's kingdom. Then, I wouldn't need to worry about Dyfnwal becoming more powerful because Mael Coluim can't control him. But then, Mael Coluim can't control anyone, and I include myself and my father in that assessment.

My father and Bishop Cathroe continue to pray as I consider all this. I sigh with annoyance, running my hand through my hair. It's beginning to turn grey.

It's then that one of the men in Bishop Cathroe's entourage meets my eye. It's almost entirely comprised of men, apart from a small collection of women, including Cathroe's wife. A bishop shouldn't wed. My father seems to have overlooked this transgression. I think the women are all nuns, well, apart from one of two, Cathroe's wife, and another woman who's equally finely dressed. I've tried to speak to the women, but the monks keep me away, implying I might take them against their will, or something like that. I don't like the interference. They're not that attractive that I'd despoil them.

Now, the monk's young face is amused, as yet unlined by age or the sun. I look away but, unable to stop myself, glance back. He continues to watch me, his posture calm, and then walks outside.

Does he mean for me to follow him? Will he speak to me about the content of my father's and Bishop Cathroe's conversation? Intrigued, I trail him, the wind, as always, blowing fiercely in this exposed location. I can't help wishing my father had found somewhere more sheltered for his retirement. It's always bloody windy or raining or, for a scant few days, so hot I can barely move for lethargy.

The man, his fine blue cloak flapping in the stiff breeze, waits for me, eyes kind and gentle.

'My lord Ildulb.' He bows slightly. 'My name is Brother Cuthbert.'

'Well met,' I respond, holding out my hand in greeting. We briefly fumble as I realise he has a palsied hand. Flustered, I try to swap hands, but he goes to grab my other hand with his full hand, and we end up smirking wryly at each other.

'I was born with it,' he offers with a shrug. 'My mother always told me it was the work of the devil, but Bishop Cathroe assures me God gifted me with it so that I could labour in his name.'

As a warrior, I wouldn't accept such as a gift from my God, but the man's clearly comforted by the thought.

'It must have made your boyhood difficult,' I respond with sympathy. I've been training with a sword and shield since I could hold them. I can't imagine living any differently, but then, I was born the son of a king.

'I adapted, but yes, it was better when Bishop Cathroe took me in. But I didn't ask you outside to speak of me.'

'Why then?'

'Bishop Cathroe has a purpose. He endeavours to bring peace to these lands. He sees nothing but strife in the history of your people.'

I indicate we should walk as we talk. It's cold but not unbearable.

'He's read the words of the great scribe, Bede. He knows how conflict has always lain at the core of your relationship with the men in the south, the English. He hopes to rectify that and employ the faith to return everyone to peace and tranquillity. You might not realise this, but the lands have been contested ever since the ancient Romans came to your island.'

I nod slowly. He's not telling me anything I don't already know. My father ensured I received a firm grounding in the history of our friendships and wars with the English and then the Norse kings. Names from the past float through my mind, great battles where the Scots won or lost – Hædfeld where the usurper Edwin was killed by the British, Nechtansmere where we vanquished the old kingdom of Northumbria, their ruling line long since dead. Smaller skirmishes and battles that have had little impact on anyone but which kings should know about and use to rile their men to battle and glory.

Our past with the men of the south is bloody and brutal. But as I say, none of this is news to me. Kingdoms have risen and fallen on the whim and luck of kings for hundreds of winters. Only with the sort of stability my father offers can kingdoms grow firm roots and stay nourished through periods of drought and flood. Mael Coluim has disrupted that.

'Bishop Cathroe follows a calling from our God. He's been commanded to bring peace. Bishop Cathroe's a great man.' The man's tone is warm; his hazel eyes bright as he imagines a future I can't envisage. There'll never be peace along the borderlands, or with the kingdoms in the south. Never.

'How does he plan on achieving this?' I question, intrigued.

'He'll journey through these lands, seek out kings, and bring you all together, in a treaty of peace and religious unity.'

'He plans on using nothing but words then?' I ask sullenly. 'He has no warriors, shields or swords.' For a moment, I was interested, but now I see Bishop Cathroe has nothing to offer that others haven't tried before. If King Athelstan of the English couldn't ensure peace at Eamont nearly twenty summers ago, with the might of his army behind him, I don't see how a bishop can accomplish more.

'Oh yes, words and the scriptures and the love of God for peace. He's a powerful man.'

I could almost laugh at the fervour in Brother Cuthbert's voice, but I have some skills in statecraft. I appreciate laughing openly in his face isn't the best way to proceed.

'Words haven't worked before,' I goad. I want to disturb the calm and serene expression he wears. He must appreciate there's little that words can resolve. The Scots, the men of Strathclyde, the men of Bamburgh, even the English, we only understand the edge of a sword. Time and again that's been proven to be the only way to win authority over others.

Brother Cuthbert smiles softly, as though expecting my answer. 'Bishop Cathroe said there would be aversion and disbelief to his plan, but he's a beguiling man. He'll succeed. I have faith in his vision and our God.'

'Why do you wish to speak to me then?'

'Bishop Cathroe fears you'll be the most difficult to win over. He knows you're a great warrior and you want to fight. He understands... your loss.' In those words, the great well of grief I rarely fall into opens up again. It's been winters, over a decade since my son lost his life on Edmund's sword. I grieve for the boy who'll never be a man. I mark the anniversaries of his birth and his death and watch jealously as those whose sons still live celebrate the joy of marriages, grandchildren and the passing of winters. My son. Murdered by the English. One day, Edmund will pay for his crime. He's lived many winters longer than my son. Every single one is an affront.

As though Brother Cuthbert can see my thoughts, he nods with understanding.

'It won't be an easy task to accomplish, but it will be for the good of all. Everyone is now a Christian, and Christians should be together, not apart.'

I stalk away, angry that Brother Cuthbert and Bishop Cathroe think the resolution is so easy to achieve. All of my life, there's been unease on this island. Kings have tried words and swords. None of the accords have been long-lasting. None of the pieces of vellum filled with fancy words and expressions of peaceful resolution have endured for a greater amount of time than it takes to burn them.

And even if that was possible, I have a blood debt to pay. With each passing winter, my son might fade from my memory, but not my desire for revenge. I'll never see the English as anything but enemies.

Luckily, Brother Cuthbert doesn't follow me as I stalk to the cliff edge.

My father finally comes to find me gazing out with fury at the windswept peaks far out to sea, cresting white for all the sea is black and ugly this day.

'The man is all piss and wind,' my father mutters darkly, immediately lifting my ire with his opening words. I'm pleased he doesn't believe Bishop Cathroe's rhetoric. 'But, he might prove useful.'

My father's voice drifts. I realise the possibilities presented have rejuvenated him since the failure of Jorvik, not the man himself.

'How?' I ask the inevitable question.

'He could do our work for us with just a few words dropped here and there if we convince him we want to go ahead with his half-cocked idea. He plans to speak to everyone of note. That he starts with me gives an advantage.'

'How, if he only wants peace?'

'I need to think about it, but for now, show some enthusiasm.'

'He thinks to be the new King Athelstan?' I mutter sourly. I've been stewing over my encounter with Brother Cuthbert. I'm angry with myself for letting his words permeate my careful façade.

'But look what King Athelstan accomplished.' My father's words are persuasive, aimed to make me think.

'It didn't last,' I argue, focusing my attention on Athelstan as opposed to his brother, the murderer.

'Only because the poor bastard died,' my father chuckles. I look at him in surprise. He means what he's saying. 'He was a brilliant man. He used his religion to accomplish monumental changes. He took back Jorvik without raising a bloody sword, which is more than can be said for his brother.'

'But he lost it,' I counter, still surly. My father lost sons, grandsons, great warriors and the allegiance of even more at the battle of Brunanburh, fighting against the might of King Athelstan. I can't believe he's forgotten, but he is bloody old. Perhaps at his age, memories fade more quickly.

'I know what happened in the end, but he didn't lose Jorvik. He died and then Olaf Gothfrithson took advantage of his brother's youth. Stop being so bloody stubborn and take a moment to consider my words. They make sense, although I know you wish they didn't.' His voice intensifies as he tries to convince me he's right and I'm wrong.

'So you plan to go along with Bishop Cathroe's "mission to bring peace" and support it?' I speak to avoid considering his regard for King Athelstan.

'For as long as it works to our advantage, and no further,' he announces decisively. 'Like the scop and his song all those summers ago, Bishop Cathroe will unite people to a common cause.'

I don't like this. My father knows that.

'What did he speak to you about while you were praying?'

For a moment, I don't think my father will answer, but then he does.

'Bishop Cathroe assured me that he has more than just words

with which to enforce his intentions.' The answer's strangely ambiguous.

'Well, what does that mean?'

My father takes another deep breath before answering.

'He's not alone. He has the support of another who would fight with sword and shield to get what he wants.'

'You said it would be a peaceful resolution, and Brother Cuthbert implied the same?' I shake my head with confusion.

'Mostly,' he's quick to reassure, not that I want peace. 'But, he has an ally, the Norse leader, Eirik Bloodaxe.'

'That bastard?' I growl angrily. 'Even here, we know of his atrocities towards his family.'

'He's the blunt weapon in the hands of a learned man, a man who promises what we want. Peace amongst our enemies so that we can overwhelm them all.'

I grimace. I didn't like it when my father spoke of peace. Now that the name Eirik Bloodaxe has been added, I like it even less. The promise of the rejuvenation of the Scots kingdom, however, is welcome. I can't dismiss the small tendril of hope in my belly. Perhaps, after all, what this island needs is a new Norse leader to triumph where all others have failed, one unconnected with Ívarr the Boneless. We can work with that.

'I'll accord Bishop Cathroe my respect,' I reassure my father. I eye the rolling waves before me. They're in turmoil, but come tomorrow, the waves will quiet, and peace will be restored, if only temporarily. When the waves roll once more, new opportunities will present themselves. I must look at Bishop Cathroe and Eirik Bloodaxe as my new opportunities to finally overwhelm Edmund of the English. Like the barnacle on the ship, clinging on desperately against the rolling sea only to be dislodged in the fiercest of storms, I will find a new means of forging my way back into a position of power and gaining my vengeance.

21

EARLY 945, DUBLIN, IRELAND

Anlaf Sihtricson, deposed king of Jorvik, now king of Dublin

The man stands before me, travel-stained and dirty but somehow triumphant. He's taken a great risk in coming here. Doesn't he fear me? He must know of my uneasy relationship with Archbishop Wulfstan of Jorvik, the conniving arsehole. With half an opportunity, I'd cut that lying, two-faced bastard down. How King Edmund tolerates him, I don't know.

The monk wears good clothes, but heavily worn, a blue cloak around his thin shoulders. He shivers as the warmth from the fire reaches him. I don't know if it's with delight or displeasure. Some of these monks are strange men, preferring to live in discomfort rather than take what's freely offered. What's true is that it's cold outside. I pity anyone who has to work in the harsh wind as winter lingers.

His flushed face and layers of clothing attest to just how frigid it is. His eyes are filled with an inner light that drives him. I almost wish I could share his zeal. But I don't, not for what he's come to discuss with me.

I've heard of this man's master, the great missionary figure,

Bishop Cathroe, and his desire to unite the lands of the British Isles and end our constant fighting. Traders using the quayside have been filled with tales of Bishop Cathroe even though it's the winter and travel from Britain is fraught with difficulty.

His idea is ludicrous. The sneaky thought in my mind questions whether this is precisely what my ancestors have been trying to do for well over fifty winters, albeit with my great-grandfather, Ívarr the Boneless, as the master?

'King Anlaf,' the monk greets me, or rather he doesn't. He gives me my Irish name, the way the people here speak of me: Amlaib. It reveals his Irish upbringing that he doesn't stumble over the name Amlaib mac Sihtric, a strange mixture of my Norse and Irish heritage. I should respect him for trying to speak to me in a way that allows everyone to understand his words. Actually it would be better if he spoke to me in English. Few here know the language, and we'd have more privacy.

'Brother Cuthbert,' I reply, switching to English to see if he'll follow along, but his response is in the language of the hall. I curse softly. Whatever he's come to say, he's determined it should be heard. That's unfortunate. I've only recently taken back this kingdom with the aid of Dyfnwal of Strathclyde, and the high king of Ireland. It took some time, but my triumph was gained through blood at my cousin's expense, although Gothfrith Gothfrithson still lives. It's only his supporters who suffered from our attack. Gothfrith was able to flee and now causes intermittent problems from where he holds Limerick in defiance of my claim to that kingdom.

'I come on behalf of Bishop Cathroe,' Brother Cuthbert intones, as though we should all know who he is. It doesn't matter that I do know who he is, I fake disinterest. He's a strange little man, alone in a hall full of warriors who would rather kill than listen to him. 'He's a great man who works to bring peace to the blighted lands of the British Isles.' He speaks well and hides his hand from view. I know he's crippled and has no way of defending himself if I do decide to kill him.

I consider that as I listen with half an ear. Anyone who knows me would understand I'm not interested in what he has to say. My attention is on the next raid and the next steps I must take to ensure Dublin is secured under my control. I must finally banish or kill Gothfrith Gothfrithson.

'He'll use words and the love of our God to plant the seeds of peace amongst the people. I'm here to prevail upon you to abandon all claims for Jorvik. For peace to flourish, Jorvik must remain in the hands of the English. It is not for the descendants of Ívarr the Boneless to rule.'

My anger stirs. What is it with these jumped-up churchmen? First, Archbishop Wulfstan of Jorvik and now Bishop Cathroe – an Irish name, I notice – tries to do the same. I might not have wanted my men to think I planned on returning to Jorvik when Dublin has only just been secured, but I certainly don't want them to think some self-important priest will dampen my enthusiasm for doing so.

'Why would I agree to that?' I ask sharply as a ripple of noise runs through my warriors. Jorvik holds an allure that can't be explained for the Norse.

'It's for the good of the people of Britain,' Brother Cuthbert extols, a strange expression on his face. I'd call it rapture. 'All the people of Britain.'

'What of my people here?' I demand.

'As soon as Bishop Cathroe has made peace in Britain, he intends to journey to Dublin and the greater Irish lands and restore peace. He has such wondrous plans,' Brother Cuthbert eulogises. I shake with suppressed rage. He expects me to share his enjoyment of such a future when no means of winning a warrior's renown would exist.

'The men and women of Ireland have more than enough bishops to guide us,' I mutter darkly. A ripple of laughter fills the hall. The bishops of Ireland have little or no say over events between the kings, high kings and petty kings.

'Of course, they do, of course,' he placates. 'But Bishop Cathroe is determined,' he announces triumphantly, gripping his weak arm firmly to stop it jumping with excitement. He deems belief is all that's needed. 'Might I take back an assurance to Bishop Cathroe that you'll heed his words until he can come and speak to you in person?' He sounds so hopeful that I feel as though I'm disappointing a small child.

'No, you may not,' I announce decisively. It takes far too long for the words to trickle through Bishop Cuthbert's thick skull. I wonder if he's also simple; only his eyes flash sternly with rebuke.

'Bishop Cathroe will be most displeased if I can't take back your guarantee. He's working hard to restore peace and order and has determined that Jorvik is with its rightful rulers, the kings of England. They're the heirs to that kingdom, not the descendants of Ívarr the Boneless.' Brother Cuthbert sneers as he says 'Ívarr the Boneless'. It's brave for an unarmed man in a hall filled with more metal and iron than it would take to kill an entire chapter house of prattling monks.

'Then Bishop Cathroe will have to be displeased. I was driven out of Jorvik, and now I'm king of Dublin. But my birthright is to hold both Jorvik and Dublin, not one or the other. My cousin ruled Dublin for me in my absence. One day, Jorvik will also be mine.'

I hear his tut of impatience even over the roar of my warriors as they acclaim our place here. I might have feared to speak of my wishes, but the men are keen to hear me promise to capture Jorvik. I can almost taste the tepid water of the River Ouse in my mouth. It's a part of my heritage; by rights, it belongs to me. If only Blakari hadn't bloody interfered, convinced by Archbishop Wulfstan that he should rule Jorvik, we'd not have turned against one another, and Edmund of the English would never have undermined us in such a spectacular fashion.

With my firm denial, Brother Cuthbert looks more determined than when first led into my hall, all muck-stained from his journey on ships and horses. I made him clean up before I spoke with him. The Norse are not a race that favour muck and filth. We bathe, we comb and we clean. Then we kill and murder and do it all over again. It's a familiar and comfortable cycle.

In the face of my belligerence, Brother Cuthbert appears more resolute.

'Then I'll stay until I can take back such a declaration. I assume you'll provide me with comfortable lodgings?' He looks hopeful but also fired up. He sees me as a challenge.

'No. I offer you neither of those things. You can go back to Bishop Cathroe and tell him the Norse warriors of Dublin bow down to no one else. We're warriors. We fight for our rights. If we want Jorvik, you can be assured that we'll damn well take it back.'

I'm standing now, my arm thrust into the air in defiance. My warriors have risen, mead cups held high, feet stamping. They're as keen to take Jorvik as me. I should have trusted them more with my hopes and desires.

Brother Cuthbert looks uneasy. I smile condescendingly.

'I promise you safe passage to the quayside and no further. Now, be gone, little fly, and tell your precious bishop that the lands of your beloved island are ripe to be plucked by the men of Dublin, and we'll be coming. Soon.'

Roars greet my words. Brother Cuthbert's dwarfed in the middle of my hall. If he's lucky, he'll make it to the quayside. But, right now, I'm not convinced of it. I signal for two of my men to accompany him. I don't wish to start a war with Bishop Cathroe. I'll safeguard his messenger, but I won't adhere to his bloody plans for

Jorvik. I've land to reclaim, and for all that I've not considered it much since the English king ousted me, now I want it back. All of it. Brother Cuthbert has reawakened my memories of the place. I'm grateful for that.

Brother Cuthbert turns as he leaves, his eyes fixed on mine. He grins. I note the maliciousness there, surprised. A monk shouldn't look so pleased with himself.

'And what of Eirik Bloodaxe?' Brother Cuthbert shouts. My blood runs cold. I'm grateful that the raucous cries of my supporters swallow his words.

What's Eirik's part in all this?

If Brother Cuthbert and Bishop Cathroe know Eirik Bloodaxe then they're welcome to him. I hear enough of his depravity to avoid the bastard like he's pox-ridden. I don't want him anywhere near Dublin, or Jorvik for that matter. My pleasure in dismissing Brother Cuthbert evaporates. I almost consider calling him back. But no. Eirik Bloodaxe is far away, in Norway. I hear almost as many stories about him from the traders as I do about Bishop Cathroe. But all of them assure me Eirik is in Norway. He won't be coming to Dublin anytime soon. I'm almost sure of that.

Suddenly, I consider Bishop Cuthbert's words. I thought he implied the Norse shouldn't hold Jorvik. But is that actually what he said? My eyes narrow.

I'll need to discover more about Eirik Bloodaxe, and how a Christian monk would even know the name of that pagan bastard.

22

945, WINCHESTER, THE KINGDOM OF THE ENGLISH

Edmund, king of the English

I face the man before me. He calls himself a bishop, and I've nothing to tell me any different. Yet there's something about him I instinctively mistrust. His words are more oiled than Archbishop Wulfstan's. His vision for the future is nonetheless more audacious than anything Wulfstan has ever suggested.

I wish I could ignore Bishop Cathroe and send him on his way. But I might do better to listen to what he has to say. If I can make myself do so.

Word came two weeks ago that a holy missionary wished to seek me out: to visit me in my royal court and speak of England and the wider island with me. The request came via a man who'd been visiting with Constantin at St Andrew's. I immediately became suspicious. What if he was nothing more than an assassin who had come to try his luck? What if he was a missionary, as he says, but one with assassins within his entourage? Constantin and I have never been good friends, never allies. My brother once respected him until Constantin turned against the alliance prepared at

Eamont. Now that he's no longer king, but remains powerful enough that Blakari Gothfrithson sought an alliance with him before his death, I know to be wary.

Desperate men will do stupid things, and amongst Constantin's followers is one such man. His son. Ildulb hates me for killing his son in battle in Cait. I wish I could take back my actions, but the boy attacked me. I was fighting for my life, just as he was. I was a boy as well at the time. Ildulb seems incapable of accepting it for what it was, a sad result of the constant battles we fight among ourselves. If his father had only adhered to the terms of the treaty at Eamont, Athelstan and I would never have been in Cait.

I'll not feel sorry or accept the blame for events Ildulb's father played just as great a hand in manipulating. He tried to raise the Scots against my brother's rule. And the Welsh. He had the scop, Taliesen, write a poem and sing it in mead halls, telling of an England without the English. Constantin badly misjudged the strength of the English on that occasion, yet he still torments us. This might be his new trick.

I fear assassins because my brother's early death made his enemies realise how much easier it could be if the most powerful person were dead. Think of all the events that could be manipulated, such as the sudden and unexpected death of a king with an heir too young to rule in his place and a brother who lacks the political acumen needed.

The thought worries me, and yet I try to accept it as a hazard of my position. I have warriors who never leave my side, who guard me whenever I leave the protection of my palaces. Commander Ordhelm ensures I'm well secured. They also guard my mother, my wife and young sons.

My first wife died, giving me my second son, a beguiling child with wild eyes who'll never know his mother but who will, hopefully, know the new mother I've arranged for him. My new wife is a pleasant woman, a beauty to look upon, but not the love of my life. The love of my life died, and I visit her grave at Shaftesbury Nunnery instead of her bed.

I try to concentrate on the words Bishop Cathroe speaks before me. He says he's a great man from the continent, and that he spent his youth in Ireland amongst the wretches who live there. His face flushes with joy when he speaks of the past. His Irish tonsure is notable.

'I've been troubled with visions of your fair island burning, the air thick with ash, the screams of widowed wives and orphaned children. The dreams so tormented me that I knew they must have been sent from God Almighty and that he'd chosen me as his humble servant to unite the British Isles in a way not seen before.'

His words conjure a beguiling picture of the future. But visions and dreams are the preserve of all holy men. I won't dismiss them out of hand. I won't heed them, either. This island has been in danger of burning ever since the Norse came. Only when they're long gone, banished forever, and those who've settled have reconciled to their new Englishness, will England be free from the fear of attack.

'How would you unite her?' I query. I want to give the impression that I'm listening to him, that his words interest me, but all I see is a conspiracy forming before me. What new ploy is this from Constantin?

Bishop Cathroe's eyes are excited because he thinks I'm impressed by his visions and dreams. He speaks so fervently, his words almost fall over themselves in their haste to leave his slick mouth.

'I'll tell you of all I've done to bring about unity. I've sent a delegation to Amlaib mac Sihtric in Dublin, asking for his word that he and the entire family line of Ívarr the Boneless will abandon all hope towards Jorvik, or York, whichever is its correct name.'

I assume he speaks of Anlaf Sihtricson, but he gabbles the strange name and looks at me as though I should be pleased he's decided in my family's favour. There should never have been any argument about that. The Norse came, tore Northumbria apart, and took York as their capital.

'And?' I ask, trying to make that one word sound like I approve of his actions for all I don't. I wish I'd managed to kill Anlaf Sihtricson but he fled from my warriors and we never found him. The next we knew, he was claiming aid from King Dyfnwal of Strathclyde. I remember it was Dyfnwal's father who aided Gothfrith who tried to take York on the death of Sihtric, my cousin's husband. Strathclyde is too welcoming to the enemies of England.

'And I've recently spoken with Lord Constantin at St Andrew's. He supports my unifying actions.'

'Constantin is no longer king of the Scots.'

'Admittedly he's not,' Bishop Cathroe acknowledges, his animated face sobering at the concession. Does he know something that I don't? 'But with the support of his son, Constantin will soon return to his rightful position, and when he does, he'll help the English hold York. He's keen to agree on a new border with you.'

I imagine he is, but it still doesn't explain what will happen with King Mael Coluim. 'Have you spoken with Mael Coluim, at the court of the king of the Scots?'

'I fear I've not, no. The king wouldn't agree to a meeting.'

Did he try speaking with Mael Coluim first or did he go straight to Constantin? Constantin's more skilled in diplomacy than Mael Coluim, but it doesn't detract from the fact Mael Coluim's king now.

'Have you heard of Anlaf Sihtricson's agreement?' I query, changing the subject slightly, and much to the liking of Bishop Cathroe whose expression returns to one of enthusiasm having been forced to admit the huge flaw in his plans.

'Not yet, but soon, very soon. I've seen it. Amlaib, or Anlaf as you know him, will be happy to renounce his family's claim to York.'

I keep my face straight at the preposterous declaration from the holy man. He must have little knowledge of the Norse warrior, but his statement shows me I might have underestimated him. He could know more than me.

'Anyway, Amlaib rules Dublin. He has no need of York.'

Bishop Cathroe lapses into silence as he drinks and eats. I take the time to consider the rest of his entourage. They're mostly men, but there are a few women amongst them. I'm sure one of the women must be his wife, from the knowing looks they share. Bishops shouldn't marry. That displeases me. But there's also another woman. She's not a nun, I'm sure of it. She's dressed with court finery. Bishop Cathroe introduced her only by her given name, Gunnhild. It's not lost on me that she has a Norse name and the look of the Norse. I wonder why she travels with the bishop? What relation is she to him? She eats carefully, her naked interest in my court apparent, as she watches all with keen eyes. Of all of his adherents, I need to watch her most closely. My mother agrees with me.

The monks all look similar but carry some deformities. One is hunched, another on crutches, one has a broken face somehow forced back together by a skilled healer but ugly for all that. Another is blind, and the last brother has ink-stained fingers. He must be able to read and write, for all his expression is slack.

Ealdorman Athelstan's quickly at my side as our conversation lapses, his intentions to discuss our guests secretly masked as he carries my youngest son to sit with me. The boy grows well, even without his mother to nourish him. I'm indebted to Athelstan's wife, my cousin Ælfwynn, for caring for him so well. He's not often at court, but this happens to be one of those rare occasions when

Edgar is, so as my son reclines in Athelstan's arms, he lowers him into mine and speaks softly.

'What do you make of this?'

Our heads almost touch as my son's limp body is transferred from his arms to mine.

'There seems to be nothing but gain in it. I think, until we know each other better, we should be friendly with him and thank him for his endeavours. He could be a powerful enemy if he has the ear of Constantin and Dyfnwal of Strathclyde.'

I look at him sharply. I wasn't aware he'd been in contact with Dyfnwal, but Ealdorman Athelstan nods quickly.

'His monks were overheard discussing the poor excuse for a court that Dyfnwal keeps. Bishop Cathroe means to make a name for himself within Britain.'

'He means to meddle,' I mutter with annoyance, trying not to disturb my son as my body tenses.

'He does, yes.' Ealdorman Athelstan has moved to my side, sheltering my son's head and making it look as though we talk about the boy, not politics. 'But we can use that against England's enemies. Send him on a tour of Winchester tomorrow. I'll take him if you want, or you could conduct it. We'll show him how well we respect his religion and work only for the good of God Almighty. We can show him the Nunnaminster and the Old and New Minster.'

Ealdorman Athelstan's smirking as he speaks. My grandfather and my half-brother were the true believers in my family. Ealdorman Athelstan and I, well, we understand the potent political force that being able to call on the great God Almighty truly is. I build churches and endow monasteries as I must, while Ealdorman Athelstan believes the monasteries should be reformed to the places of worship they were before the attacks of the Viking raiders. All of which we do in the name of money and power. But no one ever needs to know that. Not if we mask our lack of faith well.

'Arrange it,' I offer, turning my attention to my son now, admiring his gentle curls and soft skin. My wife joins our small group. She's desperate to have children, and dotes on the youngest of my sons. The elder is less keen to engage with her, but in time, he'll love his stepmother, just as I must.

She smiles tenderly at young Edgar. I reach out to brush a stray lock of hair from her cheek. She grabs my hand as I do so and the smile on her face is so loving that I almost forget all about Bishop Cathroe. Æthelflæd's a gentle soul, and should we have children, I doubt she'll ever give them up to be fostered, as I've done with Eadwig and Edgar.

Ealdorman Athelstan nods smartly and walks away, leaving Lady Æthelflæd and me to admire my son – our son, I should get used to saying. The child will never know his true mother; perhaps it's best to present Æthelflæd in that guise.

Bishop Cathroe and his entourage are quickly muffled in the court's noise. I stand and take my son from the great hall. Tonight, he'll sleep in the royal nursery with his nurse and his foster mother close at hand. I'll only be a few rooms away from him. Should he wake at night, I can tell him stories of the old times and lull him back to sleep. I enjoy being a father.

It's a great pity that my half-brother, Athelstan, decided against fatherhood, but then, if he hadn't, I'd not be king. That gives me something to think about as I leave the feast in my hall and walk through the sprawling wooden palace to the royal nursery, accompanied by Commander Ordhelm and three of his warriors. My mother sits within the nursery, stroking my older son's head as he slumbers in his bed. She smiles softly at me. I wish I could join her and delight in having my sons at home and together for a short space of time, but politics are being discussed in the hall. I need to decipher just what it is that Bishop Cathroe plans to accomplish despite his conciliatory words.

He's spoken with Constantin of the Scots, Dyfnwal of Strathclyde and Anlaf Sihtricson in Dublin. Now he's here, with me. What sort of man is he to interfere as he does? What foolish bravery does he think to have to walk amongst the warring kingdoms of this island without fear? Archbishop Wulfstan has wrought his mischief by turning men against one another. Is that what Bishop Cathroe intends to do as well? Who holds his loyalty? Who does he hope to benefit, because, despite his fervent words, I don't believe it's for the good of the people on this island.

I must discover all I can about him.

I must know if he means harm to England, or to me and my family. I also need to determine Gunnhild's identity. Her presence here is most unsettling.

* * *

The following day, Bishop Cathroe awaits me in the king's hall. He bows as I enter. I note that every member of his entourage escorts him. We'll be a large body of people to move through the crowded streets of Winchester.

Ealdorman Athelstan's already there, speaking to the bishop. I eye the women who escort the bishop. Once more, it's Gunnhild who draws my eye. She wears a cloak that's lined with rich pelts. Her clothing sets her apart from all the others.

'My lord king, you honour me,' Bishop Cathroe oozes as I greet him. He speaks English well, but it's not his native tongue. Occasionally, he stumbles over how he pronounces some of the words.

'It's always a pleasure to share the monuments raised to the glory of God with firm believers,' I reply quickly. I don't miss the pained smirk on Ealdorman Athelstan's lips.

Behind me, Commander Ordhelm and his men space themselves out. Warriors have already been dispatched to the Nunnaminster, the Old and New Minsters to ensure nothing untoward befalls us. No one is allowed entry into those hallowed places until after our visit.

'Shall we?' I indicate we should walk. 'It's not far.' They arrived on horseback, but I know they came from Southampton. The request to meet with me might have come from the far north, but they journeyed by ship, not horseback. A fast rider sent to and from Southampton overnight informs me that their ship awaits them. The man also discovered that the ship belongs to Gunnhild, or rather, Lady Gunnhild. I knew she was more than she seemed. Now I need to uncover more about who she is. I don't imagine Bishop Cathroe will be forthcoming. Perhaps then, my sister, Eadburh, a nun within the Nunnaminster, may be able to discover more for me. I've sent word to her via our mother of my intentions today. We're not close siblings, but then she's spent almost all of her life within the Nunnaminster.

It's there that we go first. My sister greets me reverentially when the abbess summons her. She may have long been a nun, but I see the finery of her clothing. My mother ensures Eadburh's always dressed as well as any other member of the House of Wessex. I don't begrudge the expense. Eadburh's eyes travel over the women who escort Bishop Cathroe.

'We would invite you to celebrate Terce with us,' she offers openly. 'We're sure you'd welcome some time away from the weariness of the world.' So polite are her words that I know no one will be able to object.

Just for a moment, I sense some unease, but it's quickly banished by Bishop Cathroe.

'You're most kind. The women of my entourage have been sorely tested. There are few nunneries in parts of this island.'

With barely a backwards glance, the few women follow my sister and mother into the holy church, and after seeing the fine windows, with glass imported from Frankia, we leave and travel to the Old Minster.

The trip concludes uneventfully. Bishop Cathroe and I have talked about much, but only in the vaguest of terms. He wept to see the grave markers of my grandfather and half-brothers. I don't believe he thought anything of my father's. Bishop Cathroe spoke highly of all he saw. He has a well-oiled tongue, that's for sure.

That night, I seek out my mother in the royal nursery once more. She's as calm as ever, her poise assured, her clothing even finer than Eadburh's.

'I have news,' she assures me, a glint in her eyes.

'Are we betrayed?'

'No, not at all. But Bishop Cathroe keeps some interesting women in her entourage.'

'Lady Gunnhild?'

'She's the daughter of the king of Denmark.'

'I knew she wasn't who she seemed.'

'That's not all, my son. She's wed to Eirik Bloodaxe, the little-loved brother of Hakon, king of Norway, and latterly, your foster brother.'

'The wife?' I exclaim, astounded.

'Yes, the wife of the infamous Norseman. Eirik Bloodaxe, as you know, is an evil man. He kills all who stand in his way. Hakon has done well to keep hold of his kingdom.'

I swallow uneasily. 'Then why is she with Bishop Cathroe?'

'I don't know. But be assured. She portends trouble. Bishop Cathroe isn't at all the benevolent man of peace he seems.'

I nod, absorbing this new piece of information. The last I heard from Hakon, his half-brother, Eirik, had been banished from Norway, evicted and told never to return. The presence of his wife with Bishop Cathroe can only mean one thing. Another Norse bastard has his eyes set on my kingdom.

I laugh, the sound bitter.

'Bishop Cathroe urges Anlaf Sihtricson to give up all claim to York, and yet, it appears, he means to aid another to take it.'

'Possibly,' my mother agrees, her expression pensive.

'I'll send word to Lord Ealdwulf at Bamburgh, and Ealdorman Uhtred, in York. All should know of this new threat.'

My mother nods again. Her eyes blazing fiercely.

'You'll win the peace you deserve,' she reassures me, her voice firm, brokering no argument. 'But your fighting days might not yet be behind you.'

23

SUMMER 945, DUMBARTON ROCK

Dyfnwal, king of Strathclyde

Preparations are well underway for the march to war. My warriors have been summoned and will stand guard at the borderlands with the English and the Scots, as Bishop Cathroe's words echo in my mind.

He'll have spoken of peace with England, of Jorvik reconciled entirely to the English and of Norse kings banished to Dublin or their homelands upon visiting King Edmund's court. His intent is far, far different, as he told me when he visited me, eyes ablaze with his fervour for the future. I'm thrilled I've been chosen as an ally to his scheme. The deposed, but soon to be restored, Constantin of the Scots and I are firm allies, along with this man I know only rumours about, Eirik Bloodaxe, although I have met that warrior's wife. Lady Gunnhild is an intriguing woman. She assures me her husband has the men and resources to accomplish all that Bishop Cathroe promises. Together, we'll reset the pieces on the *tafl* board of who holds power on this island.

My part will be to attack King Mael Coluim. Constantin and his son will raise a force from the east to do the same. The Norse will join with Ildulb, coming ashore at St Andrew's. Then, when Constantin is once more king, we'll topple the independent kingdom of Bamburgh. Once Bamburgh is also under our combined control, we'll go further south. Jorvik will be taken from the English king. Eirik Bloodaxe will rule there.

I spare no thought for Anlaf Sihtricson in Dublin. He was too weak to hold Jorvik, and has proven to be a poor ally, reneging on his promises to repay me for my assistance in getting him to Ireland with his surviving warriors. Eirik Bloodaxe, Bishop Cathroe assures me, is a very different proposition to the weak Anlaf. It is, Bishop Cathroe told me, time to look beyond the family of Ívarr the Boneless. Eirik Bloodaxe, the son of a king of Norway, will rule here with the same lethal intent that's seen him removed from Norway by Hakon, once one of King Athelstan of the English's creatures.

With Lord Ealdwulf gone from Bamburgh, and King Mael Coluim ejected from the kingdom of the Scots, both hopefully killed in the fighting, the three of us will share the spoils. My kingdom will be powerful.

My son directs the warriors with great skill. One day, he'll rule well. He'll be a great king. Constantin once said we should ally with the English, and we did for a time, but I know that Edmund of the English means harm to me. He sees Strathclyde as the latest battleground with the Scots, and I'll not allow it. He might even hate me for assisting the Norse ejected from Jorvik, mirroring my father, who once did the same.

Bishop Cathroe couldn't have chosen a more auspicious time to present his vision of the future, even if he couches it in terms of visions from God. King Mael Coluim made his intentions clear at his inauguration when he had me swear fealty to him for my land. But Strathclyde shouldn't be part of the Scots empire. When we triumph, Constantin will see me as his equal.

When I sought Edmund out myself, having been to Mael Coluim's inauguration, I was surprised by his unwillingness to listen. Edmund demanded my kingdom should become part of the English lands, similar to Jorvik, in exchange for Strathclyde being safe and secure. Edmund promised me a new wife as part of the resurrection of the agreement gained at Eamont. I was outraged.

Over the last two years, I've laboured to strengthen the borders with the English to ensure I have enough warriors to call upon should Strathclyde be threatened. I'm pleased with my forethought. My enemies move around me, some seen and some unseen. Only on Constantin, Eirik Bloodaxe and Bishop Cathroe do I rely.

My son's loud in his support. Bishop Cathroe will lull the English king into a false sense of security. He's a well-spoken man, clever with his words. I can't see how his sincerity can be doubted. I wish I could act with such guile.

'The warriors are ready,' my son informs me, entering the hall in full battle gear. He stands strong and true, his weapons and byrnie polished and impeccable. He's tall and well built, with thick cords of muscles on his arms, which are evident beneath the tight material of his tunic. He possesses the arrogance of a man assured of his skills. Some say he looks like me, but I see a great deal of my father in him. Not that my father was much of a warrior. But even I can admit he was more of a warrior than I am. I eye my son with pleasure. I wonder if my father ever felt such pride in me.

'You'll march with them?' I say, although I already know this to be the plan. He nods.

'We have supplies for two months.'

His place is to watch the borderland with England. At some points, the actual border has long been disputed, stretching almost as far as Jorvik but on other occasions, as now, falling back behind the old, crumbling Roman wall, the one that is more complete and far to the south. Not the other one. My son and his men will shelter in one of the old ruined forts along that wall. From there they'll watch England and react if we're threatened, which I suspect will happen, even if not immediately. King Edmund might be deceived by Bishop Cathroe and his lies, but in time he'll have to march north. If that doesn't happen, then my son will bring his warriors to join me, Ildulb and Eirik.

My kingdom will rise again from the ashes of my father's failure at Brunanburh and become strong once more. We're a proud people. For too long, we've been independent. We'll not be subject to any external force ever again.

My councillors agree, as does my son.

'Keep safe, son,' I offer gruffly, my throat suddenly tight. I know I don't order him to his death, but even so, it's hard to send a much-loved son to war.

'If the English come, we'll beat the bastards,' he assures in his strong voice so everyone hears it within my hall. I raise his arms above his head and let my people acclaim him. He'll be a great warrior. I know it.

Once he's gone, my task is to join the attack against King Mael Coluim. I will prevail. My son will be proud of me. A smirk touches my lips. I feel alive with the surety of victory.

24

945, ST ANDREW'S, THE KINGDOM OF THE SCOTS

Constantin, deposed king of the Scots

My passive existence is at an end. Warriors parade through my church. Ildulb leads them as my priest blesses them.

King Mael Coluim's rule is soon to end. My son, with the aid of Dyfnwal of Strathclyde and Norse warriors under the command of Eirik Bloodaxe, will fight back against Mael Coluim, killing him in the process. Then, united, we'll take Bamburgh from Ealdwulf and install Eirik Bloodaxe at Jorvik. The three of us will rule as allies. The English will face our might.

I dismiss my unease at finally meeting Eirik Bloodaxe face to face. He's a large man, rippling with malice and muscles. He doesn't speak my language, although his wife does, and others amongst his entourage. Eirik says little, spending his time honing his blades. I know Ildulb senses my unease, but with the aid of Bishop Cathroe, I'm convinced the rumours of Eirik's foulness can be dampened. We'll rule together.

I watch the young warriors with envy and delight, wishing I were a younger man. The slaughter field of Brunanburh, or *Dun*

Bruide as it's written in my language, left me disgruntled and weak, sick with myself for forcing such destruction not only on my family but on my people. But Mael Coluim's dismissive treatment of me in recent years has ensured I'm acclaimed by many as the rightful king, even by men such as Blakari Gothfrithson. He might be dead now, but he knew I was the man to aid him in his efforts to hold Jorvik. That failure hasn't reduced the potency of my claim to rule the kingdom of the Scots.

My fears and failures from losing at Brunanburh have drifted away from me as though caught in the current of a winter-swollen river. With them gone, so too has my fear and misgivings about sending young men to war in my place. There'll be death and injury, but these warriors have given their oaths freely. Now they're mine to command.

It's reported that Mael Coluim has one thousand five hundred warriors. I find the number ludicrous. Mael Coluim would never be able to summon so many, let alone command them to do his wishes. He's a weak ruler. He showed that when he usurped my kingdom and left me to live. He should have killed me then. Not now.

I have over a thousand men, a huge number in a small outpost of the Scots lands. They hasten to support me. They know the future lies with my family. There are over three hundred Norse amongst that number, under the direct command of Eirik Bloodaxe. To the west, King Dyfnwal will bring his warriors, who must surely be close to a thousand. He, Eirik and Ildulb will counter Mael Coluim together.

Bishop Cathroe has used his words to great effect, although I fear his deceitfulness towards the English might have been too apparent to Edmund. There are troubling rumours the English ship-warriors take to their ships while others march northwards as well. I suspect the rumours are true. Not content with Jorvik, the

English plan to invade the northern kingdoms of Strathclyde and the Scots. I wish I knew which one was Edmund's focus. While we move against Mael Coluim, the English could already be undoing our intentions. We need to hurry.

Bishop Cathroe has promised me the restoration of my kingdom if I support him and his attempts to place Eirik Bloodaxe as ruler over the kingdom of Jorvik.

While Bishop Cathroe labours in the name of God Almighty to bring peace to our island, admittedly after a war first, he does so under the influence of Gunnhild, the wife of Eirik Bloodaxe. She believes she has a right to rule Jorvik, and through her, Eirik can reign there. She's also at St Andrew's, ordering her husband's warriors as though they owe their allegiance to her. I'd have liked a wife as vigorous and domineering as she is. No doubt, the children she raises with Eirik will be great kings and allies for my son and his sons after him.

I appreciate the opportunity to move against King Mael Coluim. With his defeat, I'll once more be a strong voice amongst the kingdoms of this blighted island, with firm allies in Jorvik, and in the shape of Bishop Cathroe and Archbishop Wulfstan.

* * *

The breeze is gentle on my old face. I'm pleased. The gait of the sturdy animal I ride is almost enough to unseat me. That would be a terrible way for the restored king of the Scots to view the battlefield where his son and allies won a great victory for him.

It's been too long since I last rode a horse. What need did I have stuck in my monastery at St Andrew's?

The battle site is over two days ride from St Andrew's, across rugged terrain that's once more mine to command. It little matters where the battle was and how long it takes me to get there as I won't be returning to St Andrew's, but travelling back to Scone to once more sit upon my royal chair.

Ildulb and his allies have vanquished my usurpation. Our warriors have won such a resounding victory against Mael Coluim that Mael's disappeared. The bodies of the dead have been scoured by Ildulb. He assures me Mael Coluim isn't amongst them. That's good and also bad. He must still live and will threaten me if he's not found quickly. I suspect he'll go south to find the English king and seek sanctuary with him. If not Edmund, he'll trouble Hywel of the Welsh with his presence. Not that Hywel will offer him any support. The Welsh do little now but secure their borders. Hywel works for internal cohesion.

With Edmund in control of Jorvik, there's no longer a need for the Norse to trouble the Welsh. The Welsh enjoy a peace that's almost too good to be true. Hywel, although a younger man than I am, has grown old in his position. He claims all of Wales for himself, but in so doing, he's made many enemies. When he dies, as all mortal men must do, his massive kingdom will crumble back to its constituent parts. He's storing trouble for his sons, but will be too arrogant to consider what happens after his death. For now, he could offer the former king, Mael Coluim, support. For that reason, I need to find Mael Coluim soon.

First, I must view the battlefield and thank my warriors for their efforts on my behalf. A bruised and bloody messenger rushed to me as soon as the battle was won. He staggered into my quiet church, disturbing my meditation. With blood dripping from an open wound on his face, landing loudly on the recently cleaned wooden floorboards he declared victory. Initially, on seeing him, I feared for my son's life, thinking Mael Coluim had overrun my force of only a thousand Norse and Scots. I worried my son lay dead on yet another battlefield. Not that Lady Gunnhild or Bishop

Cathroe shared my concern. They listened impassively as I was reassured of the victory gained in my name.

Ildulb, as good as his word, has annihilated any opposition with the aid of the Norse.

I'll take back what was stolen from me.

With the honour due to an old man, my bodyguards ride beside me, Lady Gunnhild and Bishop Cathroe remaining at St Andrew's. If my warriors feel impatient at my slower speed, they mask it well. Only Ildulb doesn't, riding towards me as we draw nearer, his face lit with inner delight at his success.

'Good, you're here, my lord king,' he announces, turning his horse to ride back the way he's come.

'Tell me of the battle, son,' I demand, hastening to keep pace. He clears his throat. His hair is wild, and his byrnie has recently been thoroughly cleaned. Speckles of thick red fluid mar it, and his sword has blood ingrained on the hilt.

'We met above the river,' he recounts, pointing along the path we're following. 'Mael Coluim had sent scouts. He knew we were here. All the same, he chose to cross the river rather than using it as a temporary refuge. I enticed him to attack up the hill,' Ildulb continues, pointing once more to where I can see a rugged outcrop, topped with exposed rock even in the growing season.

'His men were no match for our defences. Many fell to their death along the sharp slopes before they even met our weapons. Others stumbled into our concealed ditches and were flattened by their fellow warriors. Overcoming the force was easy. They were ill-disciplined and unable to mount an effective attack against us.'

I see now where Ildulb forced the confrontation. I release a whistle of surprise. The outcropping is no place for a battle. The bodies of the dead remain visible across its exposed surface, slashes of red against the paler flesh of the dead and the starkness of exposed rock. Mael Coluim must have been delusional to believe he could fight his way up such a steep hill and unseat his enemy.

'He allowed you to dictate the battle in such a way?' I question. Mael Coluim has even less fighting acumen than I thought. I notice that Eirik Bloodaxe has ridden to join my son. His face is expressionless, and he appears unwounded. Whether he takes pride in all we've accomplished, I'm unsure. No doubt, his thoughts are centred on Jorvik. I don't see Dyfnwal. Where is the king of Strathclyde?

'Whether it was Mael Coluim or his men that ran wild, it little matters now. They're dead or apprehended and Mael Coluim is gone.'

'Mael Coluim's still not been found?' I check. Ildulb shakes his head.

'We've men searching to the south and the north, but no, Mael Coluim's disappeared.'

'He'll have gone south,' I announce. I turn towards the hazy borderlands, shrouded in lazy summer sun. As soon as I'm reinvested in my kingdom by visiting Scone, I'll travel these lands and reassure my people they're safe again. I've been stuck inside my monastery for too long.

'I agree, but I also thought it unwise not to search north. He might hope to seek out alliances with the men of the islands.'

In the distance, I see horsemen crawling over the grasslands and the hills. One man, riding swiftly northwards, not veering from his path, catches my eye. I point him out to Ildulb, who shields his eyes against the sun with his weathered hand. He rests his head on one side but offers no explanation.

'We'll know his news soon enough,' he mutters and leads on towards the encampment. My warriors stand smartly to attention as I ride between them, trying to keep my seat. I'll be pleased to slide from the back of the horse and rest. My body's become frail. Men cheer me and proclaim me as Constantin, the king of the Scots. I smile, feeling young for the first time in nearly a decade.

Still, I see no men from Strathclyde. I open my mouth to question Ildulb about our other ally, only the horseman approaches. The closer he gets, the more I can see, and the question dies on my lips. I recognise Denewulf, and his crooked nose, with a jolt. His expression is bleak. His clothing filthy. At some point today, he's ridden through a deep river. Patches of slime adhere to his left shoulder, although he remains unaware.

I wave Denewulf before me. A man in such a rush must have important news for his king. He shows no surprise on seeing me with Ildulb and Eirik Bloodaxe, or of the banners proclaiming me as the king of the Scots. His eyes are harsh, his breathing ragged, as though he were the horse being ridden and not vice versa.

Denewulf's voice is flat and devoid of emotion despite his words being incendiary.

'The English are heading north,' he announces, loud enough for all to hear.

We've had a victory here. But we still have another battle to fight.

I eye Ildulb. He grunts but shows no other emotion. I do notice that Eirik's eyes flash with fire.

'We'll win again,' Ildulb reassures, disappearing from my presence, his voice ringing through the encampment as he issues his orders in my name.

The kingdom of the Scots is mine. Now we must face yet another king of the English to ensure my kingship. Some things, it seems, never change.

25

SUMMER 945, THE KINGDOM OF THE SOUTH WELSH

Hywel, king of the South Welsh

War. It always comes down to war. Men will never disappoint me in their inability to live peacefully.

King Edmund of the English has sent word he marches on Dyfnwal's kingdom of Strathclyde. He intends to quell it and bring it under his control following the successes at York last year, and Dyfnwal's refusal to restore the accords agreed at Eamont with his father, Owain. Edmund doesn't ask for my support. I wouldn't give it. He knows that. I won't take my people to war over something that doesn't involve us. Whether the kingdom of Strathclyde is under English command or not, as long as it doesn't affect my kingdoms and people, I'll allow it to exist in peace.

Edmund's messenger Wihtred cautions against Bishop Cathroe, but the name's a mystery to me. I've never heard of him. Edmund, Wihtred advises, suspects Bishop Cathroe's in league with a new Norse warrior, Eirik Bloodaxe, along with his wife. Edmund advises that the Scots kingdom is at war amongst itself because of Bishop

Cathroe. Edmund's messengers tell me a great deal about Bishop Cathroe. I'm unsure how much to believe.

The rapid change in events is astounding. Edmund, Constantin, the descendants of Ívarr the Boneless and Mael Coluim have existed in a world of strange shifting alliances for the last two years. I thought war would return to this island, but not in such a way. I believed it would be an attempt by Anlaf Sihtricson to besiege York. I never imagined a new Norse interloper would become involved.

It changes everything and nothing. Conflict won't come to the Welsh. I refused to offer support to Anlaf Sihtricson when he first fled from York. I've never questioned that resolve, even though Anlaf is once more king of Dublin and could attack my exposed coastline that faces his. No, Anlaf's too busy keeping Gothfrith Gothfrithson and his nephew at bay to think about my kingdom.

Despite my strength, I suspect a show of force will be required in the coming days. I intend to send Owain to the north of my kingdom. He'll ensure no one imperils my borders with an ill-conceived attack. My two other sons will watch the coastlines. There's no harm in being prepared.

Wihtred states that King Edmund assures me the Welsh kingdoms are of no interest to him. The border between the Welsh and the English has grown increasingly quiet over the last few years. No longer do men bedevil me with claims of attacks from the English. Instead, alliances are forming between English and Welsh neighbours. Soon, I imagine it'll be difficult to determine who was once English and who Welsh. That's what peace can do. I applaud it, just as Edmund does with the remnants of the Five Boroughs, the Danelaw as it's becoming known. He upholds their laws and accepts their heritage is different to his English subjects. The Norse jarls living there almost fall over themselves to help him and keep their positions.

Edmund's intentions towards the kingdom of the English

surpass even those of Athelstan. Athelstan was a Christian warrior. It's taken the warlike skill of his brother to ensure Athelstan's vision of a combined England continues after his death. It's been subjected to compromise, but has also been accomplished with violence.

It's a pity the other kings on our island can't see the same good in Edmund as me. They continually rebel against his aims. War will devastate Strathclyde. Constantin and Dyfnwal will both lose a great deal. Mael Coluim's part is more difficult to determine.

I anticipate messengers will soon reach me from Constantin or Dyfnwal, or even this mysterious Bishop Cathroe, demanding my involvement. How little these men know me. Edmund informs me of his actions. Ours is an alliance of near-equals. Constantin and Dyfnwal will demand my involvement. Bishop Cathroe will no doubt lie about his intentions. I'll not give my support to any of them.

My son, Owain, walks into my inner sanctuary, his expression apologetic. I follow him outside. He's preparing to ride out, no doubt he comes to bid me goodbye before heading north.

'Father,' he says once we're outside, and the warm summer day fills my senses with the sounds and smells of growth and rebirth.

'Son,' I reply, smiling.

'We have a visitor. Anlaf, son of Sihtric, has landed on your shores. He comes in person from Dublin.'

'What does he want?' I grumble, sounding like a small child and earning a rebuking glance from my son. I've already refused to ally with Anlaf. Why would he seek me out again? Why would he risk leaving Dublin? Who holds Dublin in his absence, or has he, once more, been careless with his kingdom? Does Gothfrith Gothfrithson rule Dublin again?

'He comes to warn you.'

I'm not expecting that answer. My gaze sharpens.

'This Eirik Bloodaxe. He plans to take Dublin and York and the land to the north of our kingdom, allowing men to journey unmolested between the two places.'

This isn't what I wish to hear.

'Anlaf seeks my support against Eirik Bloodaxe?' I press.

Owain shakes his head. 'No, he only wishes to speak with you. Then he'll leave. From what I can gather, Eirik Bloodaxe isn't a... pleasant man.'

I stop, considering what I should do. If Anlaf has taken the trouble to journey across the fractious dividing sea, I should heed his words. I should respect a man who comes in person to warn another who isn't even his ally. Indeed, a man who has refused to become his ally.

My son's brought horses with him. I quirk an eyebrow at him.

'I didn't bring him here,' he squeaks in shock.

'Where is he?'

Owain nods towards the coastline, hazy in the distance. It'll be a journey of half the afternoon, no more. 'I left my warriors guarding him and his men. Do you want your household guard?' But already, my men fall into line behind me. Sometimes I forget they're even there, I've grown so used to their presence. My son mounts as my animal's brought to me. Together, we move down the steep slope upon which my monastery is housed. Owain's talkative, telling me of Anlaf and his men. I listen with half an ear. If Anlaf gives me intelligence on Eirik Bloodaxe, should I send it to Edmund as he's warned me against him?

By rights, if I want peace to prevail, as I think I do, it's my duty to tell him, but a perverse part of me considers what would happen if I didn't. Could I rule his kingdom If he fell in battle?

Owain's arranged for Anlaf to wait for me in the hall of one of my supporters, close to the coastline. In the far distance, I hazard I can make out the sail of the ship that's brought him here. I wonder if he means to leave just as quickly as he arrived. Dismounting and entering the elegant wooden building, I'm welcomed by Gruffudd, and then Anlaf Sihtricson is before me, drinking Gruffudd's mead and eating his fish.

Anlaf stands and hastily wipes his mouth. He's a large man but not the biggest I've ever seen. He has a warrior's wide stance. His face is serious. He has fine blond hair, tied back in a thong and fraying slightly on top of his head. I always think it cruel when men lose their hair unevenly. His clothes are beribboned with bright threads. I assume he didn't come across the sea so well dressed. If he did, he expected to be welcomed peacefully. His boots are high around his lower legs. His cloak's swung half aside. Perhaps he's an arrogant arsehole like all the Norse.

'My lord king, this is Anlaf Sihtricson, king of Dublin,' Owain introduces. 'Lord Anlaf, this is my father, King Hywel of the Welsh.' I notice that Owain uses the tongue of the English. That surprises me.

We appraise one another.

I offer a handshake, but Anlaf steps forward, gripping my arm tightly before whispering, 'It's good to meet you, finally.' He speaks with an accent, but his English is good. Now I understand why Owain introduced us as he did. Anlaf's bristly beard rubs my ear. I can smell mead on his breath. The touch is so intimate it almost feels as though I face him in battle.

'And you,' I offer, stepping away from his half-embrace and gesturing that we should sit at the table refilled with plates of abundant dark bread and freshly grilled fish. Gruffudd keeps a good table because he collects my taxes from the harbour. He takes his payments however he can, not averse to accepting food instead of silver. He then converts this into silver for my treasury. He's an honourable man and impeccably honest. He also has a wife who can cook anything. He brags more about her than his fine house and great wealth.

Anlaf pats his stomach with appreciation and resumes eating.

'I'd forgotten how hungry being on the open sea makes me,' he offers as an explanation, but I gesture for him to take his fill. Good food can ease the most difficult of meetings.

I help myself to a portion of bread and grilled fish and watch the rest of Anlaf's delegation in Gruffudd's hall. None of the men appear to be more menacing than typical Norse warriors. Perhaps his intentions are as he says. He means to warn me about Eirik Bloodaxe. After all, Eirik could threaten Anlaf if he's not dealt with. Anlaf has as much to lose as Edmund of the English.

'I'm sure you're wondering why I'm here,' Anlaf says when he's finished eating.

I nod. I'm curious.

'Eirik Bloodaxe endangers the stability of this island. I know you're an ally of Edmund's. I hope you'll get word to him or assist one of my men in seeking him out. I know this Bishop Cathroe's allied with Eirik and speaks of his Christian duty to bring peace. The bloody fool.'

His words, delivered with anger, surprise me despite Owain's warning.

'What will Eirik do?' I query.

Anlaf appraises me intently. 'He calls himself a king in the northern lands but has no kingdom to call his own since his brother, King Hakon, had him removed from Norway. You might know Hakon. He was one of Athelstan's foster sons. No doubt you've met him on one of your many trips to the English court.' The words are evenly spoken. Has Anlaf learned to respect Athelstan and Edmund? That would be another surprise garnered from this meeting. 'Eirik plans on taking Jorvik as well as Dublin. He'll amass thousands of men with his promise of wealth and war. He'll be any of your lands. I hear they thought it was too rocky and your warriors too bloody and fleeting to bother. I intend to keep to the same agreement.'

My son observes Anlaf. I've turned away as though his words aren't for my ears, and they're not. Owain will rule on my death, alongside his brothers. He, and they, need to consider alliances and allies, as well as enemies.

I hold my hand out to Anlaf, and grasp his forearm as warmly as he did mine at the beginning of our meeting.

'We part as friends then, and your men may travel north.'

'We should trade,' he counters.

I pull back and appraise him. 'We should, yes. Gruffudd's the man to negotiate with.' I stand. As pleasant as it's been talking with Anlaf, I've much to consider. 'I pray we don't have cause to meet again,' I respond. His head quirks to one side.

'As do I.' But he settles to his food once more. I know he's not going, not yet. I need to return to my monks, laws and books. Despite what Anlaf has told me, the routine of ruling my kingdom concerns me and not what others are prepared to fight over. They're welcome to spill one another's blood. My intentions do not lie with war.

But still, the news of a new Norse pretender wishing to cause devastation is unwelcome. As ever, conflict is never far from raging to warfare. Men will never learn the value of peace.

26

945, THE NORTHERN BORDER BETWEEN ENGLAND AND THE KINGDOM OF THE SCOTS

Athelstan, the ealdorman

The knowledge I ride almost the same path as eight summers ago isn't lost on me. Then, I rode to do battle at Brunanburh. Now I travel further north. First, we must go almost to Brunanburh, the site of the greatest slaughter of our enemies, within sight of the sea, where King Athelstan was victorious against the combined might of the Norse and the Scots.

I can't believe only eight summers have elapsed since then. It feels a lifetime ago and yet only yesterday. I remember the fear and the excitement, the flush of youth that told me I was invincible!

So much has changed since then, and also so little.

I ride to war with Edmund, not Athelstan. Both men are different and yet similar. Athelstan was always a little dour, his confidence clear to see. He presented himself as a man who was dwarfed by responsibilities for all he accepted and strove to fulfil the legacy left by his aunt in Mercia.

Edmund, far younger than Athelstan, has less seriousness about him but also lacks Athelstan's serenity. It's taken him a long time to realise he possesses the skills to rule as his brother did. Olaf Gothfrithson's reclaiming of York when he'd barely warmed his arse on the throne set his kingship back years.

I journey knowing that Edmund's a great warrior and commander of men. He dreams of the same future his brother did, of a united England, but he'll not rely on treaties and the spoken word. He'll write his writ in blood.

Edmund will make the other kingdoms on our island bow down to his superiority, or he'll defeat them. His current intention to subjugate Strathclyde is audacious. I also know it will be successful. Edmund will drive Dyfnwal and his family from Strathclyde. Then Edmund will have a voice in the north to stop the encroachments of the Norse, the Scots and the men and women of Strathclyde.

But as we ride through the wild countryside between the slaughter field of Brunanburh and the border with Strathclyde, I feel an unexpected spark of fear. It feels almost as though something in our plans has been thwarted, even before they've begun. A messenger appears before us. Edmund summons me to listen to what this man has to tell us. I fear it will not be welcome news.

The messenger is a Norseman, that much is evident from the inkings on his arms. He rides poorly, and I don't miss that it's a stocky animal, one the Welsh ride, but why?

'My lord king.' His words are respectful, although Commander Ordhelm stands close enough to end his life with a swift movement from his drawn seax. The man, long hair pulled back from his face, smiles at the sight of the blade. 'I mean no harm. Indeed, I've been sent with the very opposite of intentions.'

'Why are you here and on a Welsh pony?' Edmund demands.

'King Hywel allowed me safe passage and aided me with a horse. He's as keen for you to hear my message as King Anlaf

Sihtricson. King Anlaf bids you know the truth of Eirik Bloodaxe and Bishop Cathroe's intentions.'

Now I'm intrigued. I can see Edmund is as well.

'Go on,' Edmund advises him, indicating that Commander Ordhelm should relax his tense posture and allow the messenger some room. If our messenger has already travelled through the lands of King Hywel, then he should be deemed as friendly despite his Norse heritage.

'Eirik Bloodaxe is reviled amongst the Norse. As you know, he's half-brother to King Hakon of Norway, raised at the English court.'

'I know this,' Edmund confirms.

'King Hakon has banished Eirik from Norway. It's said he killed Hakon's brothers. We don't know the truth of that. But now his wife, Gunnhild, the daughter of the Danish king, has attached herself to Bishop Cathroe. While Bishop Cathroe calls for peace on your behalf, he builds an alliance with Constantin, Dyfnwal and Eirik. The three men intend to rule Jorvik, Strathclyde, Bamburgh and the kingdom of the Scots.'

'They mean to remove King Mael Coluim and Lord Ealdwulf?'

'They do, and then you, my lord king.' The messenger doesn't smile as he speaks.

'So why are you here?'

'My lord king, Anlaf Sihtricson wishes you to know this. He's a friend to England.'

'Is he now?' Edmund muses.

'He is, my lord king, yes. He'll pledge you his aid, in exchange for relinquishing Jorvik to him.'

Edmund chuckles, but there's no malice there. 'King Anlaf thinks much of himself?' he suggests.

'He is almost your cousin. His father was wed to your half-sister, Edith,' the man offers, his eyes flashing with amusement.

'Then, as good cousins, please offer King Anlaf Sihtricson my

Commander Ordhelm, with the messenger, rides down the hill. Edmund stays mounted.

'It appears King Anlaf Sihtricson's caution was correct. We must send word to York and Lord Ealdwulf once more, but only after I've spoken to King Mael Coluim.'

'I don't like this,' I mutter. I sensed something was amiss. It seems that a great deal is wrong.

'Me neither, but we'll see what Mael Coluim can tell us.'

As though summoned with the words, the messenger and Commander Ordhelm appear, bringing King Mael Coluim with them up the steep slope. Mael Coluim appears broken, his body sagging and his horse ridden ragged in the stiff breeze of the day.

'My lord king. It's good to see you,' he demures, I realise he speaks in the language of the English. He bows respectfully, but remains in his saddle.

Behind Mael Coluim, a ragtag collection of men and women stream over the hills. Some ride, some work. Some are within a creaking wooden cart. No doubt the wounded. I'm astounded that women and children are also part of the flood of people.

'My lord king Mael Coluim.' Edmund does him the honour of giving the honorific. 'I'm surprised to find you, here. There has been a battle?'

'Yes, we were defeated by Ildulb, son of Constantin, and Eirik Bloodaxe.' Mael Coluim speaks calmly. As his words continue, I realise he must be furious. 'I received intelligence Ildulb intended to move against me. Alas, we were defeated by a combined force of him, Dyfnwal and their Norse allies, under Eirik Bloodaxe. I thought the rumours circulating about Bishop Cathroe were little more than that. But I was wrong.' He's angry at the admission. 'They have the greater numbers, but for now, Constantin's more intent on reclaiming Scone than supporting Eirik or Dyfnwal. I would align my warriors with your attack on Strathclyde and weaken the alliance.' Mael Coluim's voice sounds hopeful, not resigned.

'You'd join with me?' Edmund questions, no doubt surprised to find yet another ally where, in the past, there's always been an enemy.

'I would, my lord king.' Mael Coluim's respectful as he speaks. 'Constantin and his son, Ildulb, and Eirik Bloodaxe have a great many supporters. Bishop Cathroe's encouraged him to bring them into play.'

'Bishop Cathroe's a charismatic man,' Edmund comments, 'to incite war in such a way.'

'I've not met the man,' Mael Coluim counters. 'I refused to welcome him to my kingdom.'

'I wish I'd been spared a visit from him,' Edmund offers wryly. 'I'm prepared to work with you,' he decides quickly. 'But only on condition that you ally with England and pledge your personal oath to me as both a man and a king. You'll be restored to the kingship as my subordinate.'

I look down at my hands to hide a smirk. Here, on this windswept hill, with three thousand men at his back carrying shields, swords and seaxes, Edmund reconstructs the treaty agreed at Eamont.

'You'll also ally with the House of Bamburgh. Lord Ealdwulf's sworn an oath of loyalty to me. We'll be united in friendship, not animosity.'

King Mael Coluim doesn't stir to anger at Edmund's suggestion. Perhaps he even expects the terms. If Mael Coluim works with Edmund and keeps to his oaths, there'll be much-needed peace. His closest neighbour, Lord Ealdwulf, will also be a party to the same agreement. The island will be held firmly in the hands of only four men: Edmund, Hywel of the Welsh, Mael Coluim of the Scots and Ealdwulf of Bamburgh. It will never have been as united, not even under King Athelstan. Edmund promised war, but he'll bring peace.

'The agreement will be formalised in vellum, with signatures to the document.'

'I agree,' Mael Coluim announces without pausing to think. His easy acceptance surprises me as much as Edmund's quick decision to ally with him.

'You don't wish to discuss this with your advisors first?' Edmund asks courteously, all the same.

'No, my advisors are all dead, killed in the battle.' Mael Coluim's voice clouds with grief. I look away from his anguish. He's lost many of his friends as well as his kingdom. No wonder he's so desperate to align with Edmund. 'We must move quickly,' Mael Coluim states, hard iron in his voice.

'We move quickly anyway,' Edmund reassures. 'We'll rest for today and resume travelling tomorrow. I'll have my scribe draw up the agreement to be signed later today. In the morning, we'll march together. Those of your people who wish to, the women and children, can remain here or travel to York or Chester for safety. I'll send some of my finest warriors with them. They'll be released to your care as soon as the land of the Scots is back in your hands and Dyfnwal has been quelled.'

With such a flow of words, Edmund immediately has hostages for Mael Coluim's good behaviour, but Mael Coluim doesn't seem to notice. His tired face is flushed with the promise of his kingdom. He's not even considered what will happen to those hostages should we fail in our endeavours.

But I know we won't fail. Edmund will soon be king of more than just England. He'll be an emperor of Britain, as King Athelstan was before him. He will resolve these conflicts with bloody means. The knowledge brings a smile to my cold cheeks.

27

945, THE NORTHERN BORDER BETWEEN ENGLAND AND THE KINGDOM OF THE SCOTS

Mael Coluim, deposed king of the Scots

My agreement with Edmund has been formalised in vellum and ink, and my oath of loyalty spoken. I bowed low as I proclaimed the words. 'I behove to be faithful to my lord, King Edmund of the English, without any dispute or dissension, openly or in secret, favouring what he favours and discountenancing what he discountenances. And from the day on which this oath shall be rendered, let no one conceal the breach of it in a brother or a relation of his, any more than in a stranger.'

I know I should fear for my future. I already wish I had more men to rally around my cause. That would make this hasty alliance with Edmund unnecessary. But I don't, and in his presence I confess to feeling safer than I have since claiming the kingship from Constantin.

I want my kingdom back. King Edmund of the English will give it to me. He might even place Strathclyde in my care as well, once we defeat Dyfnwal. All I must do is attend upon him at his court in Winchester once or twice a year and promise not to attack his borders. It seems too simple after the two years of self-doubt and problems I've encountered with Constantin. He and his son have caused nothing but difficulties for me. When Edmund rides into the kingdom of the Scots at the head of his war band, he'll meet Constantin, Ildulb and the Norse under Eirik Bloodaxe in battle. We'll ensure Constantin, Ildulb and others of their family are killed. It might cause conflict within the kingdom. But, if Ildulb and Constantin are dead, there'll be no one for their supporters to rally around, especially if more of their sons and brothers are killed in the coming battle. It's Constantin and Ildulb who present a threat to me should they live.

What should I do if Constantin and Ildulb escape? How will I geld their ambitions and make myself strong? I wonder if many of my people will appreciate the alliance with the English king. They will recall Athelstan's attack on Cait. We all remember it. But again, that was Constantin's fault. He should have been loyal to his ally. I'll remind men and women of that. And, in the meantime, should my enemy escape, I'll hunt them down. This time, I'll wield the weapon that ends their lives.

First, Edmund needs my assistance to capture Dyfnwal's kingdom of Strathclyde. Despite our recent devastating defeat, my remaining men are ready to prove themselves. Vengeance against Ildulb, Constantin and the Norse drives them on. Many were once allies or friends of the House of Constantin. But no more. Now they serve me, and each night, as we ride towards Strathclyde, surrounded by the voices of the English, they call and shout to each other what they'll do to punish those who supported Ildulb and Constantin.

Restoring my kingdom with King Edmund's aid will cause few problems, especially if I bring Strathclyde with it, which I hope to do. Once Ildulb and Constantin are dead, my people will not take long to appreciate the wisdom of my actions.

Between the two forces, the English and the men of the Scots, there are well over three thousand warriors. Dyfnwal's force will be smaller. Those he does have will be clan warriors. They'll not possess the skills of the English king's warriors. Provided Edmund's men can avoid the spears and arrows of these clan warriors, I don't foresee the battle resulting in a meeting of shield walls. It's not the way the men of Strathclyde wage war. It never has been. That's why the Norse were able to almost starve them to death over fifty winters ago. The warriors of Strathclyde retreated inside their peaked capital at Dumbarton Rock and waited to die from hunger rather than face a battle they couldn't hope to win. I can't imagine anything has changed since then except the name of their king.

Edmund and his ealdormen state they'll fight against the warriors of Strathclyde as soon as they arrive at the remnants of the second ancient wall stretching across our island. It's ruined and tumbled down in places, but the grassy banks and ditches remain. They'll provide the means to hold higher ground and achieve some tactical advantages. I've advised that the enemy army will be long gone before we even reach that point. Edmund remains incredulous at my confidence, but then, he doesn't know the way the warriors of Strathclyde wage war against one another and others. His experience against them at Brunanburh saw them in an unusual situation. This time, they'll be in their own kingdom.

But I'm proved wrong when we reach the second ancient wall. Warriors do wait for Edmund, but not many of them. They stand beneath a sagging banner of the kingdom of Strathclyde. I'm sure Edmund could overwhelm them, but he doesn't act hastily.

I squint into the bright sunlight, trying to determine who leads the Strathclyde warriors.

'Dyfnwal's son,' I inform my overlord, recognising the familiar cast of his face, having been allowed close to Edmund through the mass of warriors who protect him. King Edmund nods, absorbing the information from atop his fine mount. He's called a halt to our advance as he considers what to do. It seems unfair to throw over three thousand warriors against such a small force.

'He knew of our plans?' Edmund questions with some consternation.

'Everyone knew you were marching north.'

'It's hard to keep such intentions a secret,' Edmund comments sourly.

'I don't see any of Ildulb's men, or any of the Norse,' I add. These are the best of Dyfnwal's men, armed and well dressed. But they're only Dyfnwal's men, wearing his emblem daubed on their clothing and weapons.

As we watch, the men rush to their horses, leaping on them to hurry northwards, with no intention to speak with Edmund. The English jeer and throw stones towards the fearful enemy. My warriors don't. They watch through narrowed eyes. They know not to trust the warriors of Strathclyde.

'We camp here tonight,' Edmund eventually announces, as the last of our enemies disappear from view. Despite the sun, the fierce wind pulls the English king's red, yellow and black wyvern banners taut, and the horses fret in the stiff breeze.

I survey the ruins of the wall. Some buildings still stand, possibly used by traders or shepherds. While most lack roofs, seeking the shelter the stones provide from the wind is still pleasant. My warriors surround me. They agree with my decision to ally with Edmund. But here, almost back within my kingdom, the reality of the agreement sits uneasily. If this is all Strathclyde has to offer, it'll hardly be a campaign to stir the hearts of the scops. I fear there'll be no battle glory to be gained. Edmund might even decide that Strathclyde doesn't need me to rule in his stead. That would reduce my triumphant return to my kingdom.

King Edmund surprises me by joining me. He's followed by Ealdormen Eadric and Athelstan.

'The scouts say the enemy ride north without even looking back.' He sounds astounded by that.

'They'll be heading for Dumbarton Rock and its peak.'

'They'll not meet us in the open, close to their border?'

'It's unlikely. They know how powerful such a position is. Their intention will be to thwart you and your warriors by standing on that high rock and pissing on you.'

Edmund's next words surprise me. 'I've sent my ship fleet to Dumbarton Rock under Ealdorman Ealhhelm's command. They'll prevent these warriors from retreating onto their outcropping.' He speaks with confidence of a plan already well advanced. 'I don't want King Dyfnwal and his son hiding away. We need to capture or banish him, or we'll spend the winter season trying to starve him from the stronghold. I don't wish to be away from home come the winter. Neither can we allow Ildulb to send reinforcements.'

'Then send some of your warriors with my son to prevent reserves arriving from the east and the kingdom of the Scots.'

Edmund's eyes blaze at the suggestion. I ignore my son's uncomfortable squirming at being mentioned. He doesn't like the English king. But he knows the area well. He'll be able to find any Scots loyal to Constantin. He might even be able to turn them from Constantin and have them reinforce my men.

There's some muttering from amongst my warriors. Would it be asking too much to send warriors from the kingdoms of Scots and English together? Surely not. They desire the same thing: to kill Dyfnwal's men.

'So our attack will be from every direction except the north?' Edmund summarises. His face is animated.

'Yes, Dyfnwal won't be able to hold off that many. He has only a small force. If we capture his son, he'll be tempted from his fortress to fight for him.'

'Good,' Edmund decides. 'Ealdorman Eadric, have fifty men ready by dawn. My lord Mael Coluim, you do the same. Your best warriors. They're to intercept any possible reserve force from Constantin, Ildulb and the Norse. They don't have to face them in full battle. They must delay any support from arriving long enough for us to reach Dumbarton Rock.'

'Agreed,' I offer, although it's not a suggestion but an order.

'The rest of the force will march at dawn as well.'

As soon as Edmund's gone, a hubbub of conversation begins. My son, Dub, glares at me.

'Am I to be your hostage?' Dub hisses angrily.

I shake my head, perplexed by his words. 'I give you a position of honour. You'll find Ildulb. If you kill him, you'll make a name for yourself.'

Dub growls and steps away.

'Dub, I've not finished speaking with you,' I murmur angrily. 'This is because I trust you,' I hiss, stressing the 'you'. Dub breathes deeply to calm his fury.

'I'll ready the men,' he mutters, still unhappy, stepping outside the protection of the tumbled-down wall into the growing wind, the smell of damp wood burning heavy in the air. I hear him calling to those who'll escort him.

I look to the rest of my warriors. 'With Edmund's support, we'll soon return to our own homes, and you'll be reunited with your families,' I state with a king's authority. Here, dirty and unkempt, they've forgotten who I am. I need to remind them that my decisions have kept us safe throughout the last two years and that I'll do so again.

But, if I expect a show of support from them, I'm bitterly disappointed. I ignore the angry glances and hollow silence and follow where Dub has gone. My warriors who'll travel with the English need to know how important their role is to the future of my kingdom. They must see our alliance as positively as possible.

I hurry towards my son. Men surround him, voices raised. I cannot get inside the circle of men who'll ride with him and the English ealdorman. Momentarily, I'm thwarted and feel useless, just as I did when Ildulb's men overwhelmed mine on the battlefield. I shouldn't have allowed him to dictate where the battle took place.

I've not had time to mourn all those who died that day. But I will. Once I've overpowered them all.

I consider barging my way through, but I don't. My son must exert his dominance over our warriors. Instead, I look back at the temporary camp's activity. To my right, Edmund issues instructions, his ealdormen deferential as they listen and rush to do whatever task they've been assigned. I wish my warriors were as respectful.

Finally, and just when I'm considering turning aside, the warriors part, some hurrying away to prepare themselves for the morning. Dub rushes back towards where I was earlier, stopping abruptly when he realises I'm already there. Flashes of emotions cross his face before he hides them. I realise he's embarrassed by my instructions and by me. It's not something a father should see.

'Father,' he stutters.

I incline my head towards him. 'You chose your men for the morning?'

Dub nods sharply.

'Assemble them,' I command. Dub falters, surprised by the resolve in my voice, and looks around helplessly to see everyone rushing hither and thither. 'They need to know how significant this initiative is,' I continue.

He doesn't speak but considers me for a long moment. Again, a flurry of emotions covers his face. He proves himself a consummate man of politics in that moment, stamping down on what he would like to say.

'Very good, my lord father.' I'm sure he'd rather warn me not to trust the English, and that the Scots who support Constantin aren't truly our enemy, but he's wrong. The Scots who support Constantin are our deadliest enemy, and in the moment of our greatest peril, the English offer the highest chance to reverse the catastrophic losses we've encountered.

Quickly, the men obey my son and return to their original position. I make eye contact with as many as I can, seeing in them the same rage that infects my son and, in others, the determined stance of men who'll fight to the death for what they believe in.

These are my most loyal warriors, the best fighters from amongst those I took to counter the threat of Constantin, his son and the Norse. That we failed isn't their fault, but mine for underestimating the strength of Constantin's support. They need to understand that. Now I must ensure they appreciate how imperative it is that they stop Ildulb from reaching Dyfnwal. If we don't, we'll be exiles from our land, with no home to call our own. King Edmund of the English will not support us if I lack all power and influence.

'My loyal warriors,' I begin, ensuring I pitch my voice so they can hear what I'm saying, provided they remain silent. 'You've been tasked with the most important element of our plan to return to our homeland, to reclaim our birthrights and win back the support and love of our friends and families.'

They stir at this.

'To ensure our alliance with King Edmund is a success, we must see the English as our allies, our fellow Scots who support Constantin as our enemy and the men and women of Strathclyde as an encumbrance. King Dyfnwal must be isolated, and if possible, Ildulb silenced once and for all. Ildulb cannot reach Dyfnwal. It will not be allowed to happen.'

The men are silent. My words aren't meant to be pleasant for them to hear.

'You know who the Scots are, who Ildulb is, and the area on the borders between the land of the Scots and Strathclyde. Your knowledge will be invaluable to the English. You need to remember that.' My voice holds menace. They're not helpless in our alliance. They're just as powerful as the English. They have the knowledge that will win the coming fight.

Silence greets my words. I swallow. I'd thought it would be easier to win their acceptance.

'Do you want Constantin as king in the land of the Scots? Do you want to lose your possessions? Because if that's what you want, you should leave now, run away to Bamburgh, perhaps even to Dublin. Those are your only opportunities if we don't make this alliance work.'

Their faces are angry, snarls and yips escaping their tight lips.

'This task will give us,' and I stress the 'us' by stabbing at my chest and then jabbing my finger angrily at them all, noting as I do that the ring with my royal seal flashes in the late evening sun, 'the opportunity to show the English that we're better than them. That we can protect and hold our land.'

The men stir now. I've told them what they don't want to hear. Now I'm filling their heads with the chance of redemption. Even Dub needs to hear this. He's as close to giving up as the rest of them.

'Your task is to stop Ildulb from reaching Strathclyde, kill whoever you can, and stop them from reinforcing Dyfnwal. Try not to kill our allies. Work with them, respect them, and if you can, use them to do your work for you. Don't keep secrets, and don't try to outfox them. You need to rejoin the army's main force with no casualties, especially English ones. Understand?' I'm almost shouting, but my fury's restrained. I want them to appreciate this situation is as unacceptable to me as it is to them.

I'm a king. I should be at Scone, not here, on some windswept hill in the middle of nowhere.

Dub meets my gaze, his eyes blazing with fury and pride. I've turned him from a petulant child to a man who'll die for me if the need arises.

'For the king,' Dub cries. The men take up the chant. My son moves forward to raise my arm high to show I'm his king. I allow myself to luxuriate in the moment. I've felt like shit since the battle and our retreat. I feel like a king once more. Long may it last.

28

SUMMER 945, WINCHESTER, THE KINGDOM OF THE ENGLISH

Eadred, prince and ætheling of the English

The court's peaceful and expectant. We await word of my brother's advances into Strathclyde. In his absence, I'm the sole ruler of England, trusted, as I wasn't last year when he attacked York and drove out Anlaf Sihtricson, killing Blakari Gothfrithson in the process. York's returned to his domain.

Unfortunately, Archbishop Wulfstan has come running from York, his robes held high about his knees in his haste, or so I imagine. I sit in my brother's place, my mother beside me, to listen to the lies and half-truths that will drop from his mouth.

'My lord prince,' he intones, refusing to bow before me, merely inclining his head.

'Archbishop Wulfstan, what's made you leave York at such a dangerous time?' I wave aside the furious stare from my seneschal. The sooner I've listened to Wulfstan, the sooner I can send him back to York.

'Precisely that, my lord prince.'

'What?' I press, momentarily confused.

'Eirik Bloodaxe, brother of King Hakon of Norway. The rumours are true. He's allied with Constantin, and his son. He'll journey to York in days. You must send more warriors.'

'Lord Constantin's engaged in a fight with King Mael Coluim. We have this day received word from my brother.'

'No, no, Eirik and his Norse warriors have left Constantin. I have it on good authority. I trust the merchant who brought me the news.' Archbishop Wulfstan's rotund face sweats profusely in the southern heat. His eyes stray to the food and drink arranged before me and my mother. I've heard he likes eating too much. I can tell from the size of his waist.

'There's no mention of Eirik in my brother's messages. Constantin has made a bid to reclaim his kingdom, but even now King Mael Coluim rides with my brother to take Strathclyde.'

'Lord Ealdwulf of Bamburgh sent word that ships have sailed past Bamburgh. He believes their destination is York.'

'Lord Ealdwulf informed you of this?' I'm perplexed and struggling to determine how Archbishop Wulfstan has decided these ships must be Eirik's.

'He sent word to York. He thought King Edmund would be there.'

'So, when he wasn't, you came here instead of sending the messenger south? The man would have been allowed safe passage. There's peace along the east coast, you know that.'

Archbishop Wulfstan looks pained as he tries to conjure a good excuse for his actions. 'I believed I'd encounter the king on the way south. I didn't know he'd taken the western roads.'

'Was Ealdorman Uhtred aware of this news from Lord Ealdwulf?'

'My lord prince,' Archbishop Wulfstan begins, but his words fade away. I'm fearful he might start to grovel. I'm surprised to discover that Wulfstan's a coward. All these years, he's tolerated

Olaf Gothfrithson, Anlaf Sihtricson and Blakari Gothfrithson, the progeny of Ívarr the Boneless, but Eirik Bloodaxe evidently terrifies him. I wave him aside to eat. I turn to my mother. She arches an eyebrow.

I call Oslac to me. He knows the lands between here and York well enough that I can send him north quickly. He heeds my words and is immediately gone from my hall. I'll have an answer soon as to what's happening in York. I fully expect Oslac to reach Ealdorman Uhtred, and then we'll know there's nothing to worry about other than in Archbishop Wulfstan's crazed mind.

For a moment, I feel a twinge of unease. My brother's taken his small collection of ships to war, circling around Hywel's kingdoms and then further north in case Dyfnwal tries to flee or call on any alliance he continues to share with Anlaf Sihtricson in Dublin.

I regard Archbishop Wulfstan carefully as he perspires freely and eats and drinks. Is he a member of this strange alliance that Bishop Cathroe has devised or is he genuinely terrified?

I need to find out. In the meantime, I'll keep Archbishop Wulfstan here.

Ealdorman Uhtred can thank me for that when I next see him.

29

945, THE BORDERLANDS BETWEEN STRATHCLYDE AND THE KINGDOM OF THE SCOTS

Ildulb, prince of the Scots

I left my father at Scone with the majority of the warriors who fought for us, Scots and Norse. Now I seek out Dyfnwal of Strathclyde. He was supposed to join us in the fight against Mael Coluim. Admittedly, his absence was hardly missed but where is he? I fear reports from my scouts reveal the truth. The English have travelled north. They threaten Strathclyde. Like his brother before him, King Edmund has realised the weakness in our alliance of Strathclyde, the kingdom of the Scots, and the Norse, assembled in the name of Eirik Bloodaxe.

I hurry to Strathclyde. Even with my few, most loyal warriors, we can reinforce Dyfnwal before Edmund threatens him. If Edmund beats us, Dyfnwal will fall below the might of the English, my father will lose an ally as soon as he's won back his kingdom. But that's not the end of my worries. I fear Mael Coluim knows of Edmund's advance. After his catastrophic failure, I suspect he's gone to find him. If Mael Coluim allies with Edmund, my father will lose his kingship again, and my most hated enemy, Edmund, the man who killed my son, will be victorious.

The heady triumphs of the last week have spiralled wildly out of control. I strove to restore my father to his kingdom and expel Mael Coluim. Now I fear our enemies have joined together. I know it will end badly if I don't help Dyfnwal. Even with the assistance of the Norse, we lack the numbers to counter an attack from the English. At Brunanburh, the English were victorious. They didn't have a numerical advantage against the Scots and the Norse, but now, with the Scots kingdom split between those who are loyal to my father and those loyal to Mael Coluim, we're severely weakened.

The landscape, over which I urge my horse, is bursting with summer growth but I can't enjoy it. My scouts ride the boundary with Strathclyde, reporting on what little they see, but the closer and closer we get to Dyfnwal's land, the quieter the countryside becomes. I fear I'm too late. I imagine Edmund and Mael Coluim sitting within Dumbarton Rock.

And yet, we see no sign of the English force. I almost begin to hope we're not too late. My scouts promise me we're close to Dumbarton Rock. 'The end of the day,' they assure me, riding onwards, through the lush valleys and high mountains, only then, one of them returns, his horse hurrying beneath him, sweating profusely and stumbling with exhaustion. I call a halt. My warriors stop their onward momentum in a clatter of wood and iron, the high whinnies of our horses showing their pleasure at being allowed to cease their onward momentum.

'What?' I demand. Denewulf's head bows low, face pale, and I perceive what I don't want to see before he speaks. The banner of Strathclyde catches in the breeze behind him. I swallow my anger and fury. Dyfnwal rushes toward me, encouraging his horse. His warriors stretch out behind him, yet they don't seem bloody, only hasty. Have they even attempted to defend their kingdom or just run away?

Dyfnwal's flustered, although he grins at seeing me.

'Lord Ildulb,' he greets.

'King Dyfnwal?' My tone's colder than a winter storm.

'I regret to inform you that King Edmund has taken Dumbarton Rock.' The words tumble from his mouth. I hear the pain of his admission.

'And Mael Coluim?'

'He's allied with him.'

'Bollocks,' I roar, the noise echoing in the stillness of the day and upwards, to where the mountain peaks seem to mock me with their steadfastness.

'What do they plan?' I demand. King Dyfnwal shrugs, his face flushed with anger.

'I escaped. They blockaded the sea and the river so we couldn't risk coming to your aid, and then they tried to reach the peak of Dumbarton Rock as well, coming at it with determination, holding each upward level. We were lucky to escape the huge numbers King Edmund had at his command, and I lost many warriors in the process, so I didn't exactly sit down and talk with them. We were only able to lose them by taking the most northerly route. They didn't expect that. You have more men coming?' he questions aggressively, looking over my shoulder as though they'll be visible.

'No, I don't. Why should I fight your battles for you? You didn't help me or my father even though you pledged to do so.'

'My son didn't seek you out?' he babbles, the fury of losing Dumbarton Rock being replaced with worry. In fact, he's so anxious, my denouncement of his failure to act goes unnoticed, and neither does he explain his absence.

'No, he didn't.'

'Not my son,' he whimpers. I swallow against his sudden grief. I understand his fears only too well.

'What do you plan?' I ask to distract him from thoughts of his son. He shrugs, wearing his defeat and sudden hopelessness like a heavy winter cloak. Those who've escaped with him struggle past, carrying whatever they can, tempting their beasts onwards. Their intention is clear. It seems it's better to be amongst the Scots than the English. I don't think my father will approve of this, but that'll be his decision.

I wait for Dyfnwal's answer.

'I need more warriors. I've lost many of the good fighters. They died to ensure their families and I lived. I must regroup. I'll be able to do that once I'm within your father's kingdom and can speak to him in person.' He sits straighter, prouder, forgetting he's a man without a son and a kingdom.

I don't have enough men to attack Edmund and Mael Coluim within Dumbarton Rock. Neither do I wish to fight for Dyfnwal's kingdom now I know Mael Coluim's in league with the English. It'll only be a matter of time before Mael Coluim attempts to reverse my father's gains. I must return to my father. I'll move my father from Scone to a place with walls and ditches and recall all the warriors I can. We shouldn't have allowed the Norse warriors to leave so quickly. I'll send my father to Dunnottar. No one will breach those lethal cliffs.

No, I reconsider quickly. I should stay here and send messengers to my father. I turn again and look towards Strathclyde in the distance. I came so close but not close enough. I imagine I can hear the voices of the English from here, raised in triumph at what they've accomplished. I can't allow them to take my father's kingdom as well.

My rage pulses deep within me. I could kill Dyfnwal for his failures, but we need him. He's the rightful ruler of the people of

Strathclyde. They don't like the Scots, nor do the Scots like them. Yet between us, the two kingdoms are bastions against the English. Together, we've always kept the English, and before the English, the Northumbrians, and before the Northumbrians, the men of Bernicia, from taking land they claim as their own but which belongs to my people or Dyfnwal's. This violation of Strathclyde affects the land of the Scots and the people of Strathclyde. We need to act together, and I need to summon Eirik and his Norse warriors back to aid us.

But for now, worry about my father makes me realise I must go to him.

Dyfnwal glowers at me with a mixture of emotions on his face. He knows he's a failure, but he also understands my thoughts. Together, Strathclyde, the land of the Scots and the Norse, no matter how much we might argue between ourselves, can present a united front against the might of the English and the disinterest of Hywel of the Welsh. Dyfnwal knows my father will support him. I'll do the same. Eirik Bloodaxe will join us. He'll have no choice in the matter. If our kingdoms are threatened, he can't hope to take Jorvik. The three of us are strong enough to counter the English threat provided we work together. I'm convinced of that.

'How far are we from King Constantin?' Dyfnwal breaks through my ruminations to question.

'How fast can you ride?'

'As fast as possible,' Dyfnwal assures me.

I nod. The solution to this catastrophe is to seek my father, and Eirik, and then attack the English who are far from home and likely to be poorly provisioned for a long campaign in the north of our island.

'My scouts are everywhere. If they find your son, they'll bring him to us,' I console him, a flicker of sympathy forcing the words from me.

He nods but swallows hard as he does so. He cares for his son, just as my father cares for me, just as I did my murdered son.

'Let's go,' I instruct. I direct my horse towards my homeland, regardless of how exhausted the animal already is. I thought recovering the kingdom of the Scots was the only task I needed to accomplish this summer, and that the real fight would come when we moved on Jorvik, together, to place Eirik Bloodaxe as king there.

I was wrong.

30

945, THE NORTHERN BORDER BETWEEN ENGLAND AND THE KINGDOM OF THE SCOTS

Edmund, king of the English

My men ride with me, proud of their accomplishments so far, knowing we're stronger than the alliance arranged against us. We hold Strathclyde, or rather, it's being retained for me by Ealdorman Eadric. He rules in my name. He and the small force under Dub's command were instrumental in assuring we took Dumbarton Rock quickly. They didn't find Ildulb but they did open up a line of attack that prevented the enemy from blocking our advance. My ships, under the command of Ealdorman Ealhhelm, blockaded the port and the river. My warriors then scaled the vast height of Dumbarton Rock. The only pity is that, somehow, Dyfnwal was able to escape.

But I know he'll be rushing to Constantin for help. Where else would he go without ships and access to the sea to reach Anlaf Sihtricson? So, we must now march on Constantin. As soon as Constantin's once more expelled from his kingdom and Mael Coluim's secure in it, I intend to allow Mael Coluim to rule Strathclyde on my behalf. To set one of my ealdormen over these people would put them at risk, and they'd be far from my assistance when we return to Winchester. I won't countenance that. It will be better to allow one of their own to rule them.

If Mael Coluim chooses to reinstate Dyfnwal, I'll agree to his demands, but only if he assures me of his loyalty and stands as a witness to Dyfnwal. Dyfnwal's weak, and will remain weak. He'll pledge his allegiance to Mael Coluim, who will in turn be true to the oath of loyalty he's sworn to me. In that way, if Dyfnwal causes problems, it'll be for Mael Coluim to contend with.

First, however, we'll overwhelm Constantin.

Unexpectedly, we ride south, retracing our journey to Dumbarton Rock from the ancient wall. Dumbarton Rock occupies a fine location. I could almost be jealous of its vistas across the sea and its high peak keeping everyone from its summit, apart from my warriors, of course. Only, to hold the peak, the king of Strathclyde must rely on men and women to send him food to eat and animals to slaughter. If the people turn against him, he'll be marooned. I much prefer the walls of Winchester and London which encircle such a huge space, keeping men and women safe within, and allowing food to grow and animals to be raised.

King Mael Coluim advises that Ildulb's warriors will expect an attack from the west. Coming from the south will surprise them. They'll never consider we'll retreat to advance. He says Ildulb will even now be travelling west. He was too slow to stop us taking Dumbarton Rock, but he need not know of our success yet. Now we have the opportunity to isolate the hoary old bastard Constantin in Scone. He was an old man at Brunanburh when I was barely a man. Now he must be even older and weaker. I don't anticipate him standing on the slaughter field. A pity. I should like to cut him down in a fair fight. He's interfered too much with affairs in England during his long life.

Mael Coluim says that, soon, we'll move north again. For now, we venture east. The surrounding lands are beautiful and stark, with vast, reaching hills, some still shrouded with snow, and harsh but lush valleys where plants and animals grow tall or fat and sometimes both. The people we encounter are fearful despite the scouts I've sent with words of assurance and the promise of payment if they provide us with the supplies we need. We make use of what remains of the ancient wall to supply shelter at night. It's not much, but it's better than sleeping on the exposed hills.

I can see why Lord Ealdwulf of Bamburgh so jealously guards this place. I'm pleased he's my ally. He'll have no argument with my brief incursion through his lands. It'll be but a matter of days, and then I'll be in the territory of the Scots once more. Lord Ealdwulf will welcome the restoration of Mael Coluim. I know King Constantin disappointed him when his father died. The English protected Lord Ealdwulf's mother, Hild, until her death. I remember her well. I never thought it would win me the regard of her son.

Not only will we attack Scone from the south. We also have Dyfnwal's son in our care, thanks to the endeavours of Ealdorman Eadric and Mael Coluim's son, Dub. We'll not kill him. I'll hold Owain as a hostage for his father's good behaviour.

* * *

A few days later, we ride north once more. The anticipation of the coming battle brings a smile to my lips. I welcome overawing Constantin. He's always been as slippery as an eel. His alliance with Bishop Cathroe, Dyfnwal and Eirik Bloodaxe was intended to unseat me from my kingdom. It will fail. York will stay firmly in English hands, as Ealdorman Uhtred guarantees my presence there, and Mael Coluim, my ally, will rule in the far north, with Lord Ealdwulf between them but also loyal to me. With King Hywel of the Welsh as my friend, there'll be peace such as my brother created after the battle of Brunanburh. The only problem will be Archbishop Wulfstan. Once, he was beloved by my brother, being rewarded the territory of Amounderness in exchange for supporting him. That loyalty has shrivelled and become self-preservation. When I'm the emperor of all Britain, I'll contend with Archbishop Wulfstan.

'Be alert,' I order my scouts, before I send them northwards. We're keen to have a proper battle. Dumbarton Rock was relatively easy to overwhelm, the only pity was that Dyfnwal escaped us. I don't foresee Constantin being as easy to defeat. I'll be disappointed if he is.

'My lord king.' One of my scouts rides towards me. Ealdorman Athelstan is at my side, and Commander Ordhelm is close by as well. Even King Mael Coluim and his son are near. I don't miss that my messenger flicks a perplexed look at Mael Coluim.

'Have you found the enemy?' I question, already deciding how best to beat them. The land here is surprisingly flat, and I can hear the gurgle of a river nearby. We'll need to find a means of holding the advantage. The river might be that means.

'Yes, my lord king.' And still he offers nothing further.

'What is it?' I question eagerly.

'You should come and see.'

I look at Mael Coluim. He smiles and moves forward, showing no concern.

'What do you think?' I ask Ealdorman Athelstan as I ride close to him.

'I don't know. Come, we'll look at what so perplexes our messenger but doesn't worry Mael Coluim.'

We ride onwards. Ahead, I realise the blue sky's shrouded with smoke. In the distance, across the wide river that is now visible, I see a settlement, the cause of the cook fires. It's small, and lacks all walls to protect it. I think it must be little more than a lord's estate. I look from my messenger to Mael Coluim. I'm expecting to encounter a mighty force of the Scots, the Norse and those who escaped from Strathclyde, and not be faced with a small settlement.

'What is this place?' I feel my forehead furrow.

'This is Scone, my lord king. Welcome,' Mael Coluim replies quickly, the ghost of a smile on his face.

'Scone, the seat of power for the kings of the Scots people?'

'Yes, my lord king.'

'There are no defences?'

'No, my lord king.'

'There are no walls or ditches.'

'No, my lord king.'

I'm agape. Scone's nothing like Winchester, or London. It doesn't resemble York. All of these places have walls to protect them. Scone lacks even the defences of Mexburh and the other forts that have ensured we could reclaim York from the descendants of Ívarr the Boneless.

'It's a ceremonial settlement,' Mael Coluim eventually advises, a wolf grin on his face. I've come seeking a battle, but there'll be no slaughter field as at Brunanburh. No. I'll be surprised if anyone even draws their blade. Disappointment engulfs me. How am I to earn my brother's reputation if I don't even get to fight the alliance that's formed against me?

'Where are the enemy?'

'As I said, they'll be to the west, or will have dispersed.'

'Will King Constantin be here?'

'Oh yes. He'll have vowed never to leave it again.'

Disappointment wars within me. I should be pleased not to fight. 'How did they beat you?' I question, because I'm confused.

'They had a much larger force, reinforced with the Norse. No doubt, Eirik Bloodaxe was keen to move south and so the cocky bastards have left Constantin alone, with no more than a handful of warriors to protect him.' Mael Coluim can't keep the grin from his face.

Ahead, a single rider nears us, bringing his horse over a narrow wooden bridge. He carries a green and blue banner, drooping beneath the heat from the sun so I can't determine if there's an animal depicted on it.

'Ah,' Mael Coluim says. 'Now Constantin means to sue for peace.'

I look from my ally to the messenger, who's now within speaking distance. His face is fearful, especially when he sees Mael Coluim and the number of men who follow me.

'My lord king, Edmund of the English,' he begins. He speaks my language well. 'King Constantin welcomes you to the land of the Scots. He hopes you come in peace.'

I can't help myself, my mouth drops in shock.

'You're welcome to Scone,' he continues.

'Thank you,' I manage to reply, still astounded.

'King Constantin will come and speak with you,' he continues. 'If you would be so kind as to please wait here.'

'I will,' I confirm, turning to glance at Ealdorman Athelstan. He looks at me with questions and dismay written all over his familiar face. I know exactly how he feels. We wait in silence, even Mael Coluim holding his tongue, although he looks inordinately pleased with himself. I consider Mael Coluim. I thought I had the reach on him, but it seems not. He's dragged me and my warriors all the way here for nothing. It would, I realise, potentially have been better to seek out Ildulb and his warriors and defeat them first.

I order my warriors to stand down. The ripple of unease murmurs from amongst them. But they can see what I can. There's no one to fight. And then King Constantin himself rides towards me.

He's surrounded by a handful of warriors and no more. As he gets closer, following the messenger with his drooping banner, I'm astounded by the changes that have befallen him since I saw him during my brother's reign. He's weak and white-haired. He's about half the man he used to be when I met him at Cirencester over a decade ago.

'My lord king, Edmund of the English.' He inclines his head respectfully. He shows no dread, but neither is he defiant. I'd force him to bend the knee, but if I make him dismount, I'm fearful he'll never mount again. Despite everything, I won't humiliate him like that.

'My lord king, Constantin,' I reply. He licks his lips and looks from me to Mael Coluim. A flicker of pure hatred touches his eyes, but he banishes it quickly.

'I assume you've come to take back the kingship?' he questions Mael Coluim.

'Mael Coluim is the rightful king of the Scots,' I interject before the two start bickering.

'Is he?' Constantin questions, although I notice his hands shake on the reins. Indeed, there's a youth holding the horse steady for him. I don't miss the similarities between the pair. He must be a grandson, perhaps even a great-grandson. Constantin looks like a man struggling to stay mounted.

'He has the warriors of this kingdom with him.' I indicate the force with the English. 'And you,' I pause, 'do not. And he has my support as well,' I continue before Constantin can deny it. A heavy silence falls. It's impossible not to feel uncomfortable to be faced with a man who couldn't pull his sword free from its scabbard without falling over. Where are his warriors? Where are the Norse? Have they already gone to York? Am I wasting time here? What did Constantin hope to accomplish? Why was he so arrogant?

'Then, I'll welcome my king to Scone,' Constantin murmurs, his eyes glinting with daggers. 'I ask to be allowed to return to St Andrew's and pledge myself to serve no one but my Lord God, and to make amends for my failings in being easily led by Bishop Cathroe.'

Mael Coluim opens his mouth to reply. His face is flushed with fury now that he faces his enemy.

I notice that Constantin makes no mention of his son or the Norse as he barters for his life.

'As the overlord of this island, I will support that,' I confirm. I'll not allow Mael Coluim to take this old man's head. That would not rest easily with me. And it'll be more of a punishment for Constantin to live with his failure.

'I thank you, my lord king.' Constantin bows his head, revealing the shimmering pate of a man who has no hair on the top of his head. I steady myself. Constantin has been an enemy of England for a long time, but Mael Coluim is now my ally, and my subordinate. To attack Constantin now would be like striking my children. He's weak and alone.

I think that will be that, but Mael Coluim's determined to assert himself.

'Where is your son, and his warriors?'

Fury flashes in Constantin's eyes, but he looks at me as he speaks. 'My son's a wayward boy. I don't know where he is.'

'Then we'll hunt him down,' Mael Coluim menaces.

I don't counter him. We have Constantin, but for many years, Ildulb has also threatened me. We'll find him. Constantin hasn't asked me to secure his son's life. He doesn't ask me now. Perhaps he hopes Ildulb will still take his vengeance against me.

'He's to the west,' Mael Coluim asserts confidently in a steely voice. Now that we've arrived at Scone, he's a man transformed. Constantin's lips tighten with fury. 'I suspect he's gone to aid Dyfnwal.'

'Take half the English warriors and find Ildulb,' I instruct Ealdorman Athelstan. 'King Mael Coluim, will your warriors join mine to intercept Ildulb?'

'They'd welcome it,' he confirms. 'Under the command of my son, Dub. I've much to arrange within Scone.'

'Very well. Ealdorman Wulfgar, attend upon King Mael Coluim and Lord Constantin in our absence. You have command of the English warriors who will remain here,' I announce. Ealdorman Wulfgar accepts the assignment without argument. 'I'll join my warriors,' I confirm.

Once more, I look to Lord Constantin, lingering to allow him the opportunity to treat for his son's life. He does no such thing. Instead, I speak into the silence.

'I was sorry to hear of the death of your son, Alpin. He was a good friend of mine.' This does occasion a response, but it's not verbal. Constantin holds my gaze, almost daring me to say more about how Alpin came to die. I consider doing that. If the rumours are correct, Constantin's daughter killed his son. I don't believe anything has gone right for Constantin since then.

But, still, he doesn't speak.

I sigh. 'We will return,' I proclaim, and turn aside from King Mael Coluim and the former king, Lord Constantin, and the unhappy conversations they're about to enjoy. I must still seek my personal enemy to finally resolve this uneasy conflict. Then, I'll assert my claim as emperor of Britain, just as my brother was before me.

31

945, THE BORDERLANDS BETWEEN STRATHCLYDE AND THE KINGDOM OF THE SCOTS

Dyfnwal, king of Strathclyde

We ride in tight formation. Ildulb's ostensibly in charge of this procession of warriors and refugees, but my people only take orders from me. That's as it should be.

The journey has been long and tiring. My people aren't used to privations. Our capital has been secure for so many winters. I still struggle to comprehend exactly what's happened. The horror of seeing the English and the Scots warriors surging up Dumbarton Rock will haunt me all my life. I prayed then, as I never had before, for some guidance from my God. His advice drove me to escape in the face of such overwhelming odds.

I could feel a failure, but I did the right thing. My people, for all their discontent, aren't necessarily unhappy with me, but rather with the English king and King Mael Coluim. Against Mael Coluim, I hear muttering and angry complaints. They thought we were allies. I confess, I might not have been entirely clear about which king of the Scots I'd forged an alliance with.

I know Constantin and Ildulb will restore me to my kingship.

It's just a matter of defeating the English, which is best accomplished by our combined forces. The English and their long-running fight with the Norse look only towards violence. I could pity them if I didn't feel them chasing me, always at my heels.

But I'm proved wrong. We're not being chased. The English, with the help of Mael Coluim, are cleverer than I thought. When we're almost within sight of Scone, where I swore allegiance to Constantin and then Mael Coluim, the English greet us, a vast force, spread across the flat landscape. Somehow, they've arrived first.

Ildulb races to me while my people cry in horror and fear as they realise we've been intercepted before reaching safety. If we couldn't win a battle while holding Dumbarton Rock, we can't win here. Not in the open, with no means of erecting any defensive structure.

'Bollocks,' Ildulb roars, his horse alert, with eyes as wild as the rider's. 'My father?' His bleached face reveals true terror. His future depends on his father's good health. If Edmund and Mael Coluim have seen fit to kill the old man, Ildulb will have lost all. If I weren't so fearful for my people and, more importantly, for myself, I could pity him.

I should have taken ship and sought Anlaf Sihtricson in Dublin before the English blocked the quayside and access to the river. I know I should.

'They'll attack us?' I state, and Ildulb nods sharply, his chest heaving with fear as he tries to devise a way to reach his father.

'We'll have to strike first,' he announces. My heart stills.

The English and Scots host combined is huge. Their numbers far overtop ours. If we meet in battle, there'll be a bloodbath. Strathclyde might never rise from the ruins of so many men dying to defend her.

I'm filled with fear and anger.

I thought my God had given me sound advice when he told me to keep my people safe and retreat in the face of such overwhelming odds. But instead, he protects Edmund and the English. Perhaps he's forsaken me.

'We should open a dialogue with them.' I say the words before I've considered with whom I'm speaking. Ildulb, already dangerous and murderous, rounds on me angrily.

'You'd run away again?' he spits. I recoil at the look on his face. Anyone else might have considered my words, but not Ildulb. 'Send your people back to the river. It'll protect them.'

I'm not sure how. The English have us surrounded. At our backs, they hold Dumbarton Rock. They must also be protecting their borders to the south. And they're before us.

Numb with worry and fear, I send word to the trail of tired and frightened men and women behind me. The only ones enjoying our summer trek are the children. They've been playing games of war against the English. I pity them for what they'll now see.

'Bring your men to the front,' Ildulb commands. I still at his harsh tone. It masks his fear, but we'll have a rift if he's not careful. He forgets I'm a king, unlike him.

I turn my horse to face him, growing angry. He meets my gaze unflinchingly. He means to be the commander here, not me.

'My men will only follow my orders,' I shout.

'Then your people will die on English swords and seaxes,' he retorts, fury showing in the thin sliver of his mouth. I recoil at the blatant hatred on his face. He might once have been an attractive man, but his life and the vendetta he carries against Edmund have made him ugly.

'My men will die fighting for me and what they believe. You have the lesser side here. Remember who's the king, Ildulb, and who the king's son.'

His bitterness manifests in a bubble of laughter pouring from

'Yes, and get to Scone. We can reinforce your father and then drive the English from your land.'

The words are spoken bravely. We assess each other for a moment longer. Those assertions, so casually stated, mask what will be almost impossible.

But enough of that.

I focus on reaching Constantin. On cleaving my way through my enemy.

Only then will my kingdom be returned to me.

I raise my sword before me, my shield as well. I turn to face the English, noting where the wyvern-daubed banner flies high.

'Attack,' I roar. I'm running, the weight of my clothing hampering my actions, but soon enough I meet the English shield wall. It's a terrible thing, as I've always heard. My warriors support me, pouring their strength into cleaving a hole through their defences. We need to get within.

My sword's useless in the confined space of man against man. I replace it on my weapons belt and heft my war axe instead.

Our shields don't overlap as the English ones do, but that's to our advantage. Neither side can call their strengths into play.

Behind me, warriors grunt and groan, a skirmish of living, breathing men. I feel the force of a war axe against my shield. Reaching around it, I lash out at my enemy, hitting home, as I hear a grunt of pain.

Above my head, the sound of spears being thrown and arrows loosed can be heard. I appreciate how strong the English shield wall is. We could flog ourselves just stopping it from advancing to cleave a path to the undefended children and women behind us.

Another crash on my shield. I'm lashing out with my weapon. Those around me do the same.

Voices rise in anger and fear. They mingle, and their intent is clear, irrespective of their language.

The ground's churning beneath my feet, and still, I've yet to kill anyone. Neither, it seems, have the English managed to slaughter huge numbers of my men, for we stand strong against them.

I heave, and strain, my axe working and, slowly but surely, I feel a give in the enemy shield wall.

Perhaps this might be easy after all.

And then, it gives way. I manage not to fall forward and brace myself to dash onwards, but there's a restraining hand on my shoulder. I look around in confusion.

The battle's disintegrated, both sides breaking apart as quickly as they came together.

'What?' I garble. It's hot today. I taste my sweat.

'Constantin and Mael Coluim,' is all I hear alongside a murmur of angry voices. I turn to look and angrily spit the sweat from my mouth.

Constantin and Mael Coluim have ridden into the heart of the battle, unarmed. Their intent is clear. They've made peace. The fighting must stop.

Bitterness fills my belly. I force myself to walk toward the two men, unsurprised when Ildulb does the same. Amongst the English, I vaguely see a huddle around the English king's banner, and then a man on a black stallion is riding towards us.

Peace between the two men who claim the kingship of the kingdom of the Scots has been secured without my involvement, and with the king of the English.

What does that mean for me?

My feet drag over the warm summer land. My strength and self-belief drain away like spilt blood into the earth as my warriors cry in thwarted fury. It's better to have died in battle than to be brought to heel by men who think they're my commanders.

Ildulb's face is filled with fury, but this time, it isn't directed at me.

I might have an ally yet.

* * *

I watch King Mael Coluim irately. He sits once more on his throne and glares at me with narrowed eyes and a haughty demeanour. He knows how much I hate him and, conversely, how much I need him.

He didn't take Strathclyde from me, King Edmund did that, but it is Mael Coluim's to gift back to me, with the agreement of the English king. I imagine he'll only do so when he's punished me, as he sees fit.

'Lord Dyfnwal,' he calls, summoning me to him. It's all I can do to walk forward calmly. I don't want to have to do this, but there's no choice. The forces of the English king and King Mael Coluim have ousted Constantin. The support he always said he could rely on has dispersed with the wind. Even Eirik Bloodaxe has long since disappeared.

Ildulb's also gone. He would have been my supporter if Constantin had stayed in power, but once more he's been banished to St Andrew's, alongside his father. I'm left begging for scraps.

Edmund has returned to England, confident he dominates every king upon our island. He walked with the air of a man who has nothing left to accomplish. I admire him, albeit grudgingly.

'King Mael Coluim.' I bow. I have to show humility here, just as Mael Coluim has done with Edmund. I watched it all, from the back of Mael Coluim's hall, as the English king agreed to gift the kingdom of the Scots back to him. What wasn't said, but was common knowledge, was that Edmund would only support Mael Coluim against Constantin if he assured Edmund that Constantin was a spent force. Constantin is to be contained within St Andrew's and never allowed to interfere in affairs outside his kingdom again.

The English king's too strong. He'll never be toppled. The descendants of Ívarr the Boneless are a spent influence, with nothing more to throw at Edmund and his warriors. Not even a new Norse warrior could rise and overwhelm him.

'It's in my power, and it's my wish to give you the care of your kingdom under my domain, but first, you must swear fealty to me.'

This is all war amounts to in the end: one man wanting to outdo another. Despite Constantin's assurance that such words can always be withdrawn without any adverse effects, I feel the relationship between Strathclyde and the Scots is about to change irrevocably, perhaps not for my kingdom's good.

I speak the words carefully, measured. 'I behove to be faithful to my lord, King Mael Coluim, without any dispute or dissension, openly or in secret, favouring what he favours and discountenancing what he discountenances. And from the day on which this oath shall be rendered, let no one conceal the breach of it in a brother or a relation of his, any more than in a stranger.' The words taste like bile but there's nothing I can do. Not now and not from my position of terrible weakness.

My people want to go home. I want to go home. I'm tied to King Mael Coluim, and in turn to King Edmund.

Damn the English king.

Damn him to hell.

33

945, ST ANDREW'S, THE KINGDOM OF THE SCOTS

Constantin, deposed king of the Scots

I'm banished once more, and this time, it feels permanent. I'll die at St Andrew's. Mael Coluim is king in my place and has won the acclaim of men who said they supported me.

My son, Ildulb, has been banished with me for all he remains the acknowledged heir to the kingdom after Mael Coluim. It is the way of our people. Mael Coluim is powerless to act otherwise, but I fear to think of the consequences of our actions. How will Mael Coluim punish Ildulb and my family when I'm no longer around to protect them? My worries consume me. I can find only one person to blame for what has befallen me and my family. Edmund. King of the English.

I always cautioned my son to let go of his anger and grief about his son's death on Edmund's sword, but now I feel as though I've erred. If Ildulb had hunted down the murderer of his son before, we wouldn't be in this situation now. Edmund would have been dead and buried, rotting in a fine grave somewhere. I'd still rule the kingdom of my birth. Mael Coluim would not hold the land of the Scots under Edmund.

I acknowledge I once agreed to accords with Athelstan, king of the English, and his father before him, but I had no intention of keeping to those agreements. Mael Coluim has been left with no choice. And King Dyfnwal? Well, for the time being, he has a kingdom but holds it subject to Mael Coluim, who owns his subject to Edmund. Edmund has built himself an empire. The English have covetous eyes. They wish to rule our entire island.

Ildulb's a sullen creature once more. He blames himself for our failure to hold the kingdom safe against Edmund. If I were a lesser man, I'd tell him he was right. But I can't denounce him for my mistakes. I should not have allowed Bishop Cathroe to spin me a tale built of little more than tendrils of cobwebs. I can't fault Ildulb for all he did. I was restored to my kingdom, if only for a short time. But now I find myself closer to death and further from my kingdom than I have been since the last time Mael Coluim banished me.

Perhaps I will retire gracefully from politics and allow my son to do the family's work. I still have my daughter and grandsons to consider.

However, I don't wish to fade away from the minds of men. This land has been mine for too long for my name to fall by the wayside, shrouded in mystery and confusion like so many of my ancestors. The shadowy kings of our past, dead and buried, forgotten about by all but the scribes who labour to bring forth a history of this land. Rumours and counter-rumours, and half-told truths. The history of the land of the king of the Scots may as well be a tale told by a scop than a churchman, with all the elaborate monsters that go with it.

And yet, I'm so very, very old now. So old and tired. Maybe my time is done.

No one remains from my youth. I'm the last of a breed which was already dying out when I was a young man of only forty winters. As I take once more to my knees on the cold floor of my church, I feel that my God has forgotten me. Does he mean to make me live forever? The first immortal king of the Scots? Does he intend to make me like Cadfan of the Welsh, a legend in my lifetime, a man who fought the enemies of the Britons, only real and in the flesh? A thing of imagination on which to pin the hopes of a lost kingdom?

I wish I knew, and yet I'm glad that, even at my age, some mysteries still keep me awake at night.

King Mael Coluim has sent an entire selection of his household troops to guard me in my isolation. It won't be needed. I'll content myself with this life. But, well, I know this conflict of kings isn't yet over, even if I'm a spent force.

There is always one more ploy to play. I only hope my final kingly act is still in motion. It's been many years since Denewulf was my sworn messenger, and yet, in this, I trust him. We were reacquainted when he served my son in the battle against Mael Coluim. Denewulf can make his way through any of these kingdoms with ease. And he will need to do so. I've gifted him with a rich treasure, but whether he manages to accomplish the task I've set him or not, I don't know. I won't see him again, either way.

King Edmund of the English might term himself as an emperor of Britain, but all men are mortal.

34

MAY 946, PUCKLECHURCH, THE KINGDOM OF THE ENGLISH

Edmund, king of the English

The celebration swirls before me as I relax beside my family. My two young sons are with me, their foster mothers hovering in close attention, but Æthelflæd and I know how to look after them. She rests her hand on her gently swelling belly, a sign of her growing pregnancy outlined against the pale blue of her delicate gown. She looks beautiful in the golden sunlight with her long blond hair cascading down her back. Her pregnancy has taken all the harsh angles from her body and demeanour. Now that she knows she can carry a child for me she's a changed woman, a more loving and caring companion.

We both hope for a girl. Two boys are only a start, and a daughter would make an excellent addition to my family. Already, I plot marriage alliances with my cousins' families in East and West Frankia and laugh at my folly.

The summer's well advanced, bees floating in the air and the smell of blooming flowers hanging heavy. For today, everyone is feasting and merry. There are jugglers and storytellers, scops and

Watching the boys is almost as much of a treat as watching the entertainers. I think she probably imagines what it'll be like when her child laughs in such a way.

The man, who looks Danish to me with his blond hair and angular build, flicks his right wrist and the dogs form a line and, with another flick, march forward. They resemble a small shield wall, complete with little scarves around their necks as though they fly the banners of their lord, and even I laugh.

I notice then that the man's left hand is missing below the wrist. He's more than likely a Dane who's fought against us in the past, and yet he looks content now. Still, I flick a glance around the performance space and ensure my warriors are on high alert under Commander Ordhelm's instructions. Their enjoyment will have to come at a later date, perhaps tomorrow when they don't have duties to perform and my family to protect. Nothing is more important to me than safeguarding my two precious sons and wife.

England might be peaceful, and I might be hopeful for the future and the laws that will be enacted to ensure the situation prevails, but I know men still hate me and would wish me dead.

Eirik Bloodaxe is at the top of that list. King Hakon, my foster brother, has sent word advising me of all he hears, and will continue to do so. Eirik Bloodaxe hasn't given up on his wife's claim to York.

Archbishop Wulfstan has finally proven to be loyal, and with the aid of the pope, has managed to have Bishop Cathroe summoned back to the continent, alongside his wife and Lady Gunnhild. We know to be watchful and wary. Ealdorman Uhtred guards York, refusing to be drawn away, as my other ealdormen have. Only Uhtred is not at Pucklechurch.

My allies amongst the Welsh are also in attendance. King Hywel, a man I thought I'd never see again, has come, and so have

Morgan and Cadfan, the only people who hold Welsh kingdoms without the oversight of Hywel.

I hope to speak with Hywel at length tomorrow. I wish to congratulate him on the success of his new laws and thank him for not interfering in the conflict that so recently troubled the English. I think that with the support we've given each other, our respective kingdoms have become far stronger than they've ever been. I also hope to find out his plans towards Morgan and Cadfan. I'm curious as to whether he'll let them stay independent.

The dogs have broken apart from their mini shield wall, and now they're skipping around the square, more like horses than dogs. The Danish man hasn't moved from his position, using sharp whistles to direct his dogs instead of his hand action.

I feel a tug on my arm and look into the overexcited eyes of my oldest son. Eadwig is an inquisitive child. I already know what he's going to ask. He wants one of the dogs, or he wants to know how to train them. I'll have to arrange to speak to the man myself. So before he can half mutter the words and because the little show seems to have ended with the dogs once more lined up and facing the other way in the square, I beckon to him. The entertainer comes toward me, surprise on his broad face.

It's then I notice his face is also scarred. He must have been lucky to step alive from whichever battle he fought. It might have been Brunanburh, but I think the man has been living with his wounds for longer than that. I muse over whom he fought for, but provided he's content now, it little matters if he once supported my enemies.

'My lord king?' he asks deferentially, his voice filled with awe. Up close, the scar is a nasty gash down half of his face. He might once have been handsome, but now he's lucky to have lived through an injury that would have killed many men. My respect for the ex-warrior grows.

'My son, he's interested in your dogs and so am I. Would you do us the honour of eating with us this evening and perhaps bringing one or two of your dogs?'

The man's mouth opens in amazement. I try not to laugh at his complete astonishment. One of the dogs nips at his heels. Eadwig's down on one knee, reaching out to touch the small creature.

'What's your name?' I remember to ask because the silence is stretching.

'Eglaf,' he stumbles. 'The dog is called Midnight,' he talks to my son. I watch with amusement as he turns to speak to him instead of to me. Even being a king seems to pale into insignificance when there's a small boy interested enough in your prize pets to speak to you.

'How old is he?' Eadwig asks, his voice high-pitched. 'And how do you get him to do that?'

Eglaf seems to recall that he was speaking to me first and turns, no doubt an apology on his lips, but I wave him on. It is, after all, my son who wants to speak to him; I was merely facilitating the meeting.

'Two, he's the oldest of them all. He leads the rest for me.' His other dogs, released from their show, run wild amongst the audience so that some of the women squeal and small children chase them. I've distracted their master too much with my request.

From the other side of the open space, I catch sight of Commander Ordhelm signalling to some of his men that they should restrain the dogs. I smile but he misses it as the next performers step to him and harangue him for the damage the dogs are causing.

Instead of allowing the dogs to run wild, I tap Eglaf on the arm and indicate the rest of his animals; I think he has ten in total. He tuts unhappily and whistles sharply to them, the noise coming from behind his tongue. Immediately, the dogs form into their smart wall, and Midnight, still cuddled by Eadwig, looks almost desperate to return with its mates. It must have a different command to follow because although the small creature turns to face the rest of the performing pack, he stays perfectly still, listening to my son with half an ear raised, his expression intent on his master.

I almost envy the man his control over the small animals.

Eglaf turns back to me, a sheepish grin on his face.

'Apologies, my lord king,' he mutters, and then a flash of joy crosses his face. 'I'd be most honoured,' he says, remembering my invitation to him.

'Excellent. Tonight then,' I confirm. He nods and tries to take it as a dismissal because the next act is seeking to set up in the open space the rest of the dogs still occupy, only Eadwig is having none of it. I can sense the man's worry that others will grow disgruntled with him.

'Eadwig, the dog needs to go back now. There are more people to entertain us.'

'But I want to stay with them,' he comments matter-of-factly. I know that stubborn cast on his face. I look around for someone to escort my son, and my brother steps in first.

'Come on, Eadwig,' Eadred offers with a smile, 'I'll come with you, and we'll meet all of the dogs if that's acceptable, good sir?' he asks, his voice filled with the possibility that Eglaf can refuse if he wants. But the bluff man grins and nods and a little procession leaves: Eglaf, flanked by his nine dogs, and then his tenth, with my son at his side and my brother at his side. It's a funny demonstration. I try not to smirk as they walk away but even Æthelflæd's chuckling.

'You might have to buy the dog,' she offers softly. I'm thinking the same. My son has found something that fascinates him and as he's as stubborn as the rest of my family, I can't imagine him not

Why is he doing this? I ask myself before the onslaught of pain finally reaches me, and suddenly, time returns to normal. The sound of the day rushes back into my ears.

The music has faltered, there's an uproar unfurling around me as Ealdorman Athelstan, Commander Ordhelm and every warrior rushes toward me. Æthelflæd's screaming, and my youngest son, woken abruptly from his nap, is howling in the arms of Lady Ælfwynn, who looks at me with wide, horrified eyes, focusing on the blood and the ragged executioner.

There'll be no recovering from this wound. I already feel myself growing weak, the warmth I've enjoyed all day shearing from my body with my blood loss.

This is what it means to die. This is the sort of death I've inflicted on so many men in battle. It seems a callous thing to have done.

The man comes ever closer, driving his seax into my side once more. When his face is so close to mine I can smell his rancid breath once more, he whispers, 'Compliments of King Constantin and his son and grandson,' before yanking the seax from my body. He plunges it into his own, shearing his throat before me so that now my poor son's howling and covered in the blood of the man who's killed his father. My wife, my poor wife, is screaming and yelling as she tries to reach me but is held firmly in place by the effects of her fear. Her eyes seek mine. I can see she's trying to speak around her scream, her words half forming and then being forgotten about as she screams and then half forming again. She's terrified. I'm cold, oh so cold.

People in the square, who've been sharing my entertainment, scream as well, and everywhere's suddenly chaos, a discordant note after the beautiful music of the musicians. My eyes alight on the man who wasn't a musician but who stood with them.

Ealdorman Athelstan reaches me and takes charge. Edgar, my

youngest son, and his foster mother, Athelstan's wife, are forcefully removed, the sounds of my sobbing child reaching my ears as I gasp for breath. I want to tell him I love him, to commend him to a better future, but he's whipped from my side as Ealdorman Athelstan bends to try and stem the flow of blood.

'It'll be alright,' he advises savagely. 'You can survive this,' he mutters, his belief absolute, but I know differently. A man can't outlive something as brutal.

I'm surprised I've lasted long enough to even speak with him again.

The body of my murderer is being trampled upon, the ground slick with my blood and his. Men will fall in that red river, and they'll have to wipe my life from them when I'm gone.

'Constantin,' I manage to mutter. Ealdorman Athelstan stills, shock written all over his face. He wants to question my words but somehow stops himself.

I have few words left. Each of them needs to be well considered.

My England. I thought it was safe, but I was wrong, a fool to think so.

'My brother?' I say. He nods and shakes his head. He might have told me I'll live, but some of him realises I won't.

Æthelflæd finally manages to move. She kneels before me. Her blue dress is red now, her happy face crushed and white, but she holds her tears back. I admire her firm resolve.

Her warm hands fill my cold ones, the only part of me to feel any warmth any more. All sensation is leaving my body. I must ensure they know.

'Constantin,' I say again loudly. They both nod. They understand what I'm saying.

'Eadred,' I also manage and, again, they understand that, as do the other men and women who've come to stand a guard around their dying king.

Ealdorman Athelstan's hands hold a pressed linen tunic against my wound, but blood leaks around the cloth and stains his hands. So clean and well maintained compared to the man who killed me, for all that Athelstan is a great warrior. He's laboured all his life for this vision of England that's just disintegrated around him again.

His oldest brother, the king he loved and admired, and now another king, almost his brother. So many men in his life, dead before they should be.

'The boys,' I manage to choke. I can feel my chest growing still but I've more to say. I must say it before it's too late.

Someone's found Archbishop Oda, and he's here, muttering words behind me, the Latin tongue almost as soothing as the music of the entertainers was long moments ago.

'They'll be safe,' Ealdorman Athelstan offers, trying to force a reassuring smile to his face and failing. 'And your new child,' he remembers, his voice. 'We'll keep England safe,' he assures me, his words trying to hold hope.

My hands are icy, but I try to lift one of them clear from Æthelflæd, to give Ealdorman Athelstan the comfort he needs, but it's too much effort. I sink back. I feel myself starting to slide from my chair. My body can no longer support itself. My head lolls to one side, giving me a tilted image of my death scene.

'I love you,' I manage to utter. A final sentence for both Æthelflæd, my sons, my growing child and my most loyal friend. I hope they know I mean them all.

And then my blood chokes my breath, and my eyesight fades to two tiny pinpricks of light before being extinguished.

I was England's second king. My brother will be the third king of the English. I hope he takes his vengeance against Constantin, the bastard former king of the Scots.

> Here King Edmund raided across all the land of Cumbria
> (Strathclyde) and ceded it to Malcolm, king of the Scots, on
> the condition that he would be his co-operator both on sea
> and on land.
>
> — ANGLO-SAXON CHRONICLE, A TEXT, FOR 945

offers, understanding on his young face. How like his father he looks. I smile sadly.

'No, it's time all knew of everything your father achieved. I fear he'll be forgotten if not. Your father was a wise man. You're very much like him.'

Edgar frowns at my words. 'He was forced to restore the losses suffered by Olaf Gothfrithson when he became king.'

'He was, yes. He had his own way of doing so,' I offer. 'It took him time to realise King Athelstan wasn't the only one capable of such achievements.'

Edgar's silent, listening intently. No doubt he ruminates on how successful he can be when his father suffered the terrible fate of being murdered.

'He was a careful man, but sometimes, those who seek to damage are able to do so. His death was a tragedy. But England became stronger because of it. And now we enjoy such peace, the Norse are either our allies or have been banished forever.'

Edgar smiles now, nodding along in time with the scop song. 'He was indeed a protector of warriors, and of England,' he announces, and I grip his arm, grateful to feel the strength within him.

'You'll make him proud,' I reassure, as though he needs to hear such words from a woman such as me. 'I was born when the Norse first raided this island. My father died defending it from our enemies. They murdered my oldest son, my youngest son spent his short adult life fighting them as well. And now you, Edgar, are truly king over a peaceful land, the land of the English. One day, your son will rule after you, and our enemy will never again overwhelm us. The kingdom of the English will long endure.'

Here King Edmund passed away on St. Augustine's day (26th May). It was widely known, how he ended his days, that Liofa stabbed him at Pucklechurch. And Æthelflæd of Damerham, daughter of Ealdorman Ælfgar, was then his queen. And he had the kingdom six and a half years: and then after him the ætheling Eadred, succeeded to the kingdom...

— ANGLO-SAXON CHRONICLE, D TEXT, FOR 946

HISTORICAL AND AUTHOR NOTES
944–946

The stories of the Brunanburh Series have not been easy to write. In trying to present an image of the British Isles as it might have been over a thousand years ago, I've delved into a huge variety of sources, and I've had to make any number of judgement calls that may or may not have been good ones. I've had to rely on sources I don't trust, either because of their bias, or simply because I've not studied them as much as I have the sources for Saxon England (and that always makes me nervous).

That said, the period this book covers is sparsely detailed in the source material, Welsh, Irish, Scottish or English (Saxon), and many liberties have been taken with the information I have discovered. The entries in the Anglo-Saxon Chronicle A version (translated to English) amount to only 110 words – the majority concerned with Edmund's battles in the north. (The A Version is believed to be the oldest version of the ASC.)

As I was finishing the revisions for this book, a new non-fiction title was released (by just, I mean, two days before). It is academic in nature, and consists of a series of essays regarding the discounted reigns of Edmund, his brother and his older son. It is fascinating. It is called *The Reigns of Edmund, Eadred and Eadwig, 939-959: New Interpretations (Anglo-Saxon Studies Book 48)*, and many of the quotations in the historical notes are taken from within it.

The Saxon period was not all about bloody battles but they are the details that have survived in the snatched glimpse of England, and the British Isles, available for the middle of the tenth century, and where they don't survive is as equally telling as where they do. There is only a small mention of Edmund's time in Strathclyde and Scotland, and for the Anglo-Saxon Chronicle, normally so keen to offer praise in battle, this makes me think it was little more than a scuffle. After all, a great poem was written about his battle against the Norse in 942. Surely, another poem would have been written if his successes had been primarily military? It has been suggested that the references to Edmund in the ASC have been heavily edited, either at that time, or later, with the suggestion that it can be 'proved' these erasures occurred before 1000 (these erasures have been discovered by examining the manuscript under UV light).

> The entries for the years 941 to 959 contain a number of erasures: at the end of the entry for 942; immediately above the year number of 943; and a small erasure at the end of the entry for 944... Three lines of text have been erased at the end of the entry for 946... the erasures seem to alter the content of some annals.
>
> — FORGETTING KINGS: THE FIRST 100 YEARS OF HISTORIOGRAPHY OF EADRED'S AND EADWIG'S REIGNS BY ALISON HUDSON

Why they have been erased is open to debate. But it highlights that what we do know has been subjected to editors and copiers for centuries.

The England that Edmund ruled was still recovering from the devastating Norse raids that his grandfather, father, aunt and cousin (Æthelflæd and Ælfwynn) and his half-brother, Athelstan, had done so much to stem. It's worth remembering that only seventy years had passed since the concerted attacks of the 870s. Those who survived the initial onslaughts will have passed on tales and stories that were still very much alive, despite the passage of time. The 'general' consensus may have still been that the Norse were enemies, and bloody ones. The attacks might not still be coming from Scandinavia, but the Norse of York and Dublin were a much closer menace.

There is debate about who Eirik Bloodaxe was and where he came from, much of it stemming from whether he was the son of the Norwegian king, or whether the man has become intermingled with that character, resulting in two men becoming only one. I have yet to form an opinion as I need to research further, and sometimes, when writing historical fiction, the evidence of the great Icelandic Sagas is more appealing than the stark 'factual' historical record. I make no apology for that. The fact that he is believed to be Hakon's brother, potentially one of Athelstan's foster sons, makes him relevant to this story. C Downham's *Viking Kings of Britain and Ireland* addresses Eirik's identity. It is believed he and his son were killed by the treachery of the ealdorman of Bamburgh in 952.

Bishop Cathroe seems to be a man of almost as much mystery as Eirik Bloodaxe and I confess to having wildly embellished his role in the events throughout Britain at this time. There is no widely accepted date for his mission throughout Britain, with some sources saying that he was related to Eirik Bloodaxe's wife and that he visited Jorvik on her wishes. This brings up a whole range of dating difficulties, as the narrative goes on to say that he visited Edmund, and Eirik and Edmund didn't hold their kingdoms at the same time, although it has been postulated that Eirik may have very briefly ruled Jorvik while Edmund lived (see Alex Woolf's argument for this). It's just another delicious half-known myth that I've exploited to give my story more form.

I've purposefully referred to Constantin and Mael Coluim's kingdom as the kingdom of the Scots. Scotland is still some way off in the future and it would be incorrect to use that terminology here (apologies for the nerdy need to be accurate). Alba, Pictland, Scotland, they are all names for the same place, but as with England and its constituent kingdoms of Northumbria, Wessex, East Anglia, Mercia and Kent, we can't make it a 'kingdom' before it actually becomes one, even if it would make the narrative easier. King Constantin died by 952. His 'retirement' lasted for many years. Whether he did or didn't manage to reclaim his kingship briefly in 944 is conjecture. His son, Ildulb, did eventually become king of the Scots after his father's death, on the death of Mael Coluim, but died in 962. He was succeeded by Mael Coluim's son. Just to set the matter straight, Edmund did not kill one of Ildulb's sons in Cait, and neither did Constantin arrange Edmund's death. This was a little literary licence. And indeed, Ildulb may have been much younger than I've portrayed him.

King Hywel of the Welsh died in 949/950. His three sons succeeded him, splitting his territories. The control over Gwynedd did not outlast his death. A single coin survives from his reign, believed to have been 'struck' at an English moneyer's. Hywel's fascination with the English did not perhaps extend as far as he might have liked.

King Dyfnwal of Strathclyde lived until 980. He may also have been a relative of Bishop Cathroe – I discovered this when the story was complete. I also discovered that the capital of Strathclyde may have moved from Dumbarton Rock after the earlier attack by the Norse. Alas, I couldn't bring myself to change this as Dumbarton Rock is a fabulous place.

Bamburgh's history is beyond confusing at this time. Ealdred, and his father are known. We don't know what happened after Ealdred's death in c.934. Ealdwulf is something of an invention. He might have been Ealdred's son, or his brother. I've followed Alex Woolf's tentative suggestions here. There was certainly an Ealdorman Uhtred at this time. I don't believe he ruled Bamburgh, or even claimed it as his to rule. Bamburgh remains a tricky proposition.

Lady Eadgifu lived until c.966. Her life almost encompasses the space between the reigns of two of the period's most famous kings, Alfred of Wessex who died in 899, and Æthelred II of England, who ruled from 975. Alfred has won fame for beating the Norse, Æthelred II for failing to do so. Lady Eadgifu would also be the grandmother to two more kings, one of them, Edgar/Eadgar (who she speaks to in the epilogue), is renowned for the peace that endured while he was king, and for proclaiming his third wife, Lady Elfrida/Ælfthryth as England's first acknowledged and consecrated queen. What happened after his death is not as peaceful. And indeed, I've glossed over his brother's brief reign in the epilogue, as he came into conflict with his grandmother and many other English nobles.

Anlaf Sihtricson (Olafr Sigtryggsson) lived a long life, dying in c.980, and his attempts to retake York continued after the death of Edmund. It has been suggested he enjoyed 'very short periods of rule in "Danish England" during the 940s and 950s', and eventually retired to become a monk on Iona. This information comes from the Irish Annals. The paper ('Going North: Revisiting the End of Northern Independence' by N McGuigan) makes the tentative suggestion that there is the possibility Olaf/Anlaf was actually the son of his father and Athelstan's sister, Edith, whom he wed in 927. What an intriguing idea.

Here, another confession, in that I 'killed' the wrong brother of Olaf Gothfrithson earlier on in the series. Blakari, not Gothfrith, should have been king of Dublin. Rognavaldr should have died outside York, not at Brunanburh. I confess, much of this confusion stems from incorrectly reading a genealogy table not once but twice – and indeed, in the original drafts I didn't make this error. Everyone makes mistakes, but I apologise for the confusion. And it has very much confused me as I now try and make right the mistake that I made. Gothfrith is invented. A pity I didn't kill him at Brunanburh instead.

Archbishop Wulfstan would continue to plague England's kings until his death in 956. He is not to be confused with the later Archbishop Wulfstan II who is very famous for castigating Æthelred II's attempts to defeat the Norse in his 'Sermon of the Wolf' to the English. The jury is very much out on Archbishop Wulfstan I. He was a bit of a bloody pain to the English kings, and indeed, another fascinating paper has been written about Archbishop Wulfstan ('The Many Kings of Archbishop Wulfstan I' by A Rabin) offering an explanation as to why he was so fickle with the English kings, and also suggesting that Wulfstan was an ally of Ealdorman Athelstan Half-King.

The story of Eadred's reign could take many books. I might return to it one day. Certainly, he faced his enemies, just like his two older brothers. The kingdom of the English was far from secure. There is also a debate to be had about whether or not he was contending with a challenging illness throughout his short life.

The commendatory oath is from Isabelle Beaudoin's 'Edmund's Oath of Loyalty in Perspective: Innovation, Emulation, and a French Prince'. It is taken from Edmund's Colyton Code, and is 'the earliest surviving text of an oath of loyalty to the king in the Anglo-Saxon corpus [of extant manuscripts] and indeed, is the first time the existence of such an oath is referred to explicitly.' Readers may know that I've previously used a different oath, found in Baxter's *The Earls of Mercia*, but this one is earlier.

York/Jorvik at this time. I had written, edited and re-edited this book many times before I discovered a resource called *British Historic Towns Atlas Volume V, York* ed. Peter Addyman. It is, alas, out of print, but I was able to find a copy in the local Society of Antiquaries Library in Newcastle (The Hancock Museum). It has proven to be invaluable. Previously, I had found some hazy maps on the internet of the York from this time, and I also have a copy of *An Historical Map of York*, which attempts to show what York might have looked like at a set period in time, I think in 1850, but the *Atlas* really shows me how York/Eoforwic/Jorvik might have appeared at this time – including developments and what might or might not have been standing as part of the ruins of the Roman base from the c.200s. There is still much that is unknown, and there are also many questions that I now have about the development of York that I never thought I would.

The resource informs that the River Ouse at the time would have been tidal, and much wider than it is now. The late-eighth-century Alcuin describes York as having high walls and lofty towers. Asser (Alfred's late-tenth-century biographer – although I'm curious as to how he'd know) suggests that York's walls were insecure and there is a suggestion that the Vikings restored the walls. Considering what we know about Asser and his ability to be less than honest, we might suspect this statement. Certainly, the remains of the walls were visible but whether they were defensible is unknown. The walls survive to this day. To paraphrase, from the western corner of the Roman fortress to fifty metres along its southwest front, parallel to the river, the Roman wall is still visible above ground. Beyond this point, its six projecting interval towers and the

Roman south/west gateway leading to the bridge over the Ouse have either been demolished to foundation level or been covered by organic-rich debris of post-Conquest date. The fortress's south corner tower at Freasgate survives to fifteen foot. It is suggested that the south-west section of the civilian settlement might not have been included in the walled defences.

My recreation of the battle for Jorvik is entirely fictional. I do sometimes wish I found the research before I wrote the scenes, and yet, how often I find the resources by some fluke also astounds me. I didn't know about this map until trying to track down an earlier one I'd find on the internet. Ho-hum.

For those who might not know, there are remnants of two Roman walls within Britain. Hadrian's Wall is the best known. The Antonine Wall, in Scotland, is less well known, and certainly the sections I've visited are much more ruined than Hadrian's Wall. Still, the fact some of it is still visible makes it a boundary or feature that would have been noted even in the 940s.

I have not made much mention of events in East and West Frankia throughout this final book in the series. This is because events there were beyond complicated at this time. Somewhat succinctly, King Louis fell out with Duke Hugh and was apprehended. Only the assistance of King Otto and Edmund allowed him to be released from captivity (Louis had married Otto's sister, and Hugh had married another one).

Edmund's second wife, Lady Æthelflæd, is not known to have had any children. Her pregnancy at the end of this book is a little literary licence. She lived for many years, and may have remarried another Ealdorman Athelstan. She is believed to have supported the rein of young Edgar.

Thank you for joining me through these founding years of the English kingdom and their alliances and conflicts with their neighbours. As little as we know of the period, it is one of those for which we actually can understand their interactions much better than in earlier, and sometimes later, periods. It's confusing that only certain periods of the Saxon era are quite so well known. I apologise for how complex it seems, when at other periods, it appears much simpler. I think it speaks to an awareness that only some of the pertinent information for these earlier/later periods has survived.

ACKNOWLEDGEMENTS

As always, I am so grateful to my editor, Caroline, for pushing me with this series. I've cursed her on many occasions. What you see before you has been rewritten multiple times, each one making it better. I wish I could run a comparison between this version and the original one. I wish you could hear my angst as I undertook the process. It has taken cake and perseverance, and I am not supposed to be eating cake any more.

I'm so grateful to Boldwood Books for championing this series. It's been a decade in the making, and I've changed my mind about elements of it in the final editing process. Special thanks to my copy editor, Ross, proofreader, Shirley, and to Claire, who is so passionate about marketing these historical stories.

Huge thanks to my support network of authors and allies, who keep me sane, and a grateful thank you to the Hancock Library for allowing me access to the atlas of York, and to York Archaeology for hosting a talk and walk about the surviving stone walls.

And, as ever, thank you to my readers. We did it. We made it to the end of the Brunanburh Series.

ABOUT THE AUTHOR

MJ Porter is the author of many historical novels set predominantly in Seventh to Eleventh-Century England, and in Viking Age Denmark. Raised in the shadow of a building that was believed to house the bones of long-dead Kings of Mercia, meant that the author's writing destiny was set.

Sign up to MJ Porter's mailing list here for news, competitions and updates on future books.

Visit MJ's website: www.mjporterauthor.com

Follow MJ on social media:

x.com/coloursofunison

instagram.com/m_j_porter

bookbub.com/authors/mj-porter

ALSO BY M J PORTER

The Eagle of Mercia Chronicles

Son of Mercia

Wolf of Mercia

Warrior of Mercia

Eagle of Mercia

Protector of Mercia

Enemies of Mercia

The Brunanburh Series

King of Kings

Kings of War

Clash of Kings

Kings of Conflict

WARRIOR CHRONICLES

WELCOME TO THE CLAN ×

THE HOME OF
BESTSELLING HISTORICAL
ADVENTURE FICTION!

WARNING:
MAY CONTAIN VIKINGS!

SIGN UP TO OUR
NEWSLETTER

BIT.LY/WARRIORCHRONICLES

Boldwood

Boldwood Books is an award-winning fiction publishing company seeking out the best stories from around the world.

Find out more at www.boldwoodbooks.com

Join our reader community for brilliant books, competitions and offers!

**Follow us
@BoldwoodBooks
@TheBoldBookClub**

**Sign up to our weekly
deals newsletter**

https://bit.ly/BoldwoodBNewsletter